THE GRAPE'S JOY

A Saint-Emilion Vineyard Mystery

Patrick Hilyer

Acknowledgements

The title *The Grape's Joy* is taken from the poem *This Bread I Break* by Dylan Thomas. Other quotations used in the book are attributed to their authors within the text. All the characters in the book are fictitious. Château Fontloube is also a purely fictional address, but many properties like it can be found in the commune of Saint-Laurent-des-Combes near Saint-Emilion. Any resemblance between Turk the dog and Enid Blyton's famous crime-fighting hero, Timmy, is entirely intentional. Clémentine is a real car.

Thanks go to Pascal Méli for his journal *Une Année à Bujan* which provided most of the seasonal structure to the vine-growing and winemaking parts of the book, and to the hundreds of winemakers whose generosity and patience have helped me acquire what little wine knowledge I possess.

Cover photo Domaine de Beauséjour, Panzoult.

In memory of Roy Shipley (1959-2010).

Crash

I'm standing on a roadside verge, facing a vast vineyard.
Behind me is the D936. The road is busy, but the stream of
traffic flowing past is silent. Each car, each truck, every
bus and motorcycle, buffets me soundlessly. I stare at the
wreckage. The van is there, lying on its side, crushed and
distorted. A stream of diesel fuel trickles into a pool of
spilt red wine from a consignment that will never be
delivered. Someone has opened the door. The cab is
unoccupied. I take a couple of steps forward and see a
woman kneeling on the tarmac holding a limp, blood-
soaked body.

I hear the policeman's voice. 'It's alright,' he says,
'he's not dead.'

I move closer and see that he's right. The man is gazing
up at the woman's face, smiling. Gradually – following the
dream's absurd logic – it dawns on me that I am the
woman, and the man is my husband, Olivier. I cradle him
in my arms, staring into his shining eyes. At first I think:
oh, thank God, it's all been a big misunderstanding; then:
Jean, you've always been a sucker for a smile.

'Yes,' I call out, 'these are vines wrapped round his
head, not thorns!'

I try to untangle a knot of coarse vine shoots that start
to sprout from his hair and beard. But the stems tighten,
biting into the skin on his forehead, cheeks and jaw,
binding and constricting his throat. His eyes show fear. His
breathing becomes restricted, as though he's sucking at his
breath through a straw. I panic, and tug and snap the
creeping vines that threaten to suffocate him. I use my
secateurs to prize out the tougher stalks that only bite
deeper into his flesh like tensioned wires on a rotten post.
In my haste, I injure him. The blood, at first only a trickle

from the cuts on his head and neck, begins to flow and spurt. His mouth fills with red froth – a gory, bubbling ferment. The fibrous tourniquet grips harder, the garrotte's loop tightens.

He is dead.

April 2008

Frost

A man not old, but mellow, like good wine.
- Stephen Phillips, *Ulysses*

I suppose it all started with a chance encounter in the vines. I'd set my alarm and stuck a piece of paper to the clock face with the word *frost* written on it. Of course, there was nothing I could do about it. I just had to know, that's all.

The forecast was right; All Fools' Day started cold. From the bedroom window, I could see the early morning mists rising from the river like malevolent wraiths. Up the slope of the *côte* they drifted, revealing a light frost under the vines. I dressed quickly, jogged downstairs and made a cup of tea while peering through the kitchen window at the glimmering dawn.

Outside, the oak door banged shut behind me, rousing a host of rooks from the horse chestnuts. The cold air caught my throat, and when I coughed the flapping hag-like birds seemed to mimic me with their calls. I hurried across the gravel and into the vineyard. As I walked, the rising sun cut through the mist, casting long shadows of the naked vines and the briskly moving shapes of my limbs. Dawn's sunlight warmed my left cheek as I gazed at the vine rows that covered the valley below me – an enchanting vista, but one that no longer inspired my soul which was as lifeless as the sleeping vines. My sullen mood improved when I found the old maximum-minimum thermometer nailed to a wooden picket. The gauge had not fallen below zero.

The calendar and the weather dictate my days. What with the warm sun, a perfect blue sky flecked with wispy cirrus clouds, and little to do in the winery, I decided to spend the morning training the vines. The *palissage* is one of my least favourite jobs; the annual task of maintaining the wooden posts that support the vine rows and tying the budding plants to their steel wires is tedious, repetitive work. After checking and tying a dozen rows my mood, in spite of the sunshine, had descended again. Thoughts, as they often do, carried me back to the past, to the people who once shared this work with me.

I thought of my father-in-law, Henri, planting these vines over forty years ago. I thought of the slow-turning cycle of the winemaker's year and the rare changes that it brought us, always unexpectedly. I thought about Olivier, Henri's only child, who grew up here, met an English girl, fell in love and married. Then I remembered the dashed hopes of the Valeix family who dreamt of financial success and the arrival of children to carry on the family winemaking tradition. But in our lives, providence was an infrequent visitor and calamities always came in threes. First, we suffered three disastrous harvests. The trio of exhausting bouts of ill health that followed (a broken ankle, a case of shingles and, to top it all, my depressive episode) only strengthened my determination to have children. But after my third miscarriage, Olivier, my beautiful Olivier, was killed.

The accident gave us no time to resolve the past or consider a future. An ellipsis, rather than a full stop, ended the story of our shared lives. Olivier's father and I mourned our loss together for over a year until he, too, passed away. The doctors said that his heart wasn't strong enough to cope with the extra effort of doing his son's work. But even at seventy-four, Henri was as strong as a Bazadaise bull. I know that he died of a broken heart, not a weak one. Without warning, I was left in sole charge of Henri Valeix Père & Fils, a company that had neither *père* nor *fils* to justify its name. Now, ten years later, I was still alone: a forty-three-year-old widow with a Saint-Emilion vineyard that struggled to sell its wines. I wondered, as I often did in my darker moments, when the third death would strike. These things always come in threes, like the chimes of the angelus that rang clearly over the empty valley to announce midday. I walked back to the house, then cycled up the hill to the village to buy bread.

I made my lunch at the kitchen table in a silence broken only by the distant yapping of a dog and the slow, deep ticking of the grandfather clock. I ate with the appetite of a vine worker. Between mouthfuls of crusty baguette, spread thickly with pork rillettes and a little mustard, I slaked my thirst with a glass of the recently bottled 2006 – a half-finished leftover from the previous day. After the food and the red wine, I felt drowsy and collapsed in the armchair by the cold grate of the fireplace, dozing until the clattering sound of the Bergerac train woke me at just after two o'clock. I could still hear the barking dog when I returned to the vineyard to continue the Sisyphean task of training vines.

A placid heat, that warmed the ground and stirred the earthy aroma of the vine roots, had replaced the cool of the morning. White contrail lines, undisturbed by the calm weather, scarred the clear blue sky. It was a truly beautiful spring afternoon, but one whose beauty hid behind my own scarred psyche. I worked quickly. By four o'clock, I'd completed the parcel of land I'd begun in the morning; by five, I was half way through the next one. I straightened my aching back, dried my face with a handkerchief and surveyed the completed vine rows. Across the field, beyond the small line of bushes bisecting it, I saw a white vehicle parked on one of the dirt tracks that crisscross the vineyard. Taking up my small bag of tools, I went to see who this unexpected visitor was.

If his Panama hat and the Jack Russell terrier that capered at his feet hinted at the man's nationality, then the GB sticker on the back of the camper van confirmed it. My father-in-law, when he saw a British car, often remarked that the English had returned to avenge their loss of the battle of Castillon and the Hundred Years' War. It always amused me to think of the middle-aged occupants of these vehicles dressed as medieval yeomen, sharpening pikes or stringing their longbows. This one didn't look much like a noble knight, so I decided not to tell him I was English.

'*Bonjour, monsieur,*' I said, feeling a tiny pang of guilt about pretending to be French.

The man crouched next to a thermos stove, attending to a boiling coffeepot that hissed and spluttered. He stood up slowly and replied to my greeting.

'*Ah, bonjour, ah, madame . . .*' he said, seemingly unable to recall sufficient schoolboy French to complete his sentence. He looked at his feet, his dog, the stove, but not at me.

Trying to catch the man's eye, I asked, '*Vous êtes anglais, monsieur?*'

'Er, *non, madame, je suis . . .* Scottish!' he responded, looking at me for the first time with a faux insulted expression.

'Oh, I'm sorry,' I said.

Before I realised that I'd given away my own nationality, I saw his face brighten and his hand extend towards me.

'Ah, but clearly *you're* English!' he said, seemingly delighted to have met someone with whom he shared a common language.

He stepped forward to introduce himself, but as he approached me he knocked his shin on the coffeepot which tumbled to the grassy floor along with the stove. In the embarrassed, fumbling seconds that followed, his hat came off to reveal the balding top of his otherwise hirsute head, the dog chased its tail in circles yapping louder than before, and the gas flame set fire to the brim of the Panama which he extinguished with slaps and expletives.

Once the kerfuffle was over, he proffered his hand, his face beaming with almost idiotic enthusiasm. I noticed his emerald-green eyes and his strong, dark features. He had a friendly, handsome face.

We shook hands.

'Andrew Maconie,' he said. 'I'm sorry if my dog was bothering you.'

'No, not at all,' I found myself saying, adding, 'I'm Jeanne, Jeanne Valeix. I was just about to tell you to go and find the municipal campsite.'

'Oh, I'm sorry,' he said again, 'I didn't realise I was trespassing. Perhaps I could get permission from the owner?'

He glanced down at my muddy boots, my scruffy jeans and frayed work shirt. When he flashed me a smile, the possibility that he liked what he saw came to me as a surprise.

I said, 'I am the owner. If you'd like to camp here you'll have to ask me,' then in a friendlier tone, 'and you'll have to buy some wine, too.'

'Well, I'd be delighted! If you let me stay I'll certainly buy some of your wine.' He paused, as though making sure I was listening. 'And perhaps you and your husband would let me pay you for the inconvenience?'

My response was curt. 'That won't be necessary. I'm a widow, Mr Maconie,' I said, cross at myself for dropping my guard but relieved that I'd corrected his misapprehension.

'Oh, excuse me,' he muttered, abashed. 'Look, let me at least offer you a cup of coffee. It won't take long to brew another pot.'

'Not if you're going to taste our wines before you buy some,' I said – coffee destroys the palate, so it's the worst thing to drink before a wine tasting.

I turned to go back to my work, grinning like a fool.

'Come up to the house whenever you're free,' I shouted over my shoulder as I ambled off, concealing the shame of my reddening face.

I showered quickly, dressed and lingered longer than usual at my dressing table with its cold mirror and scattered collection of cosmetics. Regarding my reflection, I saw a woman who looked ten years older than I felt. Sadness had begun to etch its creases and lines in all the wrong places. The grey hair appearing at my temples conspired with the crow's feet scratching at my eyes, and my complexion had changed from rosy to ruddy after twenty years of exposure to Atlantic winds and scorching summer sunshine. Often, when I was a child – as my mother never tired of telling me – awe-struck strangers would comment on the beauty of my hazel eyes. But now, the windows to my soul were veiled by the cruel shadows of mourning.

Managing four hectares of vines though had kept me fit. And, never having experienced the physically deleterious effects of motherhood, I'd always kept in pretty good shape. I applied my makeup, amazed at the rejuvenating power of foundation, mascara and lipstick, and found my train of thought taking me along an unfamiliar branch line. What if I did have a future? What if there was someone out there for me? Not the mysterious Scotsman in the camper van, perhaps, but someone nonetheless. I'd certainly caught Andrew's attention. Could I consider the possibility that I still looked good for forty-three? Again, my musings had got the better of me, but at least this time they came to me as a daydream rather than a waking nightmare. I consoled myself that at least a charming man had noticed me. Better to be looked-over than overlooked, I thought. The bell in the courtyard rang three times. Harbouring a feeling of apprehension, I hurried downstairs to greet my visitor.

Andrew stood by the cellar door, still wearing the broad smile and the Panama. I noticed the glint of a gold premolar that did nothing to diminish his rather conspicuous, rakish charm. The terrier was on a leash now, tied to one of the rusty iron hoops set into the wall.

'Don't mind old Turk—' Andrew began, but I interrupted him and said that the dog was welcome in if he was a competent ratter (our old cellars are a haven for rodents). 'Hear that, Turk? Our favourites – wine for me and rats for you!'

Fearing that my guest was about to burst into a rendition of *My Favourite Things*, I quickly unlocked the ancient door and stood aside to let him in.

'Well, this is marvellous, Jeanne,' he began. 'Is this your tasting room?'

'Yes,' I replied, 'although really it's what we call the caveau – a sort of wine cellar-cum-shop for our private buyers.' Then, instantly regretting my affected airs, I added, 'We have a formal tasting salon in the château as well.'

'The château?' Andrew quizzed.

I backtracked. 'Yes, but it's not exactly a stately home or a moated castle.'

'Okay,' he said with a shrug, and began to examine the label on one of the many bottles that I'd left untidily on the tasting table. 'And who's *we*?'

'Oh, me and the staff,' I lied, taking the bottle from him. I rely on a few people to help with the house, the garden and the winery, but I can no longer afford a permanent team. 'Anyway, most Bordeaux wine properties tag the word *château* to their names,' I said, moving the conversation away from my personal situation. 'Even the most humble shack can be called a château.'

'I'd hardly call this place a humble shack,' he said, eyeing the grand limestone façade of the house through the open door.

'No, it's very comfortable. I'm terribly lucky,' I lied, again. 'Now, let's see if you like my wine.'

I wasn't surprised when Andrew enthused so much during the tasting. He was too polite not to and was, I thought, genuinely impressed by my wines. He liked the spice of the 2007, drawn from the barrel; he appreciated the subtlety of the 2006; and he adored the 2005's concentration and fruit. Despite describing himself as a wine philistine, he seemed to have a remarkably adept palate and didn't dribble too much when using the spittoon. He bought a couple of half cases and settled up in cash. Of course, every winemaker likes a paying client, but during our conversation, between the slurping and sipping at the tasting bar, I'd grown particularly fond of Andrew. Our chat had begun with the inevitable question.

'So how did a young Englishwoman come to own a vineyard in France?'

I gave Andrew my oft-told potted history, omitting the tragic childless widow theme that concludes the story. 'I came here, after getting my degree, to work during the harvest,' I began. 'My husband's father owned Fontloube then. I was seduced by the place and fell in love with Olivier. I went back to England to start my Law Society Finals, but I soon decided to come back here and become the wife of a *viticulteur*. My first vintage was 1987 – not a great year, as it turned out.'

Next came the usual follow-ups.

'And how was it for you, integrating into French life? You speak such good French – was it hard to learn?'

British people always want to know these things. Sometimes I suspect they want to hear tales of terrific struggle and ultimate regret, to justify their settled but boring suburban lives – like asking someone with a tattoo if the needles hurt or enquiring of a celebrity if they hate being recognised in the street. But the rich and famous enjoy their fame and fortune, the tattooed enjoy their body art and ex-pats here, despite the challenges, love living in France – even me, and I do have a sad story to tell.

'I married into this life,' I told him. 'I got a French surname and even changed my given name. I'm really called Jean, but it's a boy's name here in France. It confuses people. The authorities couldn't work out why my husband wanted to marry a man. So I became Jeanne Valeix and soon learned to speak French in a house where no one spoke English. Anyway, that's me. What about you, Andrew? What's your story?'

'Oh, my story's quite ordinary compared to yours,' he said, eyeing me over the rim of his tasting glass. He took a small sip and hesitated. I couldn't decide whether he was contemplating the flavour of the wine or concocting his story which, after spitting into the *crachoir*, he began.

'I'm, oh, in my fifties, let's say. I grew up in Dumfries and Galloway, studied English at Edinburgh, became a local journalist, did some freelance work for The Scotsman, you know, did some teaching.'

'And then?' I asked, pouring him a measure of the '06.

'Then,' he paused and sniffed. 'Mmm, that's good. Then I married, got some of my poetry published, had a couple of kids, you know, the usual stuff.'

'A poet? I'm impressed,' I enthused. 'Would I have read any of your work?'

'Not unless you've looked very, very hard for it. I'm what's known as one of Scotland's lesser-known poets.'

I decided not to admit to my love of poetry and literature and changed the subject.

'Okay, so what brings you to France then?'

'Well, poetry actually – or rather, the lack of it. You see, since my divorce last year I've had – well, we've all had – a rather rough time. I'm suffering from the proverbial writer's block.'

'And you've come to the French countryside to find your muse,' I said, not too cynically, I hoped.

'Aye, that's it,' he said, accepting another glug of wine and raising the glass as if to make a toast. 'O for a beaker full of the warm South,' he intoned, 'full of the true, the blushful Hippocrene, with beaded bubbles winking at the brim, and purple-stained mouth.'

I humoured him. 'Bravo, Andrew. One of yours?'

'No, John Keats. But I'd give a barrelful of the blushful Hippocrene for a sip of his talent, though.'

'Oh, well,' I said, trying to sound sympathetic, 'see if a sip of the 2005 inspires you, and tell me more about your children.'

'Thanks. Well, it's been tough over the last year or so,

see. Talking about my kids makes me maudlin, I'm afraid. Do you mind if we don't?'

'No, of course not,' I said, sensing the man's mood changing. 'As long as you don't mind me not telling you about how I lost my husband.'

'Oh God,' he said apologetically, 'No, not at all. I'm sorry.'

'Don't worry about it, Andrew. So, which one did you want to buy?'

I handed Andrew his purchases at the door and said goodbye. I was fumbling with the keys when, from half way across the court, he called out, 'Oh, by the way, my dad was like you, you know.'

'What do you mean?' I said, locking the door. He walked the few paces back to the caveau and put the boxes down on the cobbled path.

'He moved countries and changed his name, I mean. He was an internee during the war. When it ended, he changed his name from Marconni to Maconie to make himself sound more Scottish.'

'Really,' I said, curious, 'and is your mother Italian, too?'

'No, she was Irish. But she was an immigrant, too, I suppose.'

'Ah, that's where you get those lovely green eyes from then,' I said, smiling.

'Aye and this is my dad's Roman nose I've got roamin' all over my face!'

'Goodnight, Andrew,' I said, trying not to laugh.

'G'night to you, too, Jeanne. But . . . it's a pity we can't carry on our chat over dinner. Are you free?'

The invitation came as such a shock that I declined by saying, too flatly, 'No, Andrew, I can't.' I made a mental note not to berate myself for this hasty refusal but foresaw a sleepless night of self-loathing ahead.

'Och, never mind,' he said. 'You've still got to let me pay you back for letting me camp though.'

14

'How are you at *palissage*, Andrew?' I asked.

He looked at me blankly.

Without waiting for him to say he didn't know what it was, I said, 'Well, meet me in the vineyard on the other side of the hedgerow at eight tomorrow morning, and we'll find out.'

With that, I returned to the house leaving the man standing in the courtyard with his wine and his little dog.

The following day began, like its predecessor, with a hard frost. Although most of the budding vine shoots would survive such a chill, experience told me that some of the tightly packed buds would have frozen and that, even this early in the growing season, the weather was already reducing my grape crop. To mitigate the frost, wealthy vine growers employ teams of workers to light fires at the ends of the vine rows, and some super-rich *vignerons* even fly helicopters over their vineyards to circulate the air and dispel the deadly chill. But, as with so many other things, blind chance would determine the health of my vines this year – and the quality and quantity of the harvest.

Having paid more attention to my work attire that morning, I strolled into the lower field wearing my best-fitting jeans and a soft cotton shirt that showed a hint of décolletage. I'd tied-up my unruly hair and applied just a touch of makeup. My evil gremlin whispered that such vanity would be punished – I'd reach the vineyard and find that the white camper van had gone – but, as I neared the line of bushes, I heard the dog's now familiar bark and saw Andrew emerge from behind the hedgerow.

'Good morning!' he called across the vine rows, sounding far chirpier than I felt.

'Hello,' I replied. 'You ready to learn about the glamorous side of winemaking, then?'

'Well, whatever it is, I'm sure it'll be a pleasure to do with you.'

'Creep!' I declared. 'Don't expect me to go easy on you just for your flattery.'

We met in the middle of the row I'd half finished the day before. Handing him a pair of gloves and some pliers, I said, 'Take these – you'll find a heavy hammer at the end of the row there. Don't cut off any fingers or crush any thumbs.'

'Yes, Miss!'

For a poet, Andrew learned quickly how to mend the broken pickets, tension the wires and tie the vine shoots to their trellises. We worked together all morning which, like the day before, turned out to be sunny and mild. It felt good sharing the work with someone, though I had to quell any romantic or adventurous thoughts about how this burgeoning friendship might develop. We chatted about vine growing and winemaking. I tried not to sound too despondent about my work, but I certainly dispelled his assumption that all Saint-Emilion winemakers were rich. He also learned that some jobs were far less enjoyable than giving wine tastings. Incredibly he managed to hit both his thumbs with the mallet (later, when he'd stopped moaning and keening, he managed to joke about his clumsiness. 'To hit one thumb with a hammer might be regarded as a misfortune,' he quipped, 'but to hit both looks like carelessness.').

By noon, we'd finished the field and made a decent start on the parcel where the van was parked. I invited my worker up to the house for lunch and set him the task of making some coffee while I drove to the boulangerie in Clémentine – my beloved tangerine-coloured 2CV – to buy the bread.

'Here we are,' I announced, returning with a crusty loaf and a thick slice of pâté de campagne.

We ate in an easy silence, punctuated by the occasional remark from Andrew who, apparently, had never tasted fresher bread or richer pâté. Turk the dog curled up quietly under the kitchen table, and after I'd poured the coffee, I allowed myself to give him a few scraps from my plate and a scratch on the back.

'Do you ever think about what you'll do next, Jeanne?' asked Andrew, apropos of our earlier conversation.

'You mean will I stay here running this place forever?'

'Aye, that sort of thing. You're still young and . . .' – young and what?, I wondered – '. . . I mean, after what you were telling me about how hard the wine business is, have you considered sharing this place with someone, expanding the operation, marketing your wine overseas?'

'Viticulteur, therapist and marketeer – is there no end to your talents?' I joked, avoiding the thorny subject of my future.

'Yes,' he said, glancing down at his half-empty cup, 'I make a lousy cup of coffee.'

'You didn't put enough water in the percolator.'

'I guess I've got a long way to go before I can call myself a winemaker, then,' he said, with a gold-toothed grin.

'Yes,' I said, examining my own empty cup, 'but you're making a good start.'

The frosty weather at the start of the month gave way to a warmer, more humid April. Realising that my permanent team consisted of just one overworked Englishwoman, Andrew offered to stay on, sleeping in his camper van at night and helping me with the vineyard work and a little gardening during the day. Gradually, we learned more about each other. I told him the sad details of how I lost my husband; he told me about his failed marriage. During the acrimonious break-up that led to his recent divorce, his son and daughter had turned against him, siding with their mother. I insisted that he let the children know where he was staying, and after some nagging, he agreed to send a postcard to his son, Archie. We became easy workmates and close friends over the following days. In the vineyard, he continued to play the schoolboy, responding with an eager 'Yes, Miss!' to my instructions. He soon started calling me Miss Jean, and when we discovered a shared love of the film *The Prime of Miss Jean Brodie*, I began addressing him as Mr Lowther in my best Morningside brogue. Whenever the subject of our ages came up we would look at each other and exclaim 'I am truly in my prime!'. I enjoyed having someone at the château and soon saw what a positive difference a full-time handyman made. The vines were in good order, now revealing their soft, pale unfurling leaves, the vat rooms and cellars were shipshape, and the lawns that flank the gravel drive to the house were cut.

In view of how well things had worked out with Andrew, I considered taking on a student apprentice and contacted the director of the viticultural school in Libourne. I doubted, however, that they would send me anyone as agreeable to work with as Andrew.

By the end of the month, we had settled into a comfortable routine. Every day after breakfast, we would work in the fields or in the winery. At noon we'd have lunch together in my kitchen. We'd go our separate ways in the afternoons, when Andrew would take the 2CV and explore the Bordeaux countryside, or keep himself busy at his camp, reading his books and (I hoped) writing again. When the swallows returned, reeling and swooping over and through the vines, I realised that three weeks had passed since Andrew's arrival.

One day, after lunch, when Andrew had poured the coffee, he passed me a large manila envelope addressed from the University of Bordeaux.

'This came for you in the post while you were at the bakery,' he said, eyeing the postmark. 'Looks like something from that wine college.'

'Nosy!' I scolded, snatching it from him. I opened the envelope and found the information that I'd requested from the University: a prospectus from the Faculty of Oenology in Libourne and a leaflet about student work placements.

'Where's the *crème*, Miss Jean?' he asked, feeding me a

line.

'The *crème de la crème*, Mr Lowther?' I teased. 'I'll fetch some from the refrigerator.'

I went over to the fridge, idly browsing the brochure, then returned to the table to pour Andrew's customary splash of cream. I handed him the prospectus. 'It's about the student placement scheme from the oenology school.'

'That's great,' he said, putting on his reading glasses.

'It works quite well for us winemakers. The students work part-time for a modest rate of pay, but they get valuable work experience, and bed and board, into the bargain.'

'Sounds terrific, how do I enrol?'

'You can't, I'm afraid.'

'Too old, eh?' Andrew asked, looking at the pictures of fresh-faced students on the cover of the booklet.

'Why, not at all, Mr Lowther, you are truly in your prime!' I corrected him, taking back the papers. 'But you have to speak, read and write French. And you have to have your baccalaureate. So that counts you out. Sorry.'

'Oh, well, it was just a thought,' he said resignedly, 'although my son would be okay – he's studying for an international baccalaureate in England.' He settled back to finish his coffee and, I hoped, tell me more about his son. Before he could continue though, the phone rang in the study.

I went next door and picked up the receiver. The young woman on the line introduced herself as Aimée Gonzalès and asked, in an educated Parisian accent, to speak to Madame Valeix.

'*Oui, c'est moi,*' I responded.

'*Ah, bonjour, madame,*' she continued, adding that she was calling from Libourne and wanted to talk to me.

I glanced at the prospectus in my hand and made the connection with my caller.

'*Ah bonjour, Mademoiselle,*' I said, then asked if she was calling about the student placement at the winery. She began to say something but was interrupted by a noisy click that sounded like the handset falling on a hard surface.

'*Ah, oui, Madame Valeix,*' she resumed, 'that is right, I'm calling about the placement.'

Her command of English impressed me.

'Okay, Mademoiselle . . .?'

'Gonzalès.'

'Mademoiselle Gonzalès. So, one of your *professeurs* told you about the English winemaker who had a vacancy, eh?'

'*Ah, oui, madame.* My *prof* told me that you might be looking for someone. I am sorry to have called you like this, how you say – unannounced?'

A confident girl, I thought. 'No, not at all. I admire your initiative. Would you be free to come and see me here at the château?'

'It would be a pleasure, madame,' she said pleasantly. 'I am free this afternoon if that is convenient for you.'

Bilingual, confident *and* polite – I wasn't going to let this one go. 'Yes, that would be fine. What time can you come?'

'Ah, *désolée*, madame, but I do not have a car,' she said, sounding crestfallen. 'Is there perhaps someone there who could come and collect me?'

'Okay, er, Aimée is it? We'll pick you up at four o'clock if that's alright?'

'Perfect,' she replied, 'At the railway station – it will be easier for you to park there.'

'At the station at four then.'

'*Merci, Madame Valeix. À tout à l'heure.*'

The line clicked dead. I hung up, realising too late that I had no idea how Aimée Gonzalès and I would recognise each other. Never mind, I reflected, let's hope there's nobody else waiting at the station.

I went back into the kitchen. 'Fancy a drive?' I suggested. The dog emerged from under the table wagging his stumpy tail. 'Okay then, Turk, let's go.'

'Can I come, too?' pleaded Andrew.

'What do you think?' I said, directing the question at the little dog who replied with an enthusiastic woof.

'Oh, alright then, Andrew, you can come, too,' I agreed. I walked out into the bright courtyard followed by a confused-looking man and a happy dog.

We went along the D670 towards Libourne with the limestone *côte* on our right and the plain of the Dordogne to our left. As usual Andrew asked me to point out the famous *cru classé* properties we passed en route – La Gaffelière, Magdelaine, Ausone ... After a few more kilometres we reached the outskirts of the town. The road took us over the railway bridge and brought us to the station, which jostled with a colourful, noisy crowd of students on their way home for the long May bank holiday weekend. I found the last remaining space in the car park. As the three of us made our way to the busy ticket office, I wondered again how Aimée and I would identify each other. I thought of making an improvised sign with her name on it, but just as I was about to ask the ticket clerk for a piece of paper, I heard a voice I recognised behind me.

'Bonjour, Madame Valeix?'

It was Aimée. I turned round to see her standing a couple of metres away holding a mobile telephone and a packet of cigarettes. 'I am sorry, madame,' she said, 'I went to buy cigarettes. Have you been waiting long?'

Andrew and I looked at the girl.

Her beauty was astounding. Boyish, cropped blonde hair framed an innocent, elfin face; but the exquisite, chocolate-coloured eyes that belied her spiky platinum locks gave her an assertive, penetrating gaze. Her look was one of contrasts: fire and ice, coffee and cream, darkness and light. She was small (I suppose *petite* is the word) with the legs of a dancer and a cheerleader's pertness. I glanced at Andrew. Her physical beauty had not escaped him, either. A stubbly chin betrayed his wonder and amazement at our pretty young visitor. He actually gaped. It's funny, but in that jaw-dropping moment, I realised that I wanted him.

Love

Wine comes in at the mouth
And love comes in at the eye;
That's all we shall know for truth
Before we grow old and die.
   - William Butler Yeats, *A Drinking Song*

'*Bonjour, Mademoiselle Gonzalès,*' I said, holding out my hand to greet her. '*Enchantée.*'

We shook hands. 'Pleased to meet you, Madame Valeix . . . and Monsieur Valeix?'

She turned to Andrew who, staring at her, seemed unable to correct the misunderstanding.

I saved him the trouble of explaining. 'This is my friend, Andrew Maconie,' I said, 'and that's his dog, Turk.'

'Pleased to meet you, Mr Maconie. I'm sorry but I thought you were—'

'I'm not married,' I interjected. 'My husband . . . well, I live alone now.'

'Oh, I see,' she said glancing between Andrew and me.

Breaking a slightly embarrassed silence, I asked, 'How *did* you recognise me, Aimée?'

'You look *so British*, madame,' she said, giving the *R* a Gallic roll. 'You really stand up in a crowd.'

'Stand *out*, I think you mean,' I said.

We both laughed at her charming slip-up.

'Yes, indeed, madame,' she giggled, 'I am afraid that my English is not so good as it should be.'

'Please, Aimée,' I said, 'call me Jeanne. And your English is impeccable.'

'Thank you, Jeanne, you are too kind.'

As we made our way towards the exit, I realised that Andrew still hadn't spoken a word. 'Come on, Andrew,' I nagged, 'say hello.'

As if distracted from a daydream, Andrew looked at Aimée and said, 'Oh, I'm sorry. Please to meet you, Miss . . . Gonzalès.'

We exited the concourse and walked over to where I'd parked the jeep, with Turk trotting behind us.

Andrew offered the passenger seat to Aimée on the return trip and sat silently in the back of the jeep with the dog. My student was a chatty passenger. I soon got to know about her background and her reasons for choosing Libourne as a place to study. She said that she belonged to a wealthy Parisian family. After studying for an accountancy degree for two trimesters she'd tired of the subject and decided to transfer to a course on viticulture and oenology. Bordeaux University was her first choice. With good academic qualifications (and, I supposed, influential family contacts) she was able to join her new faculty halfway through the year.

'I have been staying with a friend since the start of term,' she explained. 'It is only a small apartment, very cramped. I was looking for accommodation when my *professeur* told me about you.'

'Well I'm glad he did, Aimée,' I reassured her. 'If everything works out there's a room at the château for you – I'll be glad of the company.'

She turned to me and said, 'Yes, that would great,' adding, a little louder, 'and where do *you* live, Mr Maconie?'

I saw Andrew, in my rear-view mirror, lean forward to make himself heard. 'I live in the vineyard,' he said.

'Oh, how romantic, Mr Maconie,' Aimée enthused, 'do you have a little cabin in the vines?'

'Andrew has a very comfortable camper van, Aimée,' I informed her.

'A van? Oh, I see, you mean a *camping car*. Yes, that

must be very convivial, living there alone with your little dog. And what do you do, Mr Maconie?'

'He's a poet,' I said.

We left the town behind. As we cruised into the gorgeous Libournais countryside, Turk let out a low growl.

When we arrived at the château, Andrew complained of feeling unwell and went to his camper van to take a couple of aspirins. I imagined that he'd spend the evening alone and, for the moment, I was right. It suited me to have Aimée to myself. We started the tour of the property by taking a pleasant walk through the vineyards, courteously avoiding Andrew's camp. She listened with interest to my descriptions of the work we'd been doing in the vines and asked pertinent questions about viticulture. Then I showed her the winery: the vat house with its mostly empty *cuves*; the barrel cellar full of last year's vintage, maturing in oak casks; and the storeroom, chock-a-block with unsold wine. We finished the tour in the caveau, sat at the tasting bar and filled out the form I'd received from the faculty.

I took Aimée's details and went through the list of tedious bureaucratic questions on the form.

'So, I suppose these papers just need to be co-signed by the college. . .' I said, on reaching the end of the questionnaire.

'Great,' Aimée said, sounding as relieved as I was to have finished the paperwork. 'I can also give you references from a couple of Paris accounting firms where I did some work experience, if that would be useful.'

'Thanks, Aimée. Yes, that'd be good.'

'So, do I get the job?'

Was she joking? I span the form round on the countertop, passed her the pen and said with a smile, 'Just sign here.'

I watched her scribble her signature and thought: aha, a nail biter – well, nobody's perfect. I put the signed form in an envelope and searched through the other papers for the faculty's address.

'Now,' I said, 'if I can just find the address . . . Oh, I must have left the letter in the study. Never mind, I've missed today's post now anyway.'

'I can drop the papers in on Monday, if you like,' Aimée suggested, 'and save you the cost of a stamp.'

'Aimée, I do believe you're still an accountant at heart.'

'Yes, I suppose I am still, how do you say, a bean counter. I can use spreadsheets, sales and purchase ledgers, accounting software . . . I would be happy to do some of this sort of work, too, if it would help you.'

'Aimée, I'm beginning to think that you're a real godsend.'

'Well,' she said getting up from the stool, 'I was named after a saint.'

'So was I, I suppose,' I sighed, handing her the letter, 'in a way.'

When we came out into the courtyard, Turk the dog trotted up to us followed by Andrew whose previously subdued mood had lightened.

'Hello there, you two,' he called cheerily. 'Is it *apéro* time yet?'

Andrew had soon adopted the French habit of taking a pick-me-up at about six-thirty. In fact, the occasional aperitif was the only social activity we'd shared in the evenings. I was pleased that he wanted to be sociable and invited him and Aimée into the house for a glass of wine.

I handed Andrew a bottle of sauvignon blanc and a corkscrew, then went to the larder to fetch some *saucisson*, a jar of garlic-infused extra-virgin olive oil and the unfinished bread from lunchtime. He poured three glasses of wine while I cut the baguette into thin slices. 'Here's to our new arrival,' Andrew said, raising his glass.

'Yes, welcome to Fontloube, Aimée,' I toasted. 'Here's to friendship and success in your studies.'

We chinked glasses and drank, and Aimée thanked us for welcoming her.

The charcuterie piqued my appetite, so I decided to

invite my guests to stay and eat. I hadn't entertained anyone for months, but I managed to concoct what I hoped was a respectable supper from the groceries in the store cupboard. Aimée went to use the phone to tell her friend not to expect her for dinner, while Andrew opened another bottle of wine.

Supper was a success. Conversing in French and English, we chatted, laughed and joked – mostly at Andrew's expense. Framed by the stone mullions of the kitchen window, the pink sunset faded to a dark, moonless night.

A third bottle followed.

Our young guest gave us a fascinating account of her immediate family, aristocratic relatives, and exotic upbringing. Her father, she told us, was a high-ranking civil servant in the French government. Her mother, once a beautiful debutante and now a Parisian socialite, had inherited her wealth. After attending posh boarding schools in Switzerland and Provence, Aimée had begun her higher education at an élite *grande école* in Paris.

'So how did you end up here in Libourne then, Aimée?' Andrew asked, pouring her some of my 1995.

'Well,' she began, taking a sip before continuing, 'I found my degree so tedious, the freedom of Paris so exhilarating, that I am afraid that I spent too much time partying for my father's liking.'

'Ah, a bit of a wild child then?' Andrew insinuated.

'Yes,' she responded quietly, 'but since being punished I have learned my lesson.'

'Punished?' I asked, suddenly concerned.

'Well, with the other stuff that was going on, my parents chose to withdraw my allowance, send me away from Paris and stop me from seeing my sister until I can prove that I have changed.' She finished the sentence in a near whisper. Two tears, which had formed on her lower eyelids, fell to the white linen tablecloth.

I couldn't imagine what she had done to merit such tough sanctions.

'It all seems a bit harsh to me, Aimée,' Andrew was the first to say. 'What did you do exactly?'

'I had a brief affair with one of my father's political adversaries, and we were photographed by a paparazzo – at a fundraising event organised by my mother.'

'Photographed?' I asked.

'Yes, we were in the WC,' she said, pronouncing it the French way, *vay-say*, 'you know, in an embrace?'

'Well,' I said, after an awkward pause, 'did your lover accept any responsibility?'

'No, she is the deputy minister for Foreign Affairs. The whole thing was hushed up, and Papa had to pay for the pictures.'

During the cheese course, the conversation moved on to more commonplace matters. When the coffee had been served, Andrew rose from the table and offered to take Aimée back to Libourne. But in view of the amount of wine we'd consumed, I told him flatly not to drive and invited our guest to stay the night. I showed Aimée to a spare room on the first floor, brought her a towel and fresh bedding, and said goodnight. Before retiring, I went downstairs to find Andrew diligently washing the dishes.

'Well, what an incredible story that was,' I said, referring to Aimée's confession.

'Incredible indeed,' Andrew agreed, although his tone was far less sincere that mine.

'What is it, Andrew?' I asked. 'You've been funny about Aimée ever since we met her this morning.'

'Funny?'

'Yes, funny.'

He looked down into the suds and carried on scrubbing. 'Oh, I don't know, Jean. I'm just not sure about her. You said it yourself, we only just met her this morning, and now she's a full-time employee, living in your house.'

I was cross, partly with myself I suppose. 'First of all, Andrew, just who works and lives here is my business. Secondly, Aimée will be here on a part-time basis with the co-operation of her college. And third, she has references, which I intend to take up. Okay?'

'Is this, like, our first row, Jean?' he said, grinning at me.

'No, not at all,' I said, calming down. 'It's just that you don't seem to want to give her a chance. But after all she's been through, I do.'

'I know, just be careful, that's all I mean.'

'I will, Andrew. And you, too; she could be a seductress.'

'It sounds like you should be the one to watch out,' he said, eyebrows raised, 'I'd lock the door tonight if I were you.'

'Don't be silly,' I said. 'And anyway, she's not my type.'

'No, she's not mine either. Don't go for teenagers. I'm old enough to be her grandfather.'

'Technically, yes, but don't do yourself down,' I told him. 'She's nearly twenty, which makes you only thirty-eight years older than she is. I'd say you were old enough to be her dad.'

'Thanks for the compliment,' he said, drying his hands on a tea towel.

'So what *is* your type then, Andrew?'

'Oh, you know, feminine, pretty . . . curvaceous.'

'A bonnie buxom lassie, then?' I teased.

'If you like,' he agreed.

'You mean like . . .' I tried to recall the name of a Scottish actress I thought fitted the bill, but Andrew cut in.

'I mean like you, Jean,' he said, looking at me.

'Och, get on with you Mr Lowther,' I joked. 'Away to your camper van! I can't be seen fraternising with the staff.'

'Aye, Jean, I'll say goodnight. But remember what I said, okay?'

'About Aimée?' I asked.

'. . . and the other thing, too,' he said. 'G'night then.' He planted a quick kiss on my cheek and strolled off into the courtyard with Turk trotting to heel.

That night was the first time I had the dream about the railway carriage. I dreamt that I was travelling by steam train in a foreign country. Masked intruders tried to break in through the window, but my brave little dog scared them away with his barking.

I woke late with a dry throat and a slight hangover. Aimée was in the kitchen brewing coffee when I came down.

'*Bonjour*, Jeanne,' she chirped. '*Bien dormi?*'

Yes, I reflected, I'd slept remarkably well. '*Oui Aimée,*' I replied. '*Et toi?*'

While she explained to me how she never slept easily in an unfamiliar bed, I noticed my wellingtons – wet, and caked in mud – standing on the doormat. 'The storm woke me,' she continued, 'and when the rain stopped, I stepped out for some fresh air. So much wine we drank last night! You should have seen the moon after the rain. It was a beautiful *croissant du lune.*'

'I see you also borrowed my boots,' I said. 'It's a pity we've no croissants for breakfast.'

'Don't move,' she told me, fixing me with her hypnotic brown eyes. 'I will go to the village and buy some.'

She rushed out through the door, then burst back in to snatch my car keys and ask, 'Shall I get some *pains au chocolat*, too?'

'Whatever you fancy, Aimée,' I replied distractedly, rummaging in the cupboard for painkillers. 'Do you need some money?' I called to her disappearing form as she flew out of the house, but she was gone. I heard the sound of the 2CV coughing itself into life, followed by the fading rasp of its engine as she drove off towards the village.

Aimée returned with a large paper bag of patisserie. We ate some of the pastries and chased them down with plenty of black coffee. When she apologised for the previous evening's frank revelations, I told her how much I admired her honesty. The painkillers, coffee and carbohydrates soon perked me up enough to drive my new recruit back to Libourne. We set off in the *deux chevaux* along traffic-free, May Day roads. When we arrived in the deserted town centre, I dropped her off outside a tall turn-of-the-century townhouse. We shook hands through the quirky flap in the car's passenger-side window. 'I'll see you on Monday then,' I shouted, raising my voice above the sound of Citroën's noisy motor.

'Yes, I can't wait,' Aimée called back. 'Have a good weekend – *au revoir!*'

'*A bientôt,*' I said, and promptly stalled the car's unpredictable engine. 'Oops!' I said, then cursed quietly to myself as I turned the ignition key. I made a U-turn in the street and saw Aimée, still standing on the pavement, waving me off, smiling.

I looked in on Andrew when I got back, half expecting him to be sleeping-off last night's excesses. But I found him sitting on a folding chair outside his camper van, reading a book called *The Nation's Favourite Poems*.

'Funny lot, poets,' he said, by way of a greeting. 'Mad, most of 'em.'

Unable to resist a taunt I said, 'Driven mad with writer's block perhaps?'

'Philip Larkin seems to blame his parents,' he volleyed back at me, rising from his seat and kissing me politely on each cheek.

'*This Be Verse,*' I said, pleased to have trumped him.

'I'm impressed. I didn't know you were a poetry reader.'

'Well, that's one poem I am familiar with,' I said, 'but not one that I'm particularly keen on.' While studying for my A-levels, I was thrilled to discover this poem with its infamous four-letter word. But when I re-read it after my first miscarriage, Larkin's cynical attack on the futility of child raising appalled me.

'No, indeed,' he said, looking down at the page. 'Anyway, what's on today's work rota?'

'The *binage*,' I announced, making an open-armed gesture at the vast spread of vines before us. Once again, my use of French received a blank look from Andrew. 'Prepare yourself,' I hinted, 'for a harrowing experience.'

'Sounds painful, Jean.'

'Only if you fall under the plough,' I called, striding off towards the winery. 'Come along and I'll show you how to drive the *enjambeur*.'

'The what?' he called, catching me up.

'The vineyard tractor,' I told him.

'Oh, goody!' he said, his expression changing rapidly from confused to delighted.

Andrew was thrilled at the prospect of driving the tall tractor-on-stilts we call the *enjambeur*. After regulating the blades of the harrow, I showed him how to navigate up and down the vine rows while turning the soil. He enjoyed driving this 'big boy's toy', as he called it. I, too, enjoy this job and marvel at how the harrow loosens and spreads the earth, banked up in winter to protect the vine roots, leaving a clean tract of freshly turned, weed-free soil behind it. I allowed Andrew to carry on with the rest of the field and stayed in the vines, checking the trellises.

We broke for lunch as usual at midday, just as a brisk wind from the east began chasing away the morning's mild weather. After lunch we returned to the tractor under an angry-looking, storm-laden sky. Andrew had only worked a couple of rows when the storm began with a flurry of sleety rain. I gestured to him to turn off the engine and get down from the cab. Hailstones began bouncing off the vines and settling in the newly ploughed spaces between the rows. I'd seen severe hail before and knew how destructive (and even painful) it can be, so I called out to Andrew, telling him to find some cover. We ran for the shelter of the camper van, which we reached just as a shower of much larger hail rained down noisily on its roof. Once inside, we sat on a sofa by the van's window and watched as chunks of ice, some as big as golf balls, began pounding my poor, delicate vines.

'I don't think I've ever seen hail like it,' Andrew exclaimed. 'I dread to think what it's doing to the vines.'

'I've seen worse,' I said, 'but at this time of year the plants will suffer very badly.'

'Can't we do anything?' he asked, staring at the cold, white carpet of hail outside.

I was despondent. 'No, hail is just one of those hazards you can't do anything about.'

There was nothing for it but to wait for the storm to pass before assessing the damage. Andrew put the kettle on for a warming cup of tea, and we shuffled out of our damp coats. I think he was keen to divert my attention from the hail-battered vines because, after passing me a steaming-hot cup of tea, he asked, 'So, changing the subject, what's the best wine you've ever tasted?'

'Well, wine's a very subjective thing,' I began, determined not to sound like a wine snob. 'Its taste depends on where you are, the company you're with, your mood—'

'Aye, but it also depends on whether the wine's any good, doesn't it?'

'Yes, Andrew, otherwise we wouldn't bother with all this,' I said looking out of the window. 'If pressed, I'd say that very little has compared to my first taste of Château Latour. Except . . .' I hesitated, recalling a distant, sweet memory.

'Except?'

'Oh, except nothing.'

'Go on,' Andrew goaded, 'except what?'

'Well, I suppose except my first taste of . . .'

'. . . what?'

'Love?'

'Now, this sounds interesting,' he said. 'But I thought we were talking about wine.'

'We are.'

'Ooh, do tell, Miss Jean.'

'Promise not to laugh?'

'Scout's honour,' he vowed.

'Well, I first came grape picking here in the autumn of '87. I worked with a mixed group of students, some friends of the Valeix clan and a team of itinerant vine workers. There was a great sense of camaraderie, lots of the usual leg-pulling and practical-joking you get during the harvest, and quite a bit of flirting ... One evening, after a few days of making eyes at each other, Olivier and I lingered in the vineyard. The others had gone back to the house for dinner, and we talked and laughed, and finished what was left of the *pinard* – the grape pickers' rough wine. He was beautiful and exciting and – I know it's a cliché – we made love in the vines. Well, that was over twenty years ago now, but I've never since tasted a wine quite like the one we drank together that evening.'

'Like Proust and his damned madeleines, eh?'

'Yes, I suppose so,' I said, returning from twenty years ago to the present and to Andrew's mesmeric smile.

'I don't know why you thought I'd laugh though, Jean. It's a lovely story.'

'Wait for it. When it was time to go back to the house, it was dark, and Olivier couldn't find his trousers. He tried to sneak back to his room, but the grape pickers spotted him in his boxer shorts – my goodness how they laughed! At first light they discovered his jeans, hanging from a trellis wire. When we arrived for work, they gave the two us a big round of applause.'

Andrew started to titter.

'You promised!' I said.

'I'm sorry, Jean,' he said, 'I can just picture your face.'

'You know,' I continued, starting to giggle, too, 'that the French for a pair of jeans is *un jean*? Poor Olivier suffered a constant barrage of mickey-taking. Which *jean* did he prefer? How many *jeans* did he have in his closet? And much worse – you can imagine. The badinage went on and on until the end of the harvest. He took it remarkably well, though. He was a lovely man.'

We both stopped laughing. I heaved a sigh that misted the window and made my eyes go misty, too.

'Come on, Andrew, cheer me up,' I suggested. 'Compose me a poem.'

'Let me see . . .' he said, thinking. 'How about this: they last not long, these days of wine and roses; as one door shuts, another one closes.'

'You horrible cynic,' I said, raising my voice and punching him playfully on the thigh. 'Call yourself a poet? You'll have to try a lot harder than that to cheer me up.'

'That hurt!' he said, rubbing his leg.

We sat in silence together, gazing at the vineyard.

'You don't really believe that do you?' I asked, referring his pessimistic rhyme.

'What? Oh, you mean the silly poem. No, of course not.'

'Well it seemed pretty accurate to me,' I said.

'Don't say that, Jean. You've got a lot going for you.'

'So you think I should count my blessings then?'

'I'd never say that to you, Jean. I know what you've been through. It's just that sometimes I think we don't recognise happiness when it comes along, see?'

'Okay Aristotle, what's the answer then?'

'I don't know. It's not easy. Perhaps, because sorrow is such a powerful emotion, when you've experienced it it's difficult to feel happy again. Like pleasure and pain, you know; how pain is a much stronger sensation than pleasure.'

'Like your squashed thumbs the other week,' I teased.

'Yes, that's right. If you break your left leg, you don't sit around thinking about how pleasant your right leg feels, do you? See, I think that if pleasure is the absence of pain then maybe happiness is just saying goodbye to your sorrows.'

Again, we sat in silence, staring out at the hail.

He said, 'I just think we should learn to recognise a good thing when we see it, hold on to it, take our pleasures where we find them.'

A sudden gust of wind blew through the vines and buffeted the van. I shivered and turned to face Andrew.

'Hold me,' I said.

We embraced cautiously. I nuzzled the soft fabric of his collar. 'I want you, Andrew,' I whispered.

I don't know which of us was more shocked by my sudden wantonness. We separated for a moment. He looked at me earnestly. 'Are you sure, Jean?' he asked, adding, 'No, what I mean is, are you *ready* for this?'

I rested my head against his shoulder again and said, 'I will be after you've kissed me, Andrew. Don't wait for me to change my mind.'

We kissed, and I thought: how strange to find happiness here, in a camper van, trapped in the arms of a man whose kiss has set me free.

Listening to the raucous cawing of the rooks and the distant traffic noise on the *route nationale*, I pulled him closer, kissed the side of his neck and asked, 'Where's the bed, Andrew?'

He stood up and held out his hand to me. 'Er, you're sitting on it,' he said.

Once he had transformed the little bench and table into a small double bed, we took off our muddy boots, leaving them untidily on the floor. I wriggled under the thick quilt and pulled him to me again, this time taking the firm flesh above his collarbone between my teeth, biting playfully. Breathing in sharply, hissing through clenched teeth, he returned my bite with his own. We exchanged hungry glances as we shuffled out of our clothes beneath the bedcovers. He positioned himself above me, and my eager body received him. The noises outside faded, replaced by the sounds of our lovemaking, our syncopated heartbeats and panting, and the just audible squeak of the van's suspension.

Afterwards we slept.

I woke up to bright sunshine and a startling rainbow, thrilled to be reacquainted with the feeling of lying naked next to someone. We made love once more.

Later, when Andrew got up to make some tea, Turk (the discrete little soul) came out from under the worktop and begged to be let out. Andrew opened and closed the door with his left hand, holding two mugs of tea in his right.

'Why do you call him Turk?' I asked.

'It's short for turkey killer,' he said matter-of-factly.

'Turkey killer?'

'Yes. See, when my parents were alive, we bred Jack Russells on their farm near Kirkudbright. The kids were . . .' he thought about it, furrowing his brow, 'eight or nine when we got Turk as a puppy. He'd broken into the barn and killed a brood of baby turkeys. Mum and Dad didn't want to sell him and risk their reputation – no one wants a killer, right? Aye, it was Archie who named him.'

I found it hard to imagine that the friendly little dog was once a killer. 'I can't believe it – little Turk?'

'Aye, I'm afraid so. He was hard to train at first, but age seems to have quelled his blood lust. He's still got bloody sharp teeth, though.'

Oh my God, I thought, I hope he can keep them off my neighbour's chickens.

'But he's not . . . dangerous?' I asked.

'Och, no. He hardly ever destroys anything now.'

I remembered an old friend's rescued mongrel. The two of them had lived together for several months until one day, without warning, it ate her living room.

'What do you mean, "hardly"?'

'Oh, don't worry, he wouldn't harm a fly. He might make a mess of your mail, though.'

'The mail?'

'Aye, he's a bugger when it comes to packaging. You know, parcels and such like. One Christmas the kids came downstairs to open their presents and Turk had beaten them to it!'

That's enough about dogs, I thought. 'So, Archie must be fifteen or sixteen now?'

'Aye, he's sixteen now. God, how time flies.'

'And his sister?'

'Er, Poppy's fourteen. She started her GCSEs this year.'

'You did write to them didn't you, Andrew?'

'What? Oh, yes. I sent Archie a postcard of Saint-Emilion telling him where I was. I even gave him your phone number. I hope you don't mind? Not that he's likely to call his old dad, though.'

'No, of course I don't mind,' I said. 'And I'm sure he will, in time. We all need time.'

By Sunday, Andrew had moved some of his things into the house. Unfamiliar clothes made their way into my bedroom. A toothbrush appeared on the bathroom windowsill. A pair of size ten walking boots arrived on the hearth. We began, gingerly, to act like a couple. The following day Aimée was due to move in, too. Over dinner, we discussed how we might break the news to her of our cohabiting. Andrew suggested keeping our relationship a secret which made me cross with him for the second time that week.

'Andrew, I want you in my house. I want you in my bed. I want you in my *life*,' I said, almost pleading. 'I know you've only just gone through a hurtful separation, but if you want us to make it, it's got to be all or nothing, okay?'

'Okay, Jean,' he said, 'I was only thinking of you. If that's what you want then that's great – we're officially a couple.'

We sat for a moment listening to the ticking of the clock. I glanced at him. 'You said you loved me last night, remember?' I asked.

'Of course, Jean, and I meant it,' he said, meeting my gaze. 'I love you, Jean Valeix.'

'And I love you, too, Andrew Maconie.'

'Good,' he said, getting up to clear the dishes and kissing me gently on the cheek, 'that's settled then.'

'Leave the washing-up till later,' I said, poking my fingers between two buttons of his shirt and stroking the coarse hairs of his chest.

'You're going to exhaust me, Jean,' he said, kissing me again, this time on the mouth.

'I intend to, Andrew,' I said, returning his kiss.

Suddenly he pulled away, wincing.

'What's the matter?' I asked, shocked.

'Oh, it's nothing,' he replied, collapsing back into his chair and kneading his lower back with both hands. 'All this bending down in the vines is murder for my spine.'

'So, come upstairs – I'll give you a massage.'

He pushed his chair back and stood, turning to face me. 'Oh, Miss Jean,' he said, 'I thought you'd never ask.'

Betrayal

But the devil always finds a way of pouring his drop
of absinthe into the glass of happiness.
- Prosper Merimée, *The Blue Room*

On Monday morning, Aimée had taken the Libourne train
to Saint-Emilion and walked the half kilometre or so to
Fontloube. When she appeared on the drive, beaming with
youthful joy, Andrew and I were in the vines tying the
long shoots together in pairs. I told her that we could have
picked her up, but she'd wanted to surprise us. Poor child,
I said to myself, hundreds of miles from home with
everything she owns in a rolling suitcase and a shoulder
bag; you've got to make something of this lost and lonely
girl.

I showed Aimée to her room, helping to carry her
luggage up the creaky staircase, and took the opportunity
to tell her about Andrew and me. She seemed a bit
embarrassed by my news – incongruously, I thought, in
view of her own far more sensational confession – and I
wondered whether there wasn't still a vestige of old-
fashioned innocence behind this assertive, modern girl's
persona. She said she was tired after the move and asked if
she could stay in her room for a while to rest. I went down
to rejoin Andrew in the vineyard.

'How's our new girl then?' he asked.

'Oh, she's fine,' I told him, noticing the leaden hue of
the northern sky. 'Looks like another storm gathering.'

'Aye, perhaps we'd be better off in the winery this
afternoon.'

'Okay,' I said, 'I'll give you your first lesson in winemaking, if you like.'

'Shouldn't you be teaching your new apprentice?'

'Oh, she's tired after carting her stuff all the way here from Libourne,' I explained. 'Let's let her sleep now. She can help you finish off later. This job will take some time.'

After a quick lunch, we went to the barrel cellar to prepare the equipment for racking last year's wine. My precious vintage had been sleeping in oak *barriques* since the winter. Now, summer's rise in temperature had stirred it from its slumber.

I told Andrew to ready himself for a lecture on *soutirage*.

'Taste this,' I said, drawing a good measure of red wine from a barrel, using a large glass pipette.

'Mmm,' he mumbled, then spat the mouthful into the drain in the cellar floor. 'Tastes a bit fizzy,' he said.

'That's the carbon dioxide coming out of solution as the wine warms up a few degrees.'

'And the flavour is flatter than it was when I tasted it a few weeks ago.'

'Well done,' I said. 'We'll make a winemaker of you yet. Now, oxygen is the enemy of wine, but we need to put just a little back in to restore the wine's generosity and fullness. What I want you to do is draw off the wine from all these barrels, putting some air into the wine and leaving the sludgy sediment behind that lurks at the bottom of each *barrique*. Okay, any questions?'

'Yes, one: how?'

We worked all afternoon, siphoning and pumping, racking the wine from cask to cask. *Soutirage* is laborious work, but it's one of the indoor jobs that I really enjoy. By the middle of the afternoon we were exhausted from the effort and giddy from breathing the CO_2-filled air of the cellar. Aimée came down to join us, much rejuvenated, at about four o'clock. I left the two of them to finish the racking while I escaped to the stockroom to prepare an order. The realisation that I was happy took me quite by surprise, but there it was. For the first time in years I had a resident team working at the château and someone to share my life with.

May brought flowers to the vine which, by June, developed into the tiny embryonic fruits that, a hundred days hence, would swell and ripen into grapes. Torrents of rain followed the previous month's hailstorms, and sunny days were few. I received a letter, signed by the director of the college, confirming Aimée's contract and pay rates.

My newly formed team worked well together, although Aimée was an understandably reluctant gooseberry. She always found an excuse to leave us alone if Andrew and I showed any sign of mutual affection. We rarely dined together, as we had done on that first night, but Aimée prepared a surprise dinner for my saint's day, *la Fête de Jeanne d'Arc*, on the 11th of May. I returned the favour by cooking a steak-and-kidney pie – apparently her favourite British dish – to mark the end of Aimée's first month. By and large, we all got on well. We divided the work in the fields and in the winery between us, and Aimée devised an efficient rota system, allowing her to spend the time she needed at her studies in Libourne. When at the château, she either worked with me, leaving Andrew free to write, or with Andrew, if I was visiting customers or catching up with paperwork. She became a valuable secretary and filing clerk, transforming the chaotic mess that had been my study into a functional office.

Andrew bought a tourist guide to the Southwest. When the sun shone, he would go out for the day in Clémentine with a bottle of Fontloube, a picnic lunch and his black Moleskine writing pad. But rather than returning home with accounts of the glorious Perigord countryside or the stark beauty of the Gironde estuary, he invariably came back with tales of the wine villages: Pauillac, Margaux, Pessac, Sauternes . . . One evening, after such an outing, I sneaked a look at his notepad, left open on the table, and read, not florid, poetic descriptions of the beauty of the vine lands, but scribbled tasting notes of the wines that he'd sampled during the day.

I'd prepared some pâté de foie gras, spread on hot brioche, which we were eating with a glass of chilled Loupiac. 'How did you get on today?' I enquired, between mouthfuls of the tasty starter.

'Writing wise?' he replied. 'I sat by the banks of the Dordogne near Sainte-Terre and caught a glimpse of a kingfisher as he flew past me. You know the way you see the stunning electric blue colour of the feathers when they catch the sunlight?'

'Sounds good. Did you capture your muse then?'

'I spent all morning writing a poem about the relationship between the bird and the river, but it was a waste of time. There were far too many "lofty boughs" and "canopies outleant". It was a sad pastiche – like a cross between Thomas Hardy and Oliver Hardy. Then I spent half an hour trying to think of a fish that rhymes with *kill*.'

'*Brill*?' I suggested.

'I don't think it's a freshwater fish, is it? Well, anyway, I tore the page out, screwed it up and threw it in the river. It'll be in the Atlantic by now.'

'You shouldn't give up so easily,' I said. 'Keats's muse was a nightingale – maybe yours is the kingfisher. You should go back to the river and try again.'

'Aye, maybe one day I will.'

'And I'll come with you,' I said, smiling at him. A barely remembered couplet from *Ode to a Nightingale* came back to me: 'That I might drink, and leave the world unseen, and with thee fade into the forest dim.'

'You fraud!' he said. 'You pretended not to recognise Keats when we first met. Or did you learn that especially for me?'

'Don't flatter yourself, Maconie,' I replied, 'I studied English Literature *and* Language at A-level, I'll have you know. I was a star pupil!'

'You're full of surprises, Jean.'

'Me?' I said, with a hint of insinuation, 'And what about

you? What were you up to this afternoon, for instance?'

'I went to the village of Pomerol and visited a couple of wineries.'

'So I see,' I said, pointing to the black writing pad.

'Hey, don't complain, Jean. I've been improving my tasting skills and doing some vital competitive analysis for you.'

'I'm not complaining, Andrew, I just hope you won't be put off drinking Château Fontloube after tasting all these fine, expensive wines.'

'No way!' he said, flicking through his notes. 'I've been to some of the most famous Pomerol properties today, and I didn't taste one wine that was any better than yours.'

'I doubt it.'

'No, seriously, I think Fontloube really could compete with some of these places who sell their wines at twice, no, *four* times the price.'

'Well let's not get carried away,' I said. 'Making good wine is one thing – selling it is quite another.'

'Aye, I know. Just a thought.'

During the third week of June the bad weather returned, bringing more storms that threatened to jeopardise my grape crop. But by the end of the week the warm summer sunshine came back, just in time for the annual midsummer celebrations. All across France, in cities, towns and villages, the (often cacophonous) sound of live music heralded the summer solstice. The *Fête de la Musique* is a one-night-only chance for musicians to claim their right to play, and Saint-Emilion's always drew a large crowd. From the top of the town, where stand the King's Tower and the collegiate church, down along the narrow cobbled streets and into the airy squares below, revellers and music-makers were making a boisterous, noisy procession. Andrew, Aimée and I decided to join the throng, so after a light supper we made our way up the hill to the mixed sounds of jazz and salsa, hip-hop and rock-and-roll. We installed ourselves in the Place du Marché in front of the monolithic church – a medieval wonder, hewn from the pale rock of the hill. We drank ice-cold beer, Aimée smoked her way through a packet of *Lucky Strikes* and Andrew puffed on a long Partagas cigar. As the evening progressed, the music improved and the tourist crowd thinned, leaving only serious music lovers (and the seriously intoxicated) to continue into the night. Daylight faded, replaced by the light show's warm halogen glow. A Gypsy jazz band launched into their opening number, rousing a bell tower full of bats that fluttered overhead, caught for a fiery, brief moment in the limelight, seemingly oblivious to the rowdy celebrations going on below. The square's time-eroded limestone façades created an amphitheatre of joyous sound. Feet tapped, hands clapped in time to the slapping beat of the guitars, and the dancing began.

Andrew ordered more beers and, inspired by the opening bars of *All of Me*, led me protesting into the mêlée. 'Quite a hooley isn't it?' he shouted, as we jived and twisted.

'Better than a ceilidh in the glens, eh?'

'Better weather, that's for sure,' he said, and following a far from well-executed spin, added, 'and better company, too!'

We danced and drank, talked loudly and sang along to the odd familiar tune. Aimée led Andrew into the square as the music softened before the finale. I sat there feeling contented, exhausted and a tad tipsy, watching my man dance with the girl who was young enough to be his granddaughter. The lilting, tender notes of Django Reinhardt's *Nuages* brought the two of them closer and, in one subtle movement, Aimée removed her red silk Hermès scarf and wrapped it round her dancing partner's waist. Slowly, hips swaying, she pulled him closer to her, before breaking away again, pirouetting gracefully and returning to face him as the notes died away, finally planting a small kiss on his cheek. He bowed and kissed her hand, then the two of them skipped back to the table, laughing bashfully at their frivolity. She certainly knew how to dance.

'You'd make a terribly good Salomé,' I said to Aimée as she sat down next to me.

'What?' she asked, missing my remark as the band launched into its final number.

'Oh, nothing,' I mouthed, smiling. Then, just for a brief moment, a guilty pang of jealousy replaced my feelings of contentment – an unfamiliar and unwelcome emotion that I discarded like a rotten fruit.

The three of us turned to watch the musicians and enjoy the end of the show.

We walked home in the cool of the short midsummer night. Rising over Castillon, the waning moon bathed the vines in monochrome luminescence and cast vague shadows of our weary bodies on the lane.

When we arrived at the house, Turk welcomed us with a friendly bark. Aimée said goodnight, kissing me on both cheeks, as was our custom. The drinking and dancing had made me thirsty, so I shuffled to the kitchen to pour a glass of water. I closed the tap, turned to leave and saw Andrew break away from a kiss that seemed far more passionate than innocent. Andrew put the back of his hand to his mouth as Aimée's high-heeled footsteps clattered up the stairs. He saw me watching him and gave a theatrical shrug complete with frown and raised eyebrows that said *don't look at me – it wasn't my fault*. He walked slowly into the kitchen still shrugging, showing his palms.

'Did I just see what I think I saw?' I asked.

'I'm afraid so, yes,' he replied, wearing an expression of shocked surprise.

'Andrew, if there's anything going on . . .'

'No, Jean, don't be silly. She's clearly just a bit drunk. I didn't do anything to provoke . . . that.'

'Andrew, you told me to be wary of Aimée – now I'm telling you.' My voice, which I'd intended to be forceful, began to quaver. 'She's a vulnerable young woman who's been thrown out by her family – if she's looking for a father figure then just make sure it's not you, okay?'

'Yes, Jean. I'm not interested in Aimée.'

'I'm not just talking about Aimée, Andrew,' I said, anger pricking my eyes. 'Don't screw this up. I've got to be able to trust you. Do you know how important that is?'

'You have to believe me. I'm yours, you know that. Yours for ever.'

He held me with his gaze. If the words sounded less than convincing, his eyes didn't seem to lie. I embraced him briefly. Looking again into his eyes, I said, 'Promise me, Andrew. If you ever betrayed me . . . I don't know what I'd do.'

'I promise.'

'Well then, I have to believe you – just don't be naïve, okay? And don't lead her on. Just . . . just be on your guard, all right?'

'Don't worry – I will. And you, too, Jean,' he said, breaking away from my arms. 'I still don't think you should trust her – she gave up studying one thing, now she's trying another. She's not reliable. Don't you think she might leave you in the lurch, too?'

'Andrew, she reminds me of myself at her age. My family wanted me to become a solicitor for God's sake, but all I wanted to do was run away to France and become a *vigneronne*. I just think she needs some structure and direction in her life. I don't think she'll let me down.'

'Listen,' he said, hesitating, 'Jean . . .'

'What?'

'Oh, nothing. Look, it's late – let's go to bed.'

We went up to bed, and I wondered if jealousy was the price we pay to trade an empty, emotionless life for the fragile security of another person's love.

The next day I rose early and finished packing a consignment for one of my favourite clients – a smart and hugely successful Bordeaux restaurant called *Chez Stéphane*.

Stéphane Lavergne was an old family friend. His father

and Henri were at school together and he and Olivier had been lifelong friends. Stéphane, and his lovely wife Isabelle, helped me enormously after Olivier's death and, again, after Henri's. He was also one of my biggest buyers. By eleven o'clock the courier hadn't arrived. I called the dispatch office and was told that the van couldn't be with me until Monday. Having promised Stéphane that the batch of 2005 wines would be with him in time for the weekend, I decided to deliver it myself.

I avoided the autoroute, crossing the river at Branne, and drove to the city through the northern vineyards of the Entre-deux-Mers. I came into Bordeaux via the Pont de Pierre, admiring the port's wonderfully sombre, self-satisfied architecture. The wealth of the 18th-century middle classes had transformed this quayside into a golden mile of palaces for rich wine merchants, and cathedral-like warehouses dedicated to the gods of commerce and agriculture. But today, bankrupted by a global wine crisis, the vineyards whose fortunes had built Bordeaux were being replaced by arable farms and the ever-increasing sprawl of the city's outer suburbs. Thank God my vineyards are still my own, I thought, at least for the time being. I reached the city centre and turned my attention to finding a parking space near the Place des Grands Hommes.

After delivering the wines, I accepted, slightly guiltily, the offer of a quick lunch. After dessert, Stéphane joined me for an espresso. I felt pampered and privileged to be drinking coffee with the chef-patron of a sophisticated restaurant, watching the other diners pretending not to eavesdrop on our conversation. I offered to pay the bill, but Stéphane refused – a quirk of doing business with him was that his shrewdness had won him the lowest possible price for my wines, yet he always paid his bills on time and was immensely generous whenever I ate at his place.

I arrived home at about three-thirty and crunched the 4x4

to a halt on the gravel drive. I spotted Andrew in the hangar, cleaning the tractor, but Aimée was nowhere to be seen.

I went indoors and filled the kettle. As I began sifting through the morning's post, I heard a door slam shut on the first floor followed by the sound of feet descending the stairs. Aimée, wrapped in a bathrobe, rushed into the kitchen and embraced me, telling me how sorry she was for kissing Andrew the night before. 'Please forgive my foolishness,' she begged, 'the dancing and all that beer made me giddy. I don't know what I was doing.'

'Think nothing of it, Aimée,' I said, smiling.

'Oh, you are so good, Jeanne,' she said. I noticed her bare feet and unkempt hair.

'Looks like you just got out of bed – sleeping off a hangover I suppose?' She looked down at the floor and asked if I was disappointed with her.

'Let's just write it off to experience, eh?' I offered, adding, ironically, 'And keep your hands off my man.'

'Very well, Jeanne. Now, let me make you some lunch.'

'Oh, don't bother about me; I've already eaten – *Chez Stéphane . . .*'

She recognised the name and gasped. 'Gosh, Jeanne, that's one of Bordeaux's best restaurants, you know.'

'Yes, I know, and they serve one of Saint-Emilion's best wines there, too.'

Feeling sleepy after my extravagant lunch, I retired to the bedroom, intending to put my feet up for half an hour. I sat on the bed to take off my shoes and noticed how neat the room was. My rush to get going early in the morning had left me no time to straighten the bed, but now it was tidy – the quilt, sheets and pillows all made up properly. As well as being a good vineyard worker and washer-up, it seemed that Andrew had learned how to do the housework, too. A cool breeze entered the room through the open window. I slid under the covers and lay on my side with my legs drawn up. I put my hand under the pillow and touched something that felt like a ball of silk. Kneeling up on the bed, I lifted the pillow to reveal a screwed-up pair of black briefs. I picked them up gingerly and shook them out. The label on the skimpy, pricey-looking knickers read: *Agent Provocateur S.* They did not belong to me. I threw the despicable item on the floor and stood up, staring at it, my hands, arms and shoulders shaking. I remembered the dance and the kiss. I thought, you got me in the end didn't you? And my evil gremlin replied, *yes Jean, it was only a matter of time.* Strangely, I felt neither angry, nor vengeful. I just felt empty, as though some invisible force had sucked out the substance of my being leaving only a vacuum where my pride had begun, tentatively, to make itself at home.

Sunlight flooded into the kitchen along with the summer sounds of industrious bees and the chattering of finches in the wisteria. There were three people in the room: one sitting at the table, one standing by the sink, and me – or rather the empty shell of my body – lingering by the door. A pair of briefs left my shaky hand and fell, softly, on the tabletop. The two people looked at it and then at me. Quietly I said, 'Please can you explain what this was doing in my bed?'

He took a step towards me, but I held out my hand to stop him. 'What?' he said.

'I'm sorry, Jeanne,' she said, looking up at me from the table. 'It was not supposed to be like this, please believe me. We were waiting for . . . the right moment.'

'What the hell are you saying?' he shouted at her.

'Don't *chéri*, remember what we said. I think it is time we all told the truth, *n'est-ce pas?*'

'You—' he said to her, cutting himself short. 'Jean, this is *not* what it seems, you've got to believe me.'

'And when can I stop believing you? When I find a half-dressed young woman's knickers in our bed after I've been out of the house all day?' I was surprisingly calm and coherent for a body without a soul.

'Just . . . Oh God, for Christ's sake, *tell* her!' he said.

'That is what I am doing. Please calm down *chéri.*' She got up from the table and went over to him, putting her arm round his waist. 'Jeanne, we didn't want to hurt you like this but, you see, for some time we have been lovers. I know it is impossible for us to remain here now, and I am sorry.'

The two of them stood there – she, smiling, he, staring blankly at the floor.

'Thank you,' my empty shell said. 'Please leave now.'

The vineyard called to me like a sanctuary during their departure. I collapsed at the end of a vine row, overcome with a sudden fatigue. I could hear my departing lodgers as they hurried between the house and Andrew's van, taking with them a few hastily packed belongings. I heard the camper van's doors slam shut, then the noise of the engine start and then fade. I was alone once more. I closed my eyes and fell into sleep's comforting embrace. My dreams took me back to the strange railway carriage. This time the intruders stood in front of me. One wore a mask that looked like Aimée; the other wore a mask of Andrew's face. He removed his mask. Behind it there was Andrew, smiling. I pulled away Aimée's mask, revealing not a face but a dark, black hole. This time there was no dog. This time the howls that echoed though the train were my own.

The lengthening shadows marked the hours I'd slept in the vineyard. I wondered if it was possible to sleep without dreaming. Feeling as lifeless as flat champagne, I pulled myself up, limbs aching and cold, and walked slowly back to the house, determined to drink myself into oblivion.

Behind the barrel cellar is a small, windowless room called the *cave.* Here, old vintages of Château Fontloube are laid down for decades, waiting for the appropriate occasion to be opened and shared, to celebrate family birthdays, anniversaries, christenings . . . Rummaging through the dusty shelves I soon found what I needed and brought the

51

bottles up to the tasting room in a wooden crate. I'd chosen the wines for their vintages: a 1987, my first year at Fontloube; a 1990, the year of my first miscarriage; a 1997, the year Olivier died; and a 1998 from the year when I buried my father-in-law. I began with the oldest: the '87. What a mediocre year that was. The wine, thin but thirst-quenching, had reached its peak many years ago. Soon the bottle was empty. The next bottle, a 1990, one of those great vintages that come round only rarely, was still drinking very well. Full, rich, complex and fruity, it seemed to mock my own barren attempts to be fruitful, and I drank it with contempt for the vine's vigorous fertility. With no food in my stomach, the alcohol had an immediately intoxicating effect. My recollections of the third and fourth bottles are hazy. I tasted the '97 (a rainy vintage that produced a dilute wine) and the '98 (a hot year with sturdy, ripe wines), but I couldn't, by that stage of inebriation, tell them apart. After swigging all I could from each bottle, I submitted to the force of gravity, and slipped onto the floor. My bizarre vertical tasting finished, quite literally, horizontally. I drifted into nothingness, still clinging to the 1998 as its dregs formed a dark red pool on the stone slabs.

Sleep dragged me back, once again, to the railway carriage. Small, ghoulish figures tapped and scratched at the window of the compartment, picking at the catches and tearing at the rubber seals. Soon they had broken in, falling upon me like rats, their quick, slimy tongues licking my face, their horrific claws scratching at my cheeks, their sharp little teeth biting into my flesh. I felt like a tortured sinner, trapped inside the final panel of a Bosch triptych, locked in a diabolical nightmare from which I could only escape by waking. The blood that gushed from my wounds settled and congealed around me. My hands touched the sticky, cold liquid. I opened my eyes.

At first it was the smell of sour wine that brought me back

to reality, then the not unpleasant sensation of having my ear licked and nibbled by a concerned Jack Russell. My throat was as dry as cork. I sat up quickly, and Turk, who had broken in through the caveau's window, jumped on my lap, panting. The rapid change in altitude made me feel so dizzy that I fell back into the frigid puddle of stale wine. Taking hold of the dog, I cradled him in my arms.

At least, I thought, I've still got one true friend.

Food

What is man, when you come to think upon him, but a minutely set, ingenious machine for turning with infinite artfulness, the red wine of Shiraz into urine?
- Karen Blixen, *The Dreamers*

I hauled myself upright and went outside into the morning's pale sunshine. Eyes adjusting to the daylight, I wondered who to hate the most. Then it came to me. Wondering if the dog might not be alone, and realising that I hoped to see Andrew's van parked in the courtyard, I had to accept that it was me. I hated myself. Evidently the little dog at my feet had returned to Fontloube on his own (from where I did not know), but the camper van and its owner were nowhere to be seen. For the moment, the throbbing pain behind my eyes and the queasy sensation in my stomach masked my sorrows, but I knew that once the hangover's physical symptoms had faded, the black feelings would return. As usual, the structure and routine of my job would offer some solace, so after eating a hasty, caffeine-fuelled breakfast, I prepared the tractor for spraying.

Several years before, we'd stopped spraying with synthetic chemicals. By using organic methods, the health of the vines improved enormously. We banished insecticides, and by allowing the wild plants and flowers to grow between the ploughed vine rows, we drastically cut down on weed-killers, too. One disease though, that stubbornly resisted our chemical-free approach, thrived in this wet and humid weather: mildew. After their decimation by April's frosts and the hail in May, my poor vines had now succumbed to this odious parasite. I filled the tanks with copper sulphate solution and drove the tractor into the vineyard.

Raining megadeath on the mildew diverted my anger, and the repetitive work of driving, spraying and turning in the vines took my thoughts away from Andrew and Aimée. The morning passed quickly, but after lunch, alone in the kitchen, recent events and their painful memories came back to mind. How, in the space of a month, had Andrew become so easily tempted to betray me? What could a word like *love* mean to a man who used it so deceptively? And why should a young, beautiful girl like Aimée desire a man nearly forty years her senior? I'd heard of multimillionaire sugar daddies taking twenty-year-old trophy wives, but Andrew wasn't wealthy. He was a recently divorced, practically penniless poet. To me he offered the hope of a future with someone kind and gentle, healthy and active. But these weren't the foremost qualities I imagined an undergraduate would look for in a partner. And why had Andrew shown such antipathy towards Aimée when she arrived? Did that first glimpse of her startling beauty provoke a temptation he knew he'd be unable to resist? If that was true, then Andrew was a psychopath, not the warm hearted, easy-going man I knew. Who was wearing the mask? Was it Andrew, Aimée, or both of them? These questions, like the barely suppressed hope that Turk's return might be followed by Andrew's, bothered me. I yearned to forget everything that had happened, but hope – vanity's last resort – continued to taunt me.

The phone's ringing in the study interrupted my bitter reflections. I picked up and heard a familiar, welcome voice.

'*Allo, Jeanne, c'est Stéphane. Ça va?*'

Stéphane's friendly baritone cheered me instantly. '*Oui, ça va, Stéphane. Comment va tu?*' I enquired, wondering if he'd called about the wine I'd delivered the previous day.

'I'm fine, Jeanne,' he replied. 'I'm sorry to call you on a

Sunday, but I wanted to congratulate you.' Such a deep, warm, comforting voice.

'That's . . . nice, Stéphane. I take it you're referring to my 2005.'

'Yes. . .' He paused, perhaps wondering what other reason he could possibly have for congratulating me. 'I sold some to one of my best clients last night.'

'Now you've got my attention. Did they like it?'

'Yes, he adored it. He's an American wine buyer. His party drank four or five bottles. And I've just sold nearly another case during lunch today.'

'That's fantastic, Stéphane,' I enthused, thinking, here comes a sale.

'I know that you probably don't have much of the '05 left, but I'd be grateful if you could let me have another few dozen bottles?'

His inflection, and the word *grateful*, should have inspired me to employ a more aggressive negotiation, but under the circumstances (my vulnerable mood and a cellar full of unsold wine) I just said, 'Of course, Stéphane, you're welcome to what I have.'

'Well, that's great, Jeanne. Send me the *livraison* when you can. Usual terms apply?'

'Yes,' I sighed, 'usual terms.'

He noticed the deflated tone in my voice. 'Listen, Jeanne,' he said, 'are you okay?'

Here we go, I thought; do I say *yes everything's fine,* or *no I've been betrayed and left to reassemble the shards of my shattered life*?

His caring, big-brotherly concern swung it.

'No, Stéphane,' I said, my voice breaking, 'I'm not.'

'*Alors*, what's wrong?'

'Oh, nothing, Stéphane. I don't want to bother you with my troubles.'

'Hey, Jeanne, you know that you're like family to us. Tell me what's happened.'

I told him how foolish I felt and gave him a brief résumé of the previous couple of months. I digressed and became less coherent. Thankfully he interrupted me.

'Listen, Jeanne, come to dinner with us tomorrow night, please. You know how busy we are in the summer, but we're closed on Mondays, so come and have a meal with us at the apartment. I've just got some excellent Toulouse goose. Do you like goose?'

I nearly declined the invitation, but the offer of dinner at the home of a double Michelin-starred chef and his charming family somehow won me over. 'Yes, I do,' I said. 'I'd love to come, Stéphane. Thank you.'

'Great, see you tomorrow at seven-thirty,' he concluded, adding, with a comforting nonchalance, 'Don't worry, everything's going to be fine.' He hung up, and I realised I was hugging the phone's purring handset.

Libourne's ring road crosses the Dordogne and joins the autoroute just south of the river, twenty-or-so kilometres east of Bordeaux. It's a boring route to the city but it's quick, even at my slow pace of driving. I left home at seven o'clock and arrived at the Lavergne's place, fashionably late, at quarter to eight. Stéphane and Isabelle live on the top floor of an unremarkable 19th-century block across a narrow street from their restaurant. Olivier and I had visited them at home many years before. Then, the apartment was a white-dusty, paint-smelling shambles of a building site, undergoing a complete renovation. When I arrived this time, clutching a bottle and a bouquet of pink and white roses, the immaculate kitchen-cum-reception room was filled with the tantalising aromas of roasting goose fat, garlic, rosemary and fondant potatoes cooking in butter. Seeing Isabelle again, after so long, gave me an emotional boost – not least because of her frank and completely unaffected welcome.

'Jeanne,' she said, taking the flowers and hugging me as old friends do, 'you look so tired, so *triste*. You mustn't be eating properly.' She called Stéphane – a man not used to being shouted at in a kitchen, I mused – demanding the *amuse-bouches* and the champagne. He arrived from the scullery bearing a platter of tasty nibbles and two flutes of ice-cold fizz.

'Here,' Isabelle said, taking the hors d'oeuvres from Stéphane and passing me a glass, 'eat and drink. I'll go and call the kids.' She disappeared into the living room while Stéphane said a quick hello before dashing back to his hob to rescue a pan of over-heating potatoes. Isabelle continued to talk to me through the open door. 'I'd forgotten what a fantastic figure you have! I swear I've put on a dress size for each of these three. You're so lucky. You English girls get sexier as you get older.' She reappeared with her trio of groomed and coiffed infants: Juliette, Corentin and Manon.

While Isabelle went to find a vase for the flowers, I gave each of the kids two kisses and a bar of chocolate. 'Here,' I whispered conspiratorially to the group, 'don't let your mother see these.' I walked over to Stéphane and handed him the bottle. 'Your wine order's in the car, Stéphane.' I said, raising my voice to be heard over the roar of the extractor. 'But I've brought you this for tonight.'

'Wow, Jeanne, a 1990 ... You're spoiling us. This should go very well with the goose. I'll decant it straight away.'

'I only hope it tastes better than it did the last time I tried it.'

'What's that?'

'Oh, never mind,' I said, forcing a smile. 'It's good to hear that business is going well.'

Stéphane removed the cork from the bottle and poured the wine carefully into a crystal decanter. 'Business is always going well. The staff, on the other hand, are just *going*.'

'Oh, dear. But I thought you had a waiting list? Aspiring young chefs ready to work for you for nothing?'

'That's almost true,' he replied, 'but keeping them once they've been trained is quite another thing.'

To avert a segue into the theme of *my* business

problems, I asked Stéphane what was for dinner.

'Simple home cooking,' he declared, taking a sip of champagne. 'Just some pan-seared king and queen scallops, sautéed with lemon and garlic; a tasty green tea sorbet; then the goose, served with fondant potatoes, rainbow chard and baby roots; a little cheese; and a plum tarte Tatin to finish. You see, it's essential to eat basic, homely food from time to time.'

'Well, I don't mind slumming it for a change,' I said, following the lead of his ironic understatement.

'Actually we usually end up eating restaurant leftovers or takeaway pizza.'

'Your leftovers win Michelin stars, Stéphane.'

He attended to his pans and wiped the perspiration from his glistening brow with a large cotton handkerchief.

'Theatre, presentation, timing . . . and the occasional bit of sleight-of-hand are what win stars,' he said, winking at me.

'And impeccable, inspired cooking, eh?'

'Okay, a bit of that as well.'

'Now then, Jeanne,' Isabelle said, returning with an expertly arranged vase full of roses. 'First you bribe my children, then you flatter my husband. What are you after?'

Whether it was the champagne on my empty stomach, or the memory of how supportive and kind the couple had been during my past tragedies, I was unable to contain my tears and the emotional outpouring that followed them. My outburst turned the evening's harmonious curtain raiser into a frozen tableau of shocked concern. 'I'm sorry, Isabelle,' I sobbed as she wrapped me in her arms. 'I shouldn't be bothering you with this.'

'Jeanne,' Stéphane said calmly, resting his hand on my shoulder, 'like I said on the phone, you are still part of the family. Come and sit down and tell us all about it.'

We sat at the kitchen table. I related the events that had led to my predicament, telling them how Andrew and I had met and how our relationship had developed. I gave a detailed account of Aimée's arrival and explained what a great asset she had appeared to be. Finally I described, with some difficulty, my discovery of their sordid treachery and confessed to my self-hatred and self-destructive mood. My recap provoked quizzical but sympathetic glances from both my hosts.

'So,' Isabelle began, matter-of-factly, 'let me understand. First you met a late-middle-aged Scotsman, then a couple of weeks later a beautiful teenage girl came to work for you. Next, the man seduces you in his *camping car* then takes up residence at the château the day before the girl moves in. Then, after only a few weeks, you discover that the two of them have been making love in your bed?'

'That's about the truth of it,' I said, still snivelling as I drained my champagne glass.

'And now you say that his dog has come back?'

'Yes, clearly Turk's fonder of me than Andrew was.'

'I see,' Isabelle continued, getting up from the table to fetch another bottle. 'Well I suggest that you put it behind you for now. You didn't give either of them any money did you?'

She refilled me glass. 'Thanks,' I said. 'No, I didn't. Apart from the first month's allowance I paid Aimée from petty cash, I didn't give them anything. That's the problem you see. I haven't got any money, and now I don't have anybody to help me at the château either."

Stéphane glanced at me with a look of surprised concern. 'But, Jeanne, you own the property, you have a Saint-Emilion vineyard and – I don't want to pry – but you must have received a significant sum after Olivier and his father . . . you know.'

I explained that the insurance money I received, as the sole beneficiary of Olivier's estate, was indeed quite a sum. But after paying-off the bank loan on the business and investing in the equipment I needed to help me run things on my own, there was only enough left to live on for three or four years. Since Henri passed away, the winery had hardly made any profit at all, and I'd had to remortgage the house just to stay afloat.

'I didn't know the wine trade was so bad,' Isabelle said.

I composed myself.

'Global recession, massive competition, the strong euro, last year's poor harvest . . . It's been incredibly difficult for small, independent winemakers. Many are selling up, especially those with debts. Thank God the bank supported me, because otherwise I'd have been declared insolvent over a year ago.'

Stéphane cut in, 'And your Saint-Emilion label isn't enough, by itself, to sell the wine?'

'Sadly, no. A few of the wealthy *classé* vineyards can charge hundreds of euros a bottle, but wineries like Fontloube are finding it difficult to sell at almost any price.'

'What about your neighbours?' he went on. 'Don't you lot get together and help one another out?'

'People were very kind, especially after Henri died, and I can still count on a couple of true friends. But everyone's up the creek and fighting for the same paddle. I'm beginning to understand how quickly and easily a widowed businesswoman can become a pariah. You know what they call me? The Chatelaine in the 2CV! Some people can't wait for me to fail.'

Isabelle took my hand. 'Do you really believe that, Jeanne?'

'I know it,' I stated flatly.

She tightened her grip and said, 'You must contact the college, Jeanne, and tell them what's happened.'

And say what, I wondered – I wish to complain that one of your students has stolen my boyfriend? I regarded my well-meaning confidante incredulously, then, giving in, I said, 'Okay, I'll call the director as soon as I can to cancel the girl's contract.'

'Look,' said Stéphane, rising to his feet, 'let's eat and see if we can find a way to help. *Food for thought* – isn't that what you English say?'

'Sort of, Stéphane, yes,' I said, and the smell of seafood

sautéing in garlic brought a smile back to my tear-smudged face.

Dinner was delicious. Golden-seared on the outside, the scallops were cooked perfectly *à point* in the middle. The thinly sliced goose was juicy and tender, and the bitter chard was a well-chosen complement to the crisp, fatty *magret*. After picking at a lavish cheeseboard (purloined from his restaurant), Stéphane treated us to a *tarte Tatin aux prunes* – his award-winning regional variation of the classic dessert. Apart from the champagne, a sip of my 1990 and a thimble-full of armagnac with the tart, I stuck to water during the meal. Isabelle poured three strong black coffees, and I thanked her for a wonderful evening.

'You're not getting away just yet,' she told me. 'Stéphane has some ideas about how to improve things at the château.'

So, they've been plotting something, I thought, probably when I visited the loo after the second glass of champagne.

'Ah, yes,' Stéphane began, tentatively. 'You know that I still keep in touch with Henri's family.'

'Yes . . .' I said cautiously.

'Well, Henri's brother, Jacques – do you remember him?'

I remembered him well. He was the dour farmer from the Corrèze who had disapproved of my marriage to Olivier. 'Yes,' I answered, 'I never got on with him. He was Henri's complete opposite. Henri was as sweet as honey, but his brother was as sour as vinegar.'

'Two things that go to make a very good vinaigrette,' Stéphane teased.

'Well, maybe. But he didn't like me and the feeling was mutual.'

'Jacques was a man governed by ideals,' he explained, 'unlike his brother who, like so many of us crazy Corréziens, was seduced by ideas.'

I'd heard the brothers' saga many times. On inheriting the family farm after the war, Jacques had begged Henri to stay with him and share the business of raising cattle and growing maize. But Henri followed his dream, bought a derelict château with a few hectares of vines near Saint-Emilion and married a young nurse from Alsace. Olivier was born, but his mother died in childbirth, marking the first of a series of Valeix tragedies. Jacques's belief – that moving, and marrying, away from their community was a dangerous folly, cursed with misfortune – was vindicated. So, years later, when Henri told his brother that his son wanted to marry an English girl, Jacques refused to attend the wedding. After much cajoling by the family, he agreed to come but would not look at or speak to me. Then, after Olivier died, Henri sold Fontloube to me, partly to cut his brother off from ever inheriting the place. Since then I'd had no contact with the rest of the Valeix clan.

'Well anyway,' Stéphane continued, 'since his stroke he barely recognises his sons. They say he won't see this year's harvest.'

'Good riddance to him,' I said, regretting the remark immediately.

'Well, perhaps. But not to his sons I hope . . .'

'No,' I admitted, ashamed of my callousness, 'Olivier's cousins were nice young lads as far as I remember.'

'. . .who now all have children of their own,' Stéphane went on. 'Two of them have sons at the lycée. I'm sure they'll be looking for work this summer. It would be a pity if they end up shovelling cow manure in the Limousin all through the holidays when they could be helping you in the vines. I could talk to Olivier's cousins . . .?'

Having a couple of boisterous seventeen-year-olds bring a bit of laughter and noise to the château was a tempting proposition. I could do with the company, and I desperately needed the help. 'Yes, Stéphane, please do,' I said gratefully. 'Talk to the Valeix's, and if they're keen then tell them to come as soon as term ends.'

'They break up this Friday. I talked to Valentin and Paul this morning.'

'Stéphane!' I said exasperatedly, 'Since when did

guardian angels start wearing chef's whites?'

'Like I said,' he said, taking my empty cup, 'you're family, Jeanne. And of course, my motives are also selfish. I want you to keep supplying my restaurant with your fabulous wine.'

We said goodbye on the landing of their apartment, and I thanked them both again for their kindness and hospitality.

'Well, I'll be off then,' I said, fumbling with my car keys. 'Oh, but don't forget about your wine, Stéphane – it's in the car.'

'Wait a second, I'll go and get the keys to the restaurant,' he said, disappearing back indoors.

'My little dog is waiting for me at home,' I said to Isabelle, while we waited for her husband to return.

'That's one thing that bothers me, Jeanne,' she said, scrutinising my face. 'Dogs and their owners hate to be separated. You know, like Snowy and Tintin, Toto and Dorothy, Dogmatix and Obelix . . . I wouldn't be surprised if your dog's owner shows up again. Just let us know if you find out what he's up to, *d'accord?*'

'*D'accord*, Isabelle,' I said, kissing her goodbye.

Stéphane came out with a large bunch of keys, and the two of us went downstairs to unload the car.

In a way Isabelle was right. It wasn't long before a certain someone came back into my life, but she was wrong in assuming it to be Andrew. In the meantime I looked forward to the arrival of my new team of Corrézien workers. The cousins, Valentin and Paul, arrived by train on the last Saturday in June. I waited for the express to chug its way out of Libourne station and had no trouble in spotting them among the disembarking passengers. I saw two strapping, handsome lads, each carrying a heavy rucksack and wearing the same smile – the smile that used to linger on Olivier's face, curling at the corners like a vine tendril, the Valeix smile.

'*Bonjour* boys,' I called to them, as they made their way

through the crowd of tourist visitors and students on their way home for the summer vacation.

'Madame Valeix?' said one, a boy with placid, soft features, not so tough-looking as his companion.

'Yes,' I said, greeting first one, then the other, with the obligatory double kiss. 'You must be . . .'

'Valentin,' said the one with the gentle looks. He turned to his friend and said, 'And this is my cousin Paul.'

'*Enchanté*, madame,' he murmured.

'He's the quiet one, Madame Valeix,' Valentin beamed. 'But he's a good worker, just like me!'

'Well, you're both very welcome. I imagine that you're hungry after your journey?'

'We're always hungry, madame,' Valentin said, as we turned and left the station.

'Less of the *madame*,' I instructed. 'Call me Jeanne, please, both of you. And this is Turk, by the way.' The dog seemed as pleased to meet our new company as I was, and the four of us set off together, in joyful mood, to buy something for lunch.

We left the jeep in the car park and went on foot to the market to buy a couple of spit-roasted chickens, bread and salad. I bought an expensive gâteau from M. Lopez on the Rue Gambetta, and on the way back to the car we stopped for coffee in the sunshine on the Place Decazes. I realised I was spoiling my new charges already, but as with Isabelle's lovely kids, I couldn't help it. Anyway, I reasoned, I'm certainly going to make them work for their keep.

We strolled back to the car park and located the jeep. The air inside was as hot as hell, so we drove home with the windows down, rejoicing in the summer sunshine. 'Maybe the dog days are here early this year, eh Turk?' I called to the terrier, who replied from his position in the back with an excited woof. Valentin sat in the front on my right, and Paul positioned himself in the middle of the back seat, listening to his cousin and me as we chatted. I was told what a coup it was for them to be working on a Saint-Emilion vineyard for the summer and how they both hoped they could come back, at least for a weekend, during the harvest.

I still hadn't cleaned the room where Aimée had stayed. I don't know why, but something prevented me from tackling the job. The boys said that they wouldn't mind sharing a bedroom, so I made up two single beds in Henri's old room. Aimée's room would remain untouched for the time being.

I reinstated the work rota which proved to be just as efficient with the Valeix boys as it had been with my previous guests. They were hard workers – and cheerful, too. By the end of their first two weeks at Fontloube, a pattern of work, mealtimes and occasional nights out, was established. It was as though the cousins had always been around. I wondered if living with two Valeix men would evoke melancholic memories of Olivier and Henri, but our situation gave me a new strength and a feeling of purpose. Apart from the fact that neither of them had a full driving licence – and I insisted on fetching them before midnight if they were out late – having Valentin and Paul at the château was a great help and a real pleasure.

Valentin's sociability made him an ideal salesman, and his patter worked wonders in the caveau. Even with English speaking buyers, when his charm and enthusiasm more than compensated for his lack of vocabulary, people just couldn't help but buy from him. I wondered if all the men of the Corrèze were genetically predisposed to entrepreneurship. After all, a fellow countryman had created the world's most famous and pricey red wine: Château Pétrus. Valentin was helpful in the house, too. He would make coffee for me, do the dishes and leave me little notes, signed with interlinked *Vs* and a kiss. In short, he was a joy to work and live with.

Paul was just as likeable. Although his shyness made him reluctant to deal with strangers, we soon grew fond of each other. Perhaps because he was less confident than Valentin, he appreciated my role of surrogate mother all the more. Happy to work on his own, he always volunteered for the outdoor jobs like pruning the excess leaf growth from the flourishing vines – an activity, he said, that did wonders for biceps and his tan. His dark, rugged looks made him popular with the local girls, and several times during that sunny first half of July, the boys returned home from an evening in the village with tales of each other's romantic conquests. I suppose it was because their personalities were so different that they got on so well. I wondered if this was what Henri and his brother had been like before the war, before their stubborn, enduring falling-out.

With two responsible family members looking after things for me at Fontloube, I found time to catch up with things in the office. I chased-up my debtors and paid-off my creditors, ordered next year's new oak *barriques* and began to think about ways of marketing my wines more successfully. I got Paul to put up brightly coloured signs at all the nearby road junctions, knowing that anyone who followed them would surely buy something from Valentin. Then I started the arduous process of looking for distributors and wine merchants in the UK. Having the boys at the château also gave me some time to myself. I took Turk for pleasant walks along the river, spent a hugely enjoyable day (and far too much money) shopping in Bordeaux with Isabelle, and wrote to my sister in England – something I hadn't done for years.

I even went to church.

Olivier's saint's day, the 12th of July, falls the day before his father's. On Saint Olivier's Day, three months or so after my husband's death, Henri and I had visited the collegiate church in Saint-Emilion to light a candle. My father-in-law, who was a thrifty man and a devotee of black humour, joked that when he was 'with the angels' I could save five francs by lighting a candle for Olivier on the 12th that would burn until the 13th for him. I had no idea how soon that day would come, but the following July I was obliged to do as Henri had instructed. Since then I hadn't been back, but with everything that had happened in the recent past, I felt the need to return.

That sunny Saturday morning would bring gridlock to the narrow streets, so I walked to Saint-Emilion. From the car park at the bottom of the town I joined the jostling bank holiday weekend visitors filing up the cobbled Rue Porte Bouqueyre. Following the human flow past the ancient *lavoir*, ducking under telephoto lenses and side-stepping the tourists, I reached the steep and narrow alleyway called the Tertre des Vaillants which brought me to the top of the town and the collegiate church.

Hot, and a little out of breath, I entered via the great west door of the nave and sat at a pew beneath the cupola to rest. Refreshed by the cool interior of the church, and awed by its sombre perpendicular architecture, I wandered along the aisle to the Martyrs' chapel. I stood at the entrance, staring at the sculpture of the crucified Christ in the arms of Mary Magdalene. Standing there, pacified by the serenity and security of the tiny chapel, I was deeply moved by the tragic theme of the statues.

'I know how you suffered,' I whispered.

I lit Olivier's candle and another for Henri that I hoped might burn until the following day.

On leaving the chapel, I spotted some faded medieval frescos on the wall of the transept that I hadn't noticed on my previous visits. The depictions showed a young maiden tempted by a horned devil, and an agonised Saint Catherine strapped to a wheel. Staring at the pictures, I heard an eerie weeping sound, echoing through the nave. At first I had the peculiar feeling that the sounds came from within me, that my subconscious had somehow recreated the anguished cries of the tempted and tortured women in the paintings. But there it was again, more loudly than before. Somewhere in the church a woman was crying. I wondered what tragedies had befallen her. Was she, like me, mourning the loss of a loved one – a husband, a parent . . . a child even? Perhaps she carried a heavy burden of regret, or suffered the burning brand of remorse. A sudden chill made me shiver. I crossed the transept and entered the cloisters to escape the girl's sad lamentations and, hopefully, to brighten my mood in the sunny quad.

Approaching the far corner I heard the echoing clickety-clack of heels on the stone slabs and moved to the side of the arcade to let the hurried visitor pass. The person stopped abruptly, inches behind me. I perceived a faint whimpering; clearly it was the girl I'd heard crying in the church. When I felt a shaky, tentative hand touch my shoulder, I knew exactly who it belonged to.

Rain

And Noah he often said to his wife when he sat
down to dine,
'I don't care where the water goes if it doesn't get
into the wine'.
- G K Chesterton, *Wine and Water*

'You!' I said, aghast.

Aimée stood before me. Her cheeks were shiny with
tears, her eyes bloodshot red. 'I am so sorry, Jeanne,' she
said, moving her hand from my shoulder and gripping my
arm tightly.

'Please let go of me, Aimée,' I said firmly.

Like a pair of broken vine stems, her arms fell limply to
her sides. She bowed her head, swaying slightly. I thought,
she's going to faint.

'I must sit down,' she said, sobbing quietly.

Aiding my adversary, I took her arm gently and led her
through the stone-arched doorway to the lawn.

We sat down on the grass in the sunshine, and I waited
for her to begin.

'I knew you would come, Jeanne, I knew it. The Holy
Mother answered my prayer.'

'Aimée,' I said coldly, 'I don't know what you think is
going on, but I came here to light a candle for my dead
husband. If I'd known that you were in the church I would
never have come.'

She looked at me, still crying, and said, 'So you think
it's just a coincidence?'

'Yes, a coincidence.' And one that I deeply regretted, I
thought.

'But you do not understand,' she ranted, 'you are not a

Catholic. I prayed to the Virgin and begged her to send someone to help me. It was a sign from God. I saw you from the Lady Chapel going out into the cloister, and I knew my prayer had been answered.'

Oh God, I thought, why did I come here today? I looked round at the four sides of the quadrangle as though searching for some excuse to leave. Finding no other device, I stood up and said, 'Aimée, you and Andrew hurt me very badly. And now, just when I'm starting to get my life together again, you confront me like this. I don't know what's wrong with you, and frankly I don't care. So please, leave me alone and go back to your lover.'

She looked up at me with the baleful eyes of a scolded child. 'That's just it,' she whimpered, 'I can't go back to Andrew. What he did to you he has done to me. I saw him with that slut, that . . . Wendy, in her caravan. He has done it again, Jeanne. He is the leopard whose spots he cannot change!'

Aimée's announcement stunned me. If what she said was true then the man that I'd fallen in love with was a serial womaniser. I needed to know more.

'Look,' I said, cautiously extending my hand to her, 'let's go somewhere else. If I'm going to hear your confession, I'd rather not hear it in church.'

Her dark eyes flashed me a questioning glance. 'What do you mean "confession"?'

'Well, not confession, perhaps,' I conceded, 'your revelation then.'

We left the church and went to a bar on the Rue du Clocher – a quieter place than the cafés on the square which, by now, would be bursting with tourists. I found a table in the shady courtyard and called for two glasses of white Graves.

Aimée told me that for the past three weeks since leaving Fontloube, she and Andrew had been living in the camper van in Saint-Emilion's municipal campsite. Since the end of term, Andrew's behaviour had become erratic, alternating between bouts of illness and drunkenness and, on one recent occasion, violence. She seemed reluctant to relate the circumstances of his sordid tryst, so I prompted her to tell me.

'And what about this woman – Wendy?'

'She is staying on the campsite during the holidays,' Aimée said quietly. 'A professor at a posh English university, apparently. She came over to introduce herself, and Andrew got on with her straight away. She charmed him with all her knowledge of literature and poetry, but I know that she's just an old slut looking for anyone in *pantalon*. The Slutty Professor, I call her.'

'So, they became friends?' I probed, ashamed of my curiosity, but desperate to know the details of Andrew's latest betrayal.

'Yes,' she went on, 'they got tipsy together on cheap *pinard* from the camp shop, and read poems to each other. When the hot weather came I caught them sunbathing in front of her caravan, whispering and giggling like convent school chatterboxes.'

I looked down into my empty glass and gestured to the waiter to bring us another round. He set the glasses down on the table and smiled at Aimée who maintained an icy, blank expression. Our waiter disappeared indoors, and she resumed her story. 'This morning I was supposed to meet a girlfriend in the market square, but she didn't show up. I walked back to the *camping car*, but Andrew was not there. I went over to the Slutty Professor's caravan and peeped through a gap in the closed curtains. Sure enough, the two of them were there on the bed. He was underneath her, and she was *accroupie* – how you say, squatting? on him. It was *dégueulasse* ... disgusting. Her horrible breasts! Such awful stretch marks! I didn't dare say or do anything, just ran here to the church.'

I regretted my sensational interest and felt bitter and slightly nauseous. Keen to dispel the mental image, I said, 'I'm sorry you had to go through all that, Aimée. Now, let's go and confront this Scottish Lothario shall we?'

'No!' she implored, grabbing my hand, 'Please, don't. I have caused you enough problems, and I have suffered enough, too. You don't know of what he is capable.' She lifted her tee shirt discretely to reveal the dark blue-and-yellow stain of a bruise on her abdomen. Seeing my look of horror she covered her face with her hands and sobbed, eliciting the interest of the waiter and the bar's *patron*.

I took her hands in mine. 'Is there anyone you can stay with, Aimée? You mentioned a girlfriend?'

She reached for her Lucky Strikes and lit one, inhaling deeply. 'She is going home for the summer, that's why we were meeting up – to say goodbye. Her flat is to be rented out until the start of next term.'

'Your family, in Paris?'

'I would rather sleep on the streets as long as my father is living at home.'

I put a ten euro note on the waiter's saucer and got up to leave. My conscience tugged at me in opposing directions. Should I turn my back on this girl who was responsible for my emotional breakdown? Or could I find some empathy with a fellow victim of Andrew's lascivious conduct. Even if I could empathise with her situation, I doubted I could find forgiveness in my heart. But I could, perhaps, provide some practical, disinterested help. Maybe she was right and some current of divine intervention had zapped me in the church. How else could I explain why I was standing there with Aimée Gonzalès, about to the invite her back to my home?

Assuming that Andrew and Wendy would still be occupied in some sweaty, post-coital discourse, I told Aimée to go and retrieve her stuff from the camper van and meet me at the gates of the campsite. I walked back to the château to get the car and drove to Saint-Emilion to collect her. As agreed, she was waiting for me outside the camp, seemingly unmolested. We returned to Fontloube watched by two curious teenage boys and an excited Jack Russell.

'Paul! Valentin!' I called, climbing out of the jeep. 'Come and meet Aimée.'

Fixing their best Hollywood smiles and puffing-up their chests, the cousins ambled over to the car and presented themselves. 'Bonjour,' said Valentin.

'This is Aimée Gonzalès, boys,' I said, without further introduction.

'Hello . . . boys,' Aimée said, glancing at me as though she expected some clarification. 'They aren't from the college, are they?'

'No, they're my husband's second cousins. They've come to work here during the holidays. This is Valentin, and this is Paul.'

'Oh, I'm sorry,' she giggled nervously, shaking hands with the boys. 'I thought maybe you were from my college in Libourne.'

'You're the girl who worked here a couple of months ago, aren't you?' Valentin asked. I'd told the boys very little about their predecessors, just enough to explain the few items of clothing and makeup that remained in Aimée's room.

'Yes, that's right,' she said, casually offering each of the boys a cigarette.

'No thanks,' Valentin demurred, 'we don't smoke. Are you moving back in then?'

She looked at me, smiling, and said, 'I don't know, Valentin—'

'Aimée is staying with us for a few days until she can find a place of her own,' I said, mirroring her smile.

'Great,' Valentin said, 'and we're so glad to see you, Jeanne. We we're starting to worry.'

Mistaking his concern to be for *my* well being, I said, 'Oh, you've no need to worry about me, I'm fine.'

'No, it's not that, Jeanne,' he said, looking at his watch. 'We thought that you might not be back in time for lunch.'

I looked at my wristwatch and realised the full gravity of Valentin's concern. It was nearly one o'clock and my poor workers had not yet been fed.

'What a disaster!' I mocked. 'And I suppose it would be impossible for you to make your own lunch, eh?' Both boys looked at me, then at each other, with eyebrows arched. 'And don't think that having two women around will mean even more pandering than you get already. I'm sure that Aimée is far less tolerant of male chauvinism than me.'

Aimée stood with one hand on the cloth roof of the car and the other on her hip, smiling condescendingly. 'Don't worry, Jeanne, I think we might teach them a thing or two about Women's Lib, eh?'

'But—'

'Right, Valentin,' I said, cutting him short. 'I'll go and get something from the market. You and Paul finish what you're doing here, then get an onion, a clove of garlic and some parsley, and chop them up finely. I'll be back in half an hour.'

Turk and I jumped in the car and sped off in the direction of Libourne.

Forty minutes later I returned to the château and burst through the door with a sack of Arcachon mussels in one hand, my keys in the other, and three baguettes wedged under my arm. Like a gaggle of hungry geese at feeding time, the youngsters, who had gathered in the kitchen, were clearly pleased to see me. I noted that Valentin had found and chopped the ingredients I'd asked him to prepare and that someone had opened a bottle of white wine.

'I heard the car on the drive, Jeanne,' Paul said, 'I thought you'd fancy an aperitif.'

How thoughtful, I mused, taking a proffered glass. Valentin took the shellfish from me and started to clean them in the sink while Aimée cut the bread into thick slices. I poured an immoderate dash of olive oil into the biggest of my heavy saucepans and added the onions and garlic which, once softened, I doused with a big glass of the wine. In went the mussels, and five minutes later we were settled at the kitchen table helping ourselves to a steaming pan of *moules marinières*.

'*Voila*,' I said dipping a crust of bread into the garlicky liquor, 'Fast food.'

'Muh-huh,' mumbled Valentin incomprehensibly, his mouth stuffed with food.

'It's delicious, Jeanne,' Aimée said. 'Thank you.'

On Tuesday morning, I decided to call my friend, Isabelle. I locked the study door and dialled her number, doodling on the notepad next to the phone.

After a couple of rings I heard, '*Allo?*'

'Hello, Isabelle,' I said, 'it's Jeanne. I hope I'm not interrupting you?'

'Not at all, Jeanne. It's good to hear from you. And no, you're not interrupting anything.'

'Good. How is everybody?'

'Fine. The children are at summer camp, and Stéphane is at the restaurant, so I'm enjoying a moment of *tranquillité*. How are you?'

I told her I was doing well and that the Valeix cousins were still thriving at Fontloube. I wanted to tell her about Aimée's reappearance, mainly because I'd made a promise to pass on any news about Andrew's whereabouts, and because I still had ambivalent feelings about harbouring my former apprentice. Strangely, I couldn't find the right words to explain what had happened at the weekend – the pilgrimage to the church and the encounter with Aimée – and I dried up.

Sensing my disquiet, she asked me outright if I'd heard from my previous housemates.

'I—' I stammered. 'Well, not heard from, no. Aimée's in trouble, and I've invited her to stay with us for a couple of days until she sorts herself out.'

'Jeanne, why didn't you call us earlier? Are you sure that you're doing the right thing?'

'It happened so quickly,' I said. 'I bumped into her at the church in Saint-Emilion. It seems that Andrew has betrayed her, too. And, worse than that, she's been physically abused – she showed me her bruises.'

'That's terrible, Jeanne. Are you sure it was Andrew who assaulted her?'

'I believe so, yes. Apparently he's been drinking, and he's taken another lover.'

'My God! Look, Jeanne, why don't I come over to talk to the two of you – she should go to the police.'

'She says she doesn't want to take it any further,' I said, realising I'd just invented that part, then adding (more truthfully), 'and she certainly doesn't want to see him again.'

'Well, if you're sure, Jeanne, but do call us if he comes to the château, okay?'

I assured her that they would be the first to know if Andrew came back into my life and thanked her again for the wonderful day out that we'd enjoyed the week before. I hung up and hesitated, staring out of the window.

Why had I lied that Aimée didn't want to involve the police? Who was I trying to protect – her or me? Or was it that I didn't want Andrew to get into trouble? The thought sickened me, and I felt ashamed of the possibility that I was protecting an abuser. It was as though there were two Andrews: the one that I had loved before, whom I wanted to keep out of harm's way, and this other Andrew: a violent, drunken philanderer, whom I still couldn't allow myself to contemplate. Looking down at the writing pad I saw that I'd sketched a large copperplate letter *A* adorned with vine leaves and tendril-like curlicues.

I turned the key in the lock and opened the door. Aimée stood in the doorway holding two mugs. 'Here you are, Jeanne,' she said, passing me my tea and smiling. 'A nice, how do you say, cooper?'

'*Cupper*, Aimée,' I corrected her, chuckling. 'Thanks.'

'I was just about to knock but my hands were full. I hope I'm not disturbing you.'

'That's okay,' I said, as we moved into the kitchen. 'I was just making a phone call. I thought you were going out to buy cigarettes.'

'Oh, yes, but I couldn't get the car to start. I think it has a flat battery.'

Like so many small jobs that needed doing, Clémentine's worn-out alternator had fallen off the bottom end of my priority list. 'You could take the jeep, if you like,' I offered.

'I can't drive big cars, Jeanne. I always end up scratching them.'

'Best not then, eh?' I said, enjoying my tea and imagining my treasured 4x4 careening through the narrow village streets with Aimée at the wheel. 'Get the boys to jump-start the 2CV, and make sure you keep it running when you get to the shop.'

Aimée banged the kitchen door shut, and I heard her calling to Paul and Valentin in the vineyard. I finished my drink and put both cups on the worktop. Oddly, though mine was still warm and stained with tea, Aimée's mug was stone cold. And it was clean.

My vineyard is a reflection of my life. It's hard work, mostly unrewarding and, above all, complicated. The mix of grape varieties, soil types and methods of cultivation means that, from the vine to the barrel, my wine is a cocktail of separate and unique ingredients, each created according to nature's whim. To make matters even more complex, I use oak barrels made from timber from two or three different forests. Each type of wood gives a subtle but unique flavour to the finished wine. Even people who claim to have no palate at all can tell the difference. A wine matured in Tronçais oak and another in, say, *chêne d'Allier* can be surprisingly different in aroma and flavour. Managing this kaleidoscope of flavours is so tricky that those who can afford to, pay their oenologists a fortune. I have to rely on my own judgement (and the expert noses and palates of a few gifted friends) to select and blend my wines.

In the early spring, a year and a half after the harvest, a

final blending produces the year's vintage. But in July, I treat myself to another of the jobs that make this work more tolerable: an early judgement of the maturing wines.

I went down to the cellar, pipette in hand, to analyse a hundred different wines in the only practical way I know – by tasting them. It was the only thing to do on such a rainy morning, the day after the *Fête Nationale*, the 15th of July. I noticed the date on the calendar pinned to the wall. It was Saint Swithun's day. Listening to the rain hammering against the caveau door, I imagined my father gazing up at the battleship-grey skies and woefully predicting the forty days of rain that would surely follow. I desperately hoped that the old adage (and the old fool) would be proved wrong because what my vines needed now, if I was going to make any wine at all this year, was lots of sunshine. What *I* needed was help; so I decided to let Aimée stay on at the château.

My weather worries were assuaged for a while as the rest of July turned out to be a sunny month. However, during the first two weeks of August the rain returned in torrents, and I feared that my vineyard slopes would be washed away and settle into a boggy tangle with the lower vines. But by the middle of the month, the sun began to shine on the blushing fruit whose colour changed, during one weekend, from green to diaphanous pink and, finally, to violet. Forty-five days later, with Mother Nature's grace, my grapes would ripen in time for an unusually late harvest.

Hot and sunny days, though, brought the threat of thunderstorms. One day, after a convivial lunch in the shade of the courtyard, Paul and Valentin had gone to work in the vineyard, and I had escaped the humid August heat by busying myself in the stockroom. Aimée, who'd been in Libourne all morning, arrived in the mid-afternoon and helped me finish off in the cellar before we hefted our secateurs and joined the boys in the vines.

Like many winemakers, I'm a neurotic. I worry about

my vines. The poor grapes had been more than usually abused by the elements this year, and I was determined to maximise the effects of the ripening sun when, like today, it decided to shine. Vigorous tufts of thick foliage had sprung up in the vine rows and formed a canopy of leaves, shading the darkening grapes from the sun. We set to work clipping the excess growth like a brigade of crazed al fresco hairdressers. As with many mundane, unglamorous tasks, the French have a wonderfully poetic word, *effeuillage*, for the process of defoliating the vines. During the *effeuillage* we clip out the diseased or immature bunches which reduces the yield of the crop, but improves the concentration and flavour of the wine. I'd lost count of the number of times I'd foreseen a disastrous harvest this year but carried on clipping and shaping, allowing the work to carry my anxieties away. Aimée and I worked silently. The boys, as usual, cajoled and laughed and joked.

Effeuillage also happens to be a slang word for *striptease*. This fact provided a source of seemingly unlimited mirth for the boys. From a few vine rows away, I heard Valentin say to his cousin how delightful it was being paid to watch two beautiful women 'doing a striptease'. Paul burst into hysterics – unusual for such a bashful boy – and I told Aimée to ignore their childishness. She winked at me conspiratorially. 'You would have to pay me a fortune to watch you two ugly yokels take your clothes off!' she called over to them. Then, taking a bunch of diseased fruit, she weighed it in her hand and launched it, grenade-style, at the boys. One of the cousins muttered a curse, and we continued our work, sniggering like a couple of naughty schoolgirls. A few seconds later a mildewy grape struck the front of Aimée's tee shirt, leaving a small splatter of green flesh and a purple stain on the white fabric. We both took cover and collected handfuls of the discarded grapes that littered the ground.

The grape fight that followed was a joyful diversion

from the day's toil. After the battle, with each side insisting that they had vanquished the other, we collapsed on the ground, happy and exhausted, shaking the grape pips from our tousled hair, and scraping the juicy flesh from our skin and clothing.

Turk, who'd chosen to ignore our puerile games, heard the distant rumbling before we did. Distracted from taunting a sand lizard in the bole of an ancient vine, he lifted his snout and growled ominously. He was already barking at the sky when the thunder reached our human ears. I looked down towards the river and saw two huge cumulonimbus clouds looming over the city, drifting inexorably towards us. I carried on working, hoping that the storm would be deflected by the *côte* and dump its load on Bergerac in the east, or be carried north up the estuary to rain on Bourg or Blaye. Apparently the dog feared the worst and continued his relentless howling. Bending down to comfort the frightened animal, I felt the first splash of rain on the nape of my neck. We all glanced at one another over the vine tops, knowing full well that the rain was on its way. Within seconds the downpour began. The sprint back to the house took us no more than a minute, but by the time we reached the shelter of the vat room we were all soaked to the skin.

With the prospect of a double date with two local girls they'd met over the weekend, the cousins were pleased to get an early finish, and they dashed up to their room to change. Aimée asked if she could take a bath and went to the house to switch on the antique water heater. I stayed in the open doorway of the winery, listening to the rain and watching the forks of lightning unite the dark sky with the vine-covered horizon. Eventually, when the cold air of the departing storm made me shiver, I followed the others into the house to change out of my wet, muddy, grape-stained clothes.

I bumped into Aimée coming out of the bathroom in a cloud of steam.

'You can have my bathwater if you like, Jeanne,' she said, passing me on the landing and wrapping her head in a towel turban. 'It is still hot and I wasn't that filthy!' she called over her shoulder.

I regarded my blurred reflection in the misty mirror, and considered Aimée's suggestion. I found the idea slightly repellent, but knowing that the antiquated heater wouldn't provide enough hot water for two baths, I thought, what the hell? After all, I used to share my sister's bathwater. I slipped out of my robe and into the warm comfort of the water. Lying there, relishing nostalgic memories of childhood bath times, I allowed myself to feel that I was part of a new, if unusual, family. Harder to come to terms with, though, was the thought that I was now the matriarch of this household. I was, well, getting old. But the idea that three young people were relying on me to guide them and care for them thrilled me nonetheless.

Listening to the sound of Aimée's hairdryer and the boys' squabbling (over their only clean shirt) I shut my eyes and sank down, letting the soapy water close in over my smiling face.

When I came downstairs, wrapped in my towelling robe, the boys had left for the evening, and Aimée was in the salon, reading a paperback on the sofa. I put a Fats Waller record on the turntable and thrilled at the opening bars of *Two Sleepy People*. Waller's slow songs are like a musical massage to me. They've always had a relaxing effect. The hot bath had eased my aching shoulders, and the music's lilting melody chased away any anxieties I harboured about my vines.

'Aimée, would you—' I began, intending the offer of a drink.

'Please,' she said, holding out her hand to interrupt me. 'Oh, I'm sorry, Jeanne,' she added, 'I'm on the last page.'

'Oops, sorry,' I mouthed and sat gingerly on the couch next to her, listening to the song's delicious intro.

She continued reading the book – a battered copy of *The*

Old Man and the Sea – and as her gaze descended to the bottom of the page she began to cry.

'Oh, Jeanne,' she said, sniffing, 'I don't usually cry like this. I feel so silly.'

'It's a sad little story, Aimée. It certainly made me cry when I first read it.'

'Yes, it is very sad. But perhaps I'm feeling homesick, too. I miss my sister.' She looked at me questioningly. 'It's awful, but maybe I'm missing *him*, too, Jeanne. He gave me this book you know. It was his favourite story.'

I recognised the book. Hemingway was one of Andrew's favourites. 'It's normal, Aimée,' I said. 'Sometimes you can feel betrayed but you never stop loving.' I passed her a box of tissues. She blew her nose noisily.

She closed the book at stared at the front cover. 'I can't imagine how the poor fisherman felt, after everything he'd been through, only to be left with nothing . . . I'd go crazy. I would drown myself in the gulf of Mexico, or let the sharks finish me off, that's for sure.'

'We all find ways to cope, Aimée. And don't forget that the old man had his friend the boy, didn't he? He was loyal to him right to the end.'

'Yes,' she sighed, 'I'd be like that boy, helping the old man to mend his nets and learning all his secrets. I've always sought the company of people older than me. The boy truly loved him, didn't he, Jeanne?'

'Of course he did, Aimée. And one day you'll find someone like that, too. Someone your own age, I mean.'

'Ha!' she exclaimed, 'People of my age are such idiots.'

'What about Valentin and Paul?' I asked, nudging her.

'Those two nincompoops! They are just kids. Like all the young men I know they are shallow, like the characters in some cheap romantic novel. I prefer older men; they have such depth. They fascinate me, like you do, Jeanne.' She moved a little closer to me on the sofa and stroked the back of my neck, allowing her slender fingers to caress my damp hair.

'Oh, I'm sure one day you'll find someone like the boy in the story, someone loyal and strong and devoted.'

'I doubt it. Why would anyone like that be interested in me?'

'You're a wonderful person, Aimée,' I said, my heart starting to race. 'I'm sure you'll find someone as beautiful and intelligent as you are.'

'I think I already have, Jeanne. Do you really think I am beautiful?'

My cheeks flushed, and I resorted to a line from *Jean Brodie*. 'You are marvellous and astonishing and desirable.'

'So . . .'

She paused, transfixing me with those languorous eyes, '. . . why don't we . . . go to bed?'

I hesitated, listening to the loud beating in my chest. 'I'm sorry, Aimée.'

Her eyes revealed how badly she had judged the nature of my feelings for her.

'Of course,' she said coolly, 'I . . . I am sorry.'

'Don't say that, Aimée,' I said, touching her shoulder. 'It's just that I can't love you like . . . like that.'

'I understand. I am not your cup of tea.'

I floundered. 'No, it's not that, you see I've never . . . you know?' I looked at her coyly and said, 'When I was a girl, I preferred geldings to mares, and I suppose I've always been the same.' I cringed and yearned for the sofa cushions to swallow me up whole, but I felt so awkward that I blathered on, stretching the horsey analogy way too far. 'And I suppose I'm still looking for a stallion . . .'

We both stared down at our hands, linked together on Aimée's lap. Thankfully, when we looked up at each other we laughed.

'I am so sorry, Jeanne, please forgive me. I hope that you find someone to love one day.'

'I think it may be too late for an old maid like me.'

The last chords of the song faded, the track changed and so did the mood. Aimée stared straight ahead as though searching for the answer to some cryptic clue. She budged up right next to me and said matter-of-factly, 'No way, Jeanne. Try positive thinking. If you believe in something, it will come true.'

'Like your prayers to the Holy Mother?' I said.

'Exactly like that, yes,' she insisted, disregarding my facetiousness. 'Just say to yourself, "before the end of the year I will meet the man of my future" and it will be so. Go on!' She looked directly at me, eyebrows raised in anticipation, willing me to make my portent. 'Go on, say it! I guarantee it will come true.'

'No, I can't.'

'*Allez!* I'll give you a reward if you do.'

'Okay, I'll say it.' I paused and swallowed. 'This year I will find the man of my future. There you are – I've said it.'

'That wasn't so bad, was it?'

'No, Aimée, it wasn't,' I said, smiling. 'Now, what about my reward?'

'A kiss,' she whispered, leaning towards me. She held my gaze until the moment when our lips touched. Her embrace was warm and sensual. When we separated I thought, you're so beautiful; how could any man refuse you?

'There,' she said, sitting up straight, 'sealed with a kiss, as you say. Now your wish is bound to come true.'

'I hope so, Aimée, but what about you? You have to make *your* wish now.'

'Oh, I've used up all my wishes already,' she said, getting up. 'The magic doesn't work for ever. And anyway, I don't believe in the future, Jeanne. Now, how about a cup of tea?'

'A cup of tea would be perfect, Aimée.'

She went to the kitchen, leaving me on the sofa to wonder what sort of teenage girl has no belief in the future.

Drugs

I am falser than vows made in wine.
- William Shakespeare, *As You Like It*

September approached, and with it the beginning of the
autumn term. It was time for the cousins to go home, and I
was sad that they were leaving. On the last Sunday of
August, Valentin's father drove from Corrèze in his van to
fetch the boys. He was, no doubt, curious to see what had
become of his cousin Olivier's property. Apart from a
thick Corrézien accent and his thickening neck and
waistline, Michel resembled Olivier outwardly. His
manner, though, was quite different. Despite being related
to me by marriage, he called me *Madame Valeix* and used
the formal *vous* to address me. But he was far from
unfriendly. The polite, quiet young man I met on my
wedding day had become a likeably ebullient farmer with
an infectious laugh and a mischievous glint in his crinkly
eyes. I asked after the health of his father, Jacques. The old
curmudgeon was, he told me, still living in a retirement
home in Uzerche.

We gathered round the long table on the sunny lawn,
wished each other '*bonne santé*', chinked glasses and
began a memorable lunch. Valentin and Paul sat opposite
Aimée and me, with Michel seated at the head of the table,
regaling us with old family tales and long-winded jokes,
the punch lines of which he seemed increasingly (and
hilariously) unable to recall. Valentin, who'd learned quite
a repertoire of cooking skills, had roasted a shoulder of
lamb on a fire of old vine roots – much to the amazement
of his father who told us that, at home, his son had never
so much as boiled an egg. Michel was just as impressed by

his nephew's newly acquired knowledge of vine cultivation. The conversation flowed as freely as the wine: a juicy, chilled Bordeaux Clairet.

By the cheese course, Michel and I were on first name terms, and when the time came to say goodbye, we exchanged kisses like old friends. Valentin's provisional licence allowed him to drive whilst accompanied by one of his parents, so he took the wheel on the journey home. He climbed into the cab, started the motor and revved the engine like an impatient racing driver. Paul and his tipsy uncle squeezed in next to each other and waved and blew kisses from the open window of the van. Valentin crunched the gears and set off jerkily down the drive, pursued by little Turk who yapped excitedly and chased his stumpy tail in circles.

The day's torrid heat (and the fruity rosé's deceptive power) made me sleepy, so I lay down on the chaise longue in the salon. Mild, flower-scented air drifted into the room through the open French windows, caressing my bare limbs and cooling my face. I dozed there for an hour or so until the smell of coffee roused me. When I heard Aimée calling me from the garden, I went out into the golden evening sunlight and joined her at the table.

I yawned unselfconsciously as she passed me a cup.

'Coffee, Jeanne,' she said, throwing me a knowing smile. 'Fresh and strong.'

'Thanks, Aimée. That's just what the doctor ordered.'

'I let you sleep. I thought you needed it.'

'Yes,' I said, suppressing another yawn, 'drinking wine in the sunshine always knocks me out. How are you feeling?'

'I'm fine,' Aimée said, grinning.

'The coffee has certainly perked you up.'

'Yes, I'm full of beans,' she exclaimed, getting up and grabbing her chair. She span round in a theatrical pas de deux, then put the chair down back-to-front, straddled it, and rested her chin on the seatback. 'Back to school tomorrow,' she said, in a singsong voice. 'I'm really forward looking to it.'

'Eager to see someone in particular?' I quizzed.

'Perhaps . . .' she said, with a sidelong glance.

'Oh, do tell.' I chivvied.

'It's a secret.'

'You're full of secrets, as well as beans then, eh?'

We both looked away, distracted by the trisyllabic call of a hoopoe, and watched the colourful bird, high in the branches of the horse chestnut tree until he fluttered away over the vineyard. 'Anyway,' I said slowly, 'I've found you out.'

She reached for her coffee, took a sip and smiled. 'What do you mean?'

'You don't like tea,' I said, leaning back like a gambler showing a winning hand.

'I do!' she said, raising her voice an octave.

'Aimée, whenever we sit down to have a cup of tea you either let yours go cold or you decide not to have one after all. The other day you even pretended to drink an empty cup!'

She continued to smile at me.

'Well?' I prompted.

'Well,' she began slowly, 'I know how much English people enjoy tea. When you first offered me a cup, I didn't want to upset you by saying I didn't like it.'

'You're so funny,' I said.

The two of us started to laugh.

'I just wanted you to like me, Jeanne.'

'People will like you because of *you*, Aimée. There's no need to pretend to be somebody else.'

'Oh, Jeanne, I know you're right. I just can't help myself sometimes.'

We sat and drank our coffee in the easy silence that followed. I drained my cup and said, 'I'll give you a lift to Libourne tomorrow, if you like. Clémentine is still playing up.'

'That won't be necessary. A friend is picking me up.'

'Ah,' I said, 'another secret, eh?'

On Monday morning, I was awoken by the sound of a car horn; I'd overslept. When I came down to the kitchen, Aimée was rushing out with her college bag in one hand, her Lucky Strikes in the other, and a slice of toast in her mouth. She gripped the cigarette packet between her thumb and palm and gave me a four-fingered wave on her way out, mumbling goodbye. I went to the doorway to see her off and spotted her lift, parked at the end of the drive. Student cars are not what they used to be, I mused, watching Aimée disappear into a black-windowed BMW. The car drove off at speed, leaving a cloud of limy dust settling slowly in its wake.

When I was six or seven, my grandmother had an allotment. I looked forward to the summer Saturday visits when I was allowed to help her harvest the fruits, flowers and vegetables that grew there abundantly. Together we would cut gladioli and chrysanthemums or gather snappy green beans, lettuces and courgettes for dinner. By July the fruits would start to ripen, and I would pluck bunches of ripe cherry tomatoes from the vine, hairy gooseberries from thorny bushes and handfuls of blackcurrants from their canes. A six-year-old doesn't think about the work that goes into a garden – the cold drudgery of winter digging, the sowing and planting and endless weeding that precede (and follow) the harvest – and, to me, Grandma's allotment was an everlasting Eden of colours and tastes. I always say that my interest in viticulture began in my grandmother's garden.

My favourite bed, whose rampant plants escaped into almost every corner of the plot, was the strawberry patch. Being an impatient and greedy child, I couldn't wait for the bright red fruits to ripen. One day, in early summer, I gorged on the under-ripe berries. The cramps of indigestion that followed my feast made me cry, and the taste memory of unripe strawberries has stayed with me ever since. The following week I was much more circumspect, but found that the fruit, rather than being sharply acidic and lacking in sugar, was juicily sweet and succulent. When the end of the summer came, I discovered something else: over-ripe strawberries are far less flavoursome and can taste – well, rotten.

It's the same with wine grapes. The fruit must be harvested at its peak. For my merlot vines, the perfect time to pick the fruit lasts only three to five days. This means I get three days, between not quite ripe and nearly rotten grapes, to bring in the crop. The maturity of the grapes at the start of September helps me to estimate the date of the harvest. Based on many years' data, my forecasts are usually accurate to within a day or two.

As Monday was the 1st of September, I took my refractometer into the vineyard to take some readings in each of the different parcels of vines. Sugar levels were still low, foretelling another late harvest – probably due to begin between the 5th and the 7th of October. An early-to-mid-week start to the grape picking meant I couldn't rely on the cousins, who would be back at school, to help me. I stowed my handy gadget and the test results in my tool bag and returned to the château feeling the onset of a headache behind my tired eyes.

I put my bag on the desk in the study and went to put the kettle on. While waiting for the water to boil, I looked through the drawer for some painkillers. I'd bought a packet at the pharmacy a couple of days earlier, but I couldn't find them anywhere. I wondered if Aimée (who was a chronic headache sufferer) might have borrowed them, and went up to her room to see if my hunch was right.

Aimée's vanity case had been left open on the bedside table. Compelled by the throbbing pain in my temples, I rummaged around in the case and soon found the packet of pills. But something else caught my eye. In amongst the collection of cosmetics, I saw a clear plastic bag containing a dozen or so pale blue capsules and a transparent sachet of white powder. Oh God, I thought, taking the bag and pouring the pills into my palm, here's yet another one of my protégée's secrets.

The painkillers eventually soothed my aching head. In the afternoon, I went to the study to contact my team of peripatetic grape pickers. I made a few calls to announce the harvest date and enjoyed hearing the foreign but familiar voices of the people who, like summer's swallows, return to Fontloube year after year. It was good to catch up with the grape pickers – the North Africans, Spaniards, Basques, and Eastern Europeans – who, over the years, have become good friends.

After making the calls and opening my mail (three bills – from the bank, the public tax office and the social security – all demanding immediate payment of debts plus interest), I turned my attention to the sales ledger for August. Valentin's salesmanship had resulted in a record-breaking take. His reluctance to use my credit card payment machine meant that the safe was full of cash and cheques, more than enough to satisfy my creditors. I filled out a paying-in slip for the cheques that came to over eighteen hundred euros. The notes added up to nearly twice that, but the figure was a couple of hundred short of the amount recorded in the books. I put this discrepancy down to the many small cash purchases that I forget to record, for bread, groceries and the like. My bank is closed on Monday, so I put the bundles of cheques and cash back in the safe, intending to deposit them later in the week.

I smiled, recalling Valentin's gift for commerce. But the smile quickly faded when my thoughts returned to the small problem of Aimée's cache of recreational drugs. I felt guilty about searching through her things, and I would have to tell her how I'd betrayed her trust. But there was no way I was allowing her to bring illegal substances into my home. I wondered, apprehensively, how I might go about confronting her.

I was staring up at the grandfather clock as the car pulled up on the drive. Seven chimes broke the silence in the kitchen. My heart rate, measured against the slow ticking of the pendulum, increased as I waited for the thud of the car's door and the crunch of footsteps on the gravel that followed. When Aimée appeared in the doorway, silhouetted by the evening sunlight, my heart and my thoughts were racing.

'*Bonsoir*, Jeanne,' she said breathlessly, dropping her bag on the table and skipping over to the sink. She filled the kettle from the cold tap and spoke to me over her shoulder. 'I've had such a good day. I think I am in love!'

I thought, here goes, there's only one way to say it.

'That's nice, Aimée,' I said dispassionately. 'Why have you got drugs in your makeup box?'

Her shoulders flinched almost imperceptibly, then froze like those of a startled cartoon character. Slowly, she resumed her activities, clicked the switch on the kettle and sighed. Still with her back to me, she replied with her own question.

'Why have you been looking through my things?' Her voice was calm like mine, but her tone concealed a threat, like the low, menacing growl of a cornered cat.

I felt defensive. The feeling irritated me, but I tried to remain detached. What I said was, 'I had a bad headache, and I was looking for my paracetamols.'

The kettle was coming to the boil. Still without turning round she spat back at me, 'Yet another hangover, eh Jeanne? You shouldn't drink so much.'

'And you shouldn't be taking this . . . stuff,' I countered, raising my voice. I got up from the table and tossed the plastic bag onto the worktop. 'Aimée, I can't have drugs in my house. You have to understand.'

She turned to face me, her expression showing no hint of feigned innocence or entreaty. 'Okay, Jeanne,' she said, 'but it's only a bit of coke and a few pills. And anyway, they're not mine. My friend – you know, the girl who went home for the holidays – she gave it to me for safekeeping.

I don't do drugs anyway.'

So calm, so confident, I thought. But something about the way she spoke suggested she was lying – the verbosity perhaps or the quickening pace. Or was it the careless repetition of the word *anyway*?

Anyway, I thought, I still don't think you've got the message.

'Listen, Aimée,' I continued. 'No drugs in the house, okay?'

'Okay,' she agreed, pausing to fill her cup with boiling water. 'I was supposed to give them back today. But in the rush this morning I forgot. I'll take them with me and give them back to her tomorrow.'

Pointing at the bag, I said, 'Fine, but don't let me ever find *this* sort of thing again.'

'Okay, but why—?'

I interrupted her, anticipating the question. 'Let me tell you a story, Aimée. Come and sit down.'

The two of us sat at the table. Aimée stirred three sugar cubes into her instant coffee.

I began. 'You know that my husband died in an accident? Well, a man drove into him, head-on, on a straight road, at nine o'clock in the morning.'

'Look, Jeanne, I don't see what this has got to do with—'

Again I interrupted. 'The driver was on his way home from an all-night party. He was high on cocaine and ecstasy.'

She stared at her cup, raised it to her lips and sipped noisily.

'What happened to him?' she asked. Her voice, in spite of the hot coffee, was cold.

'He nearly died, Aimée. He was in intensive care in Bordeaux for several weeks. He ended up a quadriplegic.'

'A quadri—?'

'—plegic,' I said. 'Someone who can't move any of their limbs.'

'You must hate him.'

93

'I don't despise him anymore. I just can't stand anything to do with drugs. Now do you understand?'

'Yes, of course,' she said, staring at her coffee again. 'But you had no right to search my things. Please, don't do it again.'

We spoke little that evening, but I discovered that the object of Aimée's affection was the driver of the BMW – a young man called Gregory. She was vague about their relationship and almost evasive about his occupation. I'd meet him, she told me, very soon. I went to bed before ten with the prospect of an early start in the morning. I was planning to go to the seaside and then to the city to deliver some wine.

I was up before Aimée. After our harsh words the previous evening, I hadn't asked her to help me with loading the delivery, but I would have been glad of an extra pair of hands. Once the 4x4 was packed with a dozen-or-so cases of Fontloube, I popped back into the house to see if she had risen. It was nine o'clock but she was still in bed, so I grabbed my bag and jumped in the jeep.

My departure coincided with Gregory's arrival. I pulled out from the drive just as a black, expensive-looking car appeared in the window, stopping only just short of the driver's door in a disharmony of screeching tyres and a blaring car horn. The BMW's side windows were opaque black, but the windscreen was clear. The face that stared at me, snarling and mouthing curses, was marked by a prominent scar that cut across the man's left eye, from his cheek to his forehead. Waving apologetically, I pulled out of the drive and navigated round the other car. I hate early morning introductions at the best of times, but I was particularly relieved that a doorstep meeting with Gregory had been avoided.

After turning right on the D670, I began an introspective monologue that would accompany me all the way to the coast.

Who was this boy she was seeing? Was he linked, in some way, to her secret stash? I didn't want to think that he was luring her into a world of drug addiction, but my prejudices pressed hard on my judgement – his BMW certainly looked like a drug dealer's car. Since Olivier's accident I've had a horror of drugs, but even while at university I never liked them. I wasn't a prude (and most of my friends had experimented with cannabis and the like) but I disliked the idea of losing control. And anyway, I much preferred the flavour of claret to the throat-burning taste of hashish – I've never been a smoker.

Of course, I'm aware of the hypocrisy. I recognise the conceit. I deliver consignments of possibly the world's most dangerous and addictive drug. I know that alcohol kills more people, in their cars and in their beds, than any other single drug; and I have thousands of litres of the stuff in my cellar. But understanding the argument can't change the way I feel about hard drugs and those who peddle them. At least, like all hypocrites, I'm not alone. Hypocrisies (and prejudices, come to that) are like haemorrhoids: most people over the age of forty have them, few like to admit it, and they're not easy to get rid of permanently.

My short-term memory kept interrupting my musings and hitting me with a double whammy of guilt and regret – the guilt I felt for rooting in Aimée's vanity case and the regret at how I'd confronted her so tactlessly. If only I'd used a softer, more diplomatic approach, I thought, perhaps our discussion in the kitchen could have been far more productive. I imagined an alternative conversation opener. It went like this: *Aimée, you know how my husband died in a car crash? Well, someone who was high on cocaine and ecstasy caused the accident. Since then I really can't abide drugs, and, you see, I'm really sorry for going in your room, but while I was looking for some headache tablets, I found this . . .*

I continued to bully my conscience like this until eventually my reasoning pulled me back to the actual events. I had to concede that, whichever way I looked at it, my discovery of her drugs and our subsequent confrontation were unavoidable. I did feel ashamed though. She was, after all, only a teenager.

One of Stéphane's highly talented ex-sous-chefs had opened his own restaurant in Arcachon. He'd built a good reputation serving posh, seafood-inspired food to the yachters and Parisian holidaymakers who dined at the marina there. Luckily for me, some of the restaurant's wealthy clients favoured a fine red Saint-Emilion with their lobsters, *noix de Saint-Jacques* and line-caught sea bass. *Le patron*, having sold out of my wine during the summer, wanted to buy some more. I drove westwards through the Gascony flatlands of Les Landes and arrived at the coast at about eleven o'clock.

Without stopping for lunch, I dropped off the consignment in Arcachon and returned to Bordeaux to make my second and third deliveries – two brasseries in the same street, both within shouting distance of the town hall. A long-running feud between the owners meant that they never spoke to each other. Neither man bought much wine, but they both paid the full delivery charge, and had done for years. Unless they declared a truce one day, I knew that my extra profit was safe because they'd never, ever find out. My next dispatch was to a country auberge near Margaux, after which I took the autoroute to Bergerac to drop off my final delivery (I never go via the D936). I arrived back at Fontloube just after six o'clock. Aimée still wasn't at home.

Clémentine still needed fixing. So, I called the garage in Libourne and requested a rendezvous. After the holidays, I was told, the mechanics had been swamped with work and couldn't possibly look at the car until Thursday morning. I said I'd be there when they opened at nine o'clock and noted the appointment in my diary. Below this entry I wrote the word *bank* and underlined it three times.

By Wednesday evening, there was still no sign of Aimée. Again, I scolded myself for the unsympathetic way I'd spoken to her on Monday night and hoped that her absence wasn't evidence of some sort of sulky protest. On Thursday morning, I was so worried about my absent lodger that I decided to call her school. After the first ring a young woman answered, '*Allo, l'Ecole d'Oenologie de Bordeaux.*' I asked to be directed to the Libourne campus. After another couple of rings, I was connected with the secretary of the school. I introduced myself and asked if Aimée had been attending lessons. The secretary told me politely to hold. After a long pause a man came on the line.

'Madame Valeix?' he began. 'Monsieur Vérac here, director of the School of Oenology. My secretary tells me that you are concerned about the whereabouts of ... Aimée Gonzalès?'

I was impressed that such a senior member of the staff was dealing with my enquiry. 'Yes,' I said, 'I haven't seen her since Monday, and I wanted to know if she had been attending her lectures.'

'Madame Valeix,' the director said slowly, sounding slightly confused. 'We have no one of that name attending the school.'

I was taken aback. 'There must be some mistake. She has been at the school since the spring term. I have a letter from you confirming her position here at my winery.' I repeated her surname and spelled it out.

'I'm looking at our enrolment list now,' he continued slowly and carefully, 'I have a Furet, a Gonet and a Guérin, but no Gonzalès, I'm afraid. I'm sorry.'

'Look, I don't know what's going on, but there must be something wrong with your system,' I insisted, the pace of my talking increasing with my cardiovascular rate. 'I have to come to Libourne this morning, so I can show you the letter if you like.'

'I would be very interested to see the letter, Madame Valeix. Please feel free to visit my office at any time.'

'Yes, okay, er,' I faltered. 'Thank you, monsieur.'

I put the phone down and stared at my diary, as though searching for some kind of order to impose itself on my chaotic mind. I read the two entries for the 4th of September, went to the safe to retrieve my cash and cheques, and put them in a large jiffy bag. I found the college's letter and stuffed it in my handbag. The jiffy wouldn't fit, so I put it on the kitchen table while I looked for my keys. Having found them, I went outside and inched the jeep slowly towards the Citroën until their bumpers kissed. I flipped both bonnets and attached the jump leads that live permanently on Clémentine's back seat. Once I'd started the engine I locked the house and left in a hurry, anxious not to miss my slot with the mechanic and impatient to find out what the hell was going on at the college. I had the letter and the car's log book in my handbag. I also had a nagging feeling that I'd forgotten something.

In less than fifteen minutes I was at the garage. I explained the problem with the car's starter motor to the receptionist and handed over my keys and the car's log book – the *carte grise*. It was only a five-minute walk to the college, but it took me twice as long as that to locate the director's office within the labyrinth of academic and administrative buildings on the campus. When, at last, I found it, there was no one at the reception desk, so I tapped on a door whose brass plaque read 'Pr. D. Vérac'. The director opened the door and invited me in. 'I wasn't expecting you so soon, madame,' he said, bowing his head ever so slightly and shaking my hand. 'Please,' he continued, gesturing to a large chair in front of a mahogany desk, 'do take a seat.'

'Thank you, monsieur,' I began, gazing at the impressive array of diplomas that the man had amassed. 'As I explained, Miss Gonzalès is apprenticed to me by your faculty, and I'd like to know if she's alright.' I handed him my letter, and he put on his reading glasses.

'I'm sorry to have to tell you this, Madame Valeix, but this letter is not from my office.' He peered at me over the rims of his spectacles and passed it back to me.

I looked again at the paper in my hand and said, 'But, I don't understand, monsieur, this is your name isn't it?' I turned the page over and tapped his signature to emphasise my point.

'Yes, that is my name, madame, but it is *not* my signature. I am a creature of habit, I'm afraid. I only ever sign documents with my own fountain pen, plus I only ever use blue-black ink. That letter has been signed with a black ball-point. Then there's the writing – the bad grammar and the spelling mistakes. Our budding winemakers find countless ways of abusing the French language, so I might reasonably suspect that this letter had been written by one of our students. The mystery, however, is that Aimée Gonzalès is not one of them.'

The official surroundings, the air of academia and Monsieur Vérac's confident and logical tone all conspired to weaken my grasp on reality; a deeply buried suspicion, suppressed for months but now clawing at the surface of my conscience, made me drop it altogether. I had to accept something. Whatever and wherever she was, Aimée wasn't enrolled as a student at Libourne.

It was only later, after I'd collected the car from the garage, that I realised what I'd forgotten. The mechanic told me that the car's starter motor and its alternator needed changing, and until he could get the new spares, I should leave the engine running if I had to stop. I was just about to say that I'd be going straight home when I remembered my planned visit to the bank. When it dawned on me that I'd left the cash and cheques on the table at home, I was half way across town. Being careful not to stall the car, I turned round in a quiet street and drove back to Fontloube.

I parked on the drive and noticed that the side door was

open and the kitchen lights were on. Aimée had returned. When I went in, she was sitting at the table, quietly reading a newspaper. She looked up to greet me, but I spoke first. 'I've just been to the college in Libourne. You're not enrolled as a student there. You never have been. You've got some explaining to do.'

I walked over to the sink, put my hand on the worktop to steady myself, and starred at her. She opened her mouth to speak, then closed it again when the phone rang.

I pointed an accusing finger in her direction. 'Stay there, Aimée,' I said.

The study door banged shut behind me. I answered the phone impatiently and heard the voice of the mechanic from Libourne. He explained that the replacement parts for my car would arrive the following Tuesday, and that they could do the work on the same day. I thanked the man and put the phone down.

When I came back into the kitchen, Aimée had disappeared. So, too, had the jiffy bag of money. I rushed out into the sunny courtyard, but she was already at the wheel of the jeep. She started the engine and, in a cloud of dusty diesel fumes, shot off towards the vines, spraying my poor 2CV with gravel. I raced to the car and got in, nearly trapping the dog in the door as he leapt in behind me. I put the key in the ignition and turned. Nothing. The car's engine wouldn't start. The two of us sat there, watching the 4x4 drive up the vineyard track that runs from the house to the main road. I pounded the steering wheel in temper and desperation. Turk put his forepaws on the dashboard and gave a high-pitched growl. Aimée reached the road, but she turned off the track too acutely, flattening the end of a vine row. She over-steered, causing the back end of the vehicle to skid in the soft earth, demolishing a stone gatepost and part of the wall that marks the boundary of the property. Well, I thought, she said she couldn't drive big cars. We watched hopelessly as she drove up the lane towards Saint-Emilion. I winced when I saw the damaged side panels, scraped and gouged with grey-white scratches.

Once again, I was alone.

I made myself a cup of tea, went to my study and telephoned the *hôtel de police* in Libourne. The officer who took my call listened patiently as I explained the theft of the car and the money. He took my name, address and telephone number, and wished me good day before ringing off. I glanced at my diary, still open on the desk, thinking: my God, only a month to go until the harvest. The Valeix boys were unlikely to be there to help, and as for Aimée, I didn't expect to see her again soon. Apart from my usual team of freelance grape pickers, it looked as though I would be doing another harvest on my own.

Absorbed in my thoughts as I was, the phone's ringing made me jump. I was surprised to hear another policeman introduce himself and curious to know why my case had attracted the attention of a *capitaine*. I thanked him politely and said that I'd already given all the details to the desk sergeant. He suggested that, in view of the subject's young age, the drugs connection and the possible accusations of fraud, he would like to interview me in person. Of course, I agreed and said that I'd be at the château all afternoon.

Captain Pierre Lefèvre arrived at two-thirty in a shiny unmarked police Peugeot. I greeted him on the drive and invited him into the salon for coffee. His greying hair and lined features seemed at odds with his athletic stance. He must play squash in his spare time, I mused, or else he runs. His face wore a somewhat defeated expression – the job clearly gave him more occasion to frown than to smile. But he scored quite well on the desirability scale.

And I had a feeling that we'd met before.

We sat opposite each other at the small table in front of the marble fireplace. Silently, he took in his surroundings and watched me fussing over the coffee cups, saucers and spoons. When I upset the sugar bowl, he reached over to help me retrieve the scattered cubes. I noticed his tanned, unadorned fingers. He didn't wear a wedding ring.

'*Alors*,' I sighed, slightly out of breath, as I passed him his cup. '*Prenez-vous du sucre?*'

'*Merci*,' he replied, with a shake of the head. 'I am, as you English say, sweet enough.'

'Your English is very good, Captain,' I said, stirring my coffee.

'Thank you, madame,' he said, 'and your French is excellent, too.'

So, I thought, that's dispensed with the pleasantries. He continued to stare at me.

To break the silence, I asked, 'Have we met somewhere before?'

He lowered his eyes, looked at his coffee cup and sniffed. 'Yes, Madame Valeix,' he replied, 'I worked on the investigation following your husband's accident.'

A vague memory returned to me of a young lieutenant who'd investigated the narcotics connection after Olivier's accident. He hadn't interviewed me, but he'd certainly visited the house to talk to Henri. 'I think I remember you,' I said. 'You were interested in the drugs element, weren't you?'

'Yes, I suppose that's my area of specialisation.'

'Ah, so that's why you're interested in this case?'

'Yes, in a way. I would be very keen to talk to the young lady who has taken your four-wheel-drive. If what you have told us is true, she has quite a list of criminal misdemeanours to answer to – theft, deception, criminal damage, possible embezzlement, and possession. We are particularly interested in the drugs angle.'

'Of course, but I don't think Aimée is a serious drug user. The stuff I found didn't look like much.'

'We are looking at all possible leads,' he said.

'Is this related to a particular case then?' I asked.

He put down his cup, leaned forward a little. 'Ours is not a big town,' he explained, 'but our proximity to Bordeaux means that, when there's a crime wave in the city, we sometimes feel the . . . ripples – is that the word?

– here in Libourne.'

'I see,' I said, 'But I can't believe that Aimée would be involved in anything like that.'

'As I said, we're looking at all the leads. Now, if you could give me a description of Mademoiselle Gonzalès, I can be on my way.'

No further questions, I thought. It seemed that the captain was more interested in Aimée, than he was in my missing car and cash. I gave him a full description of the girl's physical appearance, and related the circumstances of her arrival and placement at the château. He seemed particularly interested in Andrew's part in the story.

In the hallway, I handed him a carrier bag containing the few possessions that Aimée had left behind, and asked him what the chances were of getting my car and money back. He said that although the jeep would probably turn up sooner or later, it was less likely that I'd ever see the cheques and cash again. He told me to contact my insurance company and gave me the crime number I'd need to make a claim. When I asked if he thought Aimée would be found, he was more optimistic. She was almost certainly using a false identity, and in view of her age, she had probably been declared missing. If so, and my description revealed her true identity, the police could then contact her parents. He promised to let me know if there were any developments on the case. I told him to visit any time, especially if he wanted to buy some wine.

Just as the policeman pulled out onto the lane, the little yellow post van arrived with the day's mail. The post lady passed me a couple of official-looking letters then wished me *bonne journée* as she sped off to her next address. I ambled back to the house, opening the envelopes, knowing full well that any news they contained would be bad. There was a letter from my bank, informing me of the charges I'd incurred for bursting my overdraft (again), and a bill from the insurance company requesting another year's payment for the cover on my two cars, one of which was now missing.

After lunch the following day, I decided to give Aimée's bedroom a good spring-clean. I lugged the Hoover into the room, cleaned the carpet, stripped the bed, then moved the bedside cabinet away from the wall in order to pass the vacuum behind it. Something caught my eye in the gap between the cabinet and the wall. Reaching in, I retrieved an unmarked A5 envelope, which I emptied onto the mattress. I stared at the envelope's contents: a cross-channel ferry ticket, a railway ticket from Calais to Libourne via Bordeaux (both dated April the 30th) and a postcard, written in a familiar hand, destined for an address in Richmond, Surrey. I examined the postcard. On the front was a blue-sky panorama of Saint-Emilion, and on the back an international stamp postmarked April the 15th. I read the message several times before the realisation sank in. It was the card that Andrew had told me he'd written during his first couple of weeks at Fontloube. The address and postmark proved that it had been sent to (and, presumably, received by) his son, Archie. It read:

Hope you and Poppy are well. I'm in Saint-Emilion in France, at the château of a nice lady called Jeanne Valeix. Not planning to move on again soon but, if I do, I'll be sure to let you know. In the meantime you can contact me here –
Château Fontloube, Saint-Emilion 33330, France. This is the phone number – 00 33 557 090 368. I'd love to hear from you. Missing you both. Love Dad. xx
P.S. Hope you like the numbers!

Aimée's railway ticket was just another piece in the jigsaw of her elaborate subterfuge, of that I was sure. But, if the morning's bizarre events had confused my already fuddled wits, the discovery of Andrew's note to his son left me completely dumbfounded. I sat down heavily on the divan and reread the postcard. There was only one thing I could do to begin to unravel the tangle of misinformed beliefs and false assumptions that now constituted my exhausted mind. I had to go and confront the man who had betrayed me – the seducing, womanising abuser, Andrew Maconie.

Truth

In vino veritas [In wine is truth].
 - Pliny the Elder

Up the *côte* I cycled, sweating like a Tour de France yellow-jersey on an alpine climb. My canine passenger, sitting in the bike's front pannier, made the ascent a leg-aching punishment. Mentally, too, the journey was a trial. I dislike (and usually avoid) confrontation, so the prospect of meeting Andrew again disturbed me. What I dislike more, though, is the feeling of being hoodwinked. So with fiendish dilemmas and unanswerable questions colliding with each other inside my head, I was on my way to see the only man who could help me solve the puzzle.

As I pedalled, I tried to put my thoughts into some sort of order. The railway ticket suggested that Aimée had arrived in Libourne on the day we first met. The following day, when I dropped her off on a residential street, I saw her in the rear-view mirror, waving, but I didn't see her go indoors. Now I knew that she wasn't attending college, but had she even been living in Libourne? If not, how could she have known that I was looking for a student apprentice? How had she recognised me in the crowded ticket hall? And why was Andrew so hostile towards her? As for the postcard, I recalled badgering Andrew to write to his children, and, evidently, he'd done so. But how had his note made its way back to Fontloube and into Aimée's bedroom?

Secrets and lies had shaped the past six months of my life. I was a mark, a dupe, a patsy, a kid left on her own to count to a hundred in a game of hide-and-seek that everyone else had abandoned. Could the disclosure of

Aimée's lies reveal some exonerating truths about Andrew, or help me recover the stolen four-wheel-drive and August's takings? Well, I could hope . . .

A tractor, emerging from a narrow lane, forced me to brake hard to avoid a gruesome entanglement with its wheels. The driver waved apologetically, and I waited at the side of the road to catch my breath, straddling the bicycle. After a few seconds, I set off again and followed the *enjambeur* out of the village, eastwards, until I arrived at the entrance to the campsite. My gremlin whispered, *go home, Jean, it's downhill all the way from here*, but my insatiable curiosity prevailed. I freewheeled through the gates and saw the familiar white camper van with its GB bumper sticker. Clearly, Andrew was still in residence.

When Turk spotted his master, he leapt from the basket and cantered over to him.

'Turk!' Andrew cried, 'Where have you been my boy!' He knelt down on the sun-scorched lawn and stroked and tousled his erstwhile companion. When he looked up at me, his face, shaded by the brim of his hat, was wet with tears. His voice was piteous. 'Jean,' he said, 'I'm so glad you've come.'

Despite my meditations during the ride to the campsite, I was unsure how to begin. Starting with the previous day's major event, I said, 'Aimée's gone.'

'I see,' Andrew replied, rising, with some effort, to his feet. 'She was with you then?'

I nodded.

'And you say she's gone? As in . . .?' he asked, adjusting his Panama.

'As in, left Fontloube,' I explained, 'taking my 4x4 and a few thousand euros of mine with her.'

'I see,' he said again. 'You'd better come inside, Jean. The kettle's on. I think it's time you knew the truth about Aimée.'

He climbed up the step and into the camper followed by Turk and me. Half-a-dozen empty bottles, that threatened to trip us up in the doorway, were sent clattering across the vinyl floor by the excited dog. As Andrew scrambled to right the toppled bottles, I looked at the interior of the van. A half-finished litre of whisky and a grimy tumbler shared the table with a random pile of official-looking documents, doctors' prescriptions and medicines. The disarray had spread to the other horizontal surfaces in the kitchen-cum-dining space. Only the gas cooker, on which a kettle was hissing to the boil, was free of papers and pills. He rummaged in the cupboard and produced a couple of clean mugs and some teabags.

I sat at the cluttered table. 'What's all this?' I asked, indicating the drugs.

'Oh, it's mostly medicine for my diabetes.'

'And the whisky?' I chided.

He sat down opposite me, smiling, disregarding my sanctimony. 'Ah,' he said, 'that's one of the reasons for the diabetes.'

I said, 'I'm sorry, I didn't know you were—'

'An alcoholic?' he quipped.

'No, I mean a diabetic.'

'Well, it's one of my new conditions. And no, don't worry, I'm not really an alky, although whisky and me do go back a long way.' He shuffled a few documents together to clear some space on the table. 'Luckily,' he said, 'I've got old Wendy to help me with all this paperwork.'

Old Wendy? 'Yes, I've heard about Wendy.'

He threw me a quizzical look, turned and paced over to the hob to silence the whistling kettle. 'Look, before we talk,' he said, pouring the water, 'I've got to make one thing clear, Jean. I'm leaving, too.'

'I'm glad I caught you then,' I said, trying to sound forthright, but hearing my voice waver, almost petulantly.

He stirred the cups and continued his theme. 'Aye, and just in time, too. I'm off tomorrow. You won't have to hear from me again, Jean. Turk can stay with you or come with me, that's up to him, but I'm off back to Scotland to stay with my sister.'

This was not what I was expecting. There was no way he was taking the dog away, nor was I going to let him escape from this bloody mess just yet. What I wanted to say to him (in true crime investigator style) was: *you're not going anywhere, Mister, until this case is solved.* However, all I could manage was a feeble 'okay'.

He put the teas on the table and sat back down. 'Now,' he said, sighing, 'what's our Aimée been up to, then?'

I described Aimée's return to Fontloube and her recent departure, leaving out my discovery of the tickets and the postcard. After relating the story, I said, 'Now, you said you wanted to tell me the truth about Aimée? That's why I'm here, Andrew – to hear the truth.'

'Where do I begin?' he said slowly, fidgeting with his cup. 'She's not called Gonzalès, you know. Her real name's Aimée Loroux. She's twenty-five, and when I knew her in London she was working for a city temping agency.'

This was not getting any clearer. The hot drink scalded my tongue, but I managed to say, 'You . . . *knew* her?'

'Yes, Jean. I'm afraid so. She was the reason for my break-up with Deborah. In fact, if I hadn't complied with my ex-wife's demands, Aimée would have been the sole co-respondent in the divorce. Very, very, stupidly, we had an affair. It was a late-mid-life fling with a beautiful office girl, an ego tripping month of madness that, foolishly, I didn't take seriously enough – until it was too late to regret it, that is.'

Where was the clarity I sought? Where were the explanations? The simple answers to straightforward questions? I asked another: 'So Aimée was your lover . . . before?'

'Yes, at first, I suppose you could say we were lovers. It started like an impossible dream, but it ended in a nightmare. To crib Ted Hughes – it wasn't long before our little cries, that had once fluttered into the curtains, began to crawl along the floor . . . I soon realised that love was not what she was looking for.'

I looked at him blankly and thought: for God's sake, I'm an emotionally damaged woman, and he's quoting *that* at me! Where was this leading? I wanted answers, not poetry. 'Go on,' I muttered.

His story flowed, he left his tea untouched, and his eyes did not leave mine for a moment. 'Unfortunately, Aimée has one or two expensive habits, and she wanted far more from me than romance. When I refused to leave Deborah, she found a way to destroy our marriage. That trick she pulled, with the knickers in the bed? She'd done that once before. The first time was more subtle, though. A diamond earring and a splash of perfume on the back seat of my car were enough to arouse my ex's suspicions – enough for her to employ a private detective, anyway. He didn't have to work too hard for his fee, but the photos he took of that girl and me won my wife a lot of money. I'll spare you the details, but my liaison with Aimée cost me my marriage, my kids and, eventually, my job. When she realised that the divorce settlement had left me without a penny, she dropped me, left her job and moved on with a very different set of people. I was living alone and drinking more than I could handle. Then my company was taken over. I lost my job.'

He took a swig of tea before continuing, 'I bought this camper with the severance money, and came to France in search of adventure and inspiration. I suppose I found both. I've never been happier than I was during those first few weeks we spent together, Jean. I thought I had everything – a beautiful woman, a wonderful place to live, a worthwhile job . . . Anyway, before she turned up in Libourne that day, I'd begun to hope that Aimée was just a painful, fading memory. And then there she was as bold as brass. She'd cut and bleached her hair and swapped her expensive clothes and high heels for cropped jeans and trainers, but she was the same girl alright, the same old Aimée. I nearly had a heart attack. Then, when she asked me what I did for a living . . .' He turned to the window, lowered his eyelids and exhaled slowly. When he opened his eyes, the park, with its neat, parched plots and white leisure trailers, held his gaze.

So, Aimée had recognised Andrew, rather than identified me, in the crowded railway station. That much was clear, but I was still confused. 'Why didn't you say anything?' I asked.

He continued to look through the glass. Then, like two strangers on a train, we realised we were staring at each other's reflection. He turned his head to look at me. 'I'm a fraud, too, Jean,' he said. 'I'm not a poet. I was in marketing – in the wines and spirits business. I did read English at Edinburgh, sure, and I've always loved literature and poetry, but I've never had anything published. I'd set a trap with my own lies, and Aimée's had sprung it. I was caught, like a rat in a cage.'

'Yes, just like a rat,' I had to say.

'I know, I know,' he said, raising his hands, palms forward. 'But that was just the start, you see. Aimée is capable of inventing any kind of fiction in order to get what she wants. I knew I had to go along with her story – if not, she would ruin everything. I'd already fallen in love with you, Jean, but I knew that one way or another, Aimée was going to come between us.'

'Why though? You said that she'd lost interest in you after the divorce. Why did she come looking for you?'

'She'd kept in touch with a girl from the office who'd told her about my redundancy. I tried to convince her that I was skint and begged her to leave, but she thought I was hoarding a big pay-off, see? Remember that first night? She visited me in here in the early hours and made her demands. If I didn't go along with her story, she'd say that it was me who'd set everything up. After all, only I knew that you were looking for an apprentice. Apparently, she had something that would prove that I'd arranged for her to come to Fontloube.'

The train and ferry tickets, I thought. At least they corroborate his story. 'But if *you* didn't tell her about the position at the château, how could she have known?'

'That's one of the things that puzzles me the most. I guess I was the only person who knew about that, but it wasn't me who told her. I swear it.'

I recalled our first conversation. Had I assumed that she was enquiring about the apprenticeship and mentioned, unwittingly, that I was looking for a student? Could she have invented a story based on my one simple misapprehension? Well, perhaps. With what she knew about me from the postcard, it was, at least, possible.

I already had the answer to my next question, but I wanted to gauge Andrew's response. 'Okay,' I said, 'but how did she find you here in the middle of rural France?'

'There are things that I still don't understand, Jean. I have no idea how she found me. She would never tell, and I still don't know.'

Ah yes, I thought, but I do. Now, let the rat explain himself. 'So why *did* you pretend to be a poet?'

'I didn't intend to deceive you. It's just that I had to reinvent myself. I wanted to be the kind of guy who's defined by what he says and does, rather than by how much money he's got. I mean, would you have put me to work in the vines if I'd told you I was a millionaire? Maybe I've been unlucky in love, but all my relationships start and end with the same dilemma: who gets what out of this? What I needed was unconditional love, and I thought I'd found it. Well, there's no fool like an old fool, I guess.'

'So you're a millionaire, then?'

'Och, no. Like I said, what with the alimony, the child support, two mortgages and the school fees, I've got nothing left. Apart from this van, and a few . . . mementoes from my previous life, I'm broke. It didn't take Aimée long to cotton on, and I've barely seen her since we left Fontloube.'

'You mean she hasn't been living here?'

'You don't think she'd want to live like this, do you?' he said, casting a glance round the cramped room. 'Not Aimée! She spent most of the summer with her so-called friends in Bordeaux. Until she got hurt, that is. Then she came crying back to me.'

'What happened?'

'She got beaten up pretty badly. I told her to go to the police but she refused. She was involved with some very dodgy people. I tried to appeal to her conscience and convince her to go home to her family, but unfortunately she doesn't have one.'

'What,' I asked, 'a family?'

'No, a conscience; her folks live in the North. I don't know where, exactly – that's all she told me. She knew she could stay here with me, but when she found out about my condition, she upped and left, and that was the last I saw of her. I didn't think she'd have the nerve to go back to you, though. But clearly her cover story, and a few more lies, gave her the perfect excuse. God, she's canny.'

My thoughts, which had been focussed on the memory of Aimée's bruises, drifted to Andrew's state of health. 'What do you mean, "condition"? Do you mean your diabetes?'

'No, not that. Listen, I know I'm repeating myself, but I want you to understand something. I don't think you'll see Aimée again, and from tomorrow I'll be gone, too, and you can get on with your life. When I told you I loved you, I meant it. When I asked you to believe me, just before you threw me out, I wasn't lying. I never slept with Aimée at Fontloube and, in my heart, I remained faithful to you ever since. There, that's it. Okay?'

Andrew's entreaty sent my thoughts racing back to the confession in the kitchen, to his look of desperate resignation and Aimée's arrogant stare. The fact that the betrayal, like almost everything Aimée had told me, was a lie, hurt almost as much as my discovery of it. Their guilty admission, however brazen and cruel, was at least (or so I had believed) the *truth*. My life had been touched by tragedy, but until Aimée arrived, I had never suffered the sting of deceit. I felt like one of those lumbering flightless birds whose existence is threatened by an invader against which it has no defence. Jeanne Valeix: the dodo in the *deux chevaux*. Deceit, I reasoned, is a deadly predator – quite literally so for the tragic jilted suicide or the clumsily murdered victim of *le crime passionnel*. Infidelity hurts, but the lie is the real killer.

And what did he mean by 'in my heart I remained faithful to you'? If Andrew had, as he insisted, been faithful to me before he left Fontloube, could I blame him for being seduced by the charms of a twenty-five-year-old goddess after I'd thrown him out? Should I feel jealous? Who was I kidding – I'm no goddess but I am, at least, human. Of course I was jealous.

My musings over, I saw that Andrew was waiting for me to respond. 'Yes, of course, but why are you telling me this? And why should I believe you *now*?'

'Because, now I've got nothing to lose, and whether you believe me or not can't change what happens next. Before the diagnosis, I hoped that with Aimée off the scene we might get together again. But now? Now, I won't put you through any more pain and—' He stopped himself, drained his cup and took the empties to the sink. He continued talking, with his back to me. 'I've hurt you enough, Jean, and I don't want to hurt you anymore.' He turned round. '*I'm away hame tae bonnie Scotland*,' he said, affecting a lilting Highland accent. A gold tooth glinted in his warm smile. His moist eyes sparkled.

'What are you saying, Andrew?'

'I'm ill, Jean, very ill. It's my pancreas. I don't understand everything the doctor says – he can't speak a bloody word of English – but I know I'm not going to get better.

The significance of Andrew's words dawned on me – *I've got nothing to lose . . . nothing can change what happens next . . .*

'You mean—?'

'Yes, Jean, the big C,' he said, his smile fading.

I looked again at my reflection. A faltering heart was pumping its five litres of blood to my stomach and bowels, fingertips and toes – to everywhere, that is, except my face, which was as pallid and deathly as baker's dough.

Avoiding my emotions, I resorted to a practical question. 'So, you'll be having treatments then? Chemotherapy? Radiotherapy?'

'Yes, of course,' he said thoughtfully, adding, 'but palliative, not curative.'

'You mean there's no cure?'

'Apparently not, no. My sister Mary is taking me in, and I'll get all the treatment I need in Scotland. I'm sorry you had to hear all this. Really, I am.'

'Your sister?'

'Yes, my younger sister, Mary. She and her husband have offered to look after me, you know. Mary's a wonderful person. You'd love her, really. But like quite a few of my family, she's a bit crazy.'

In spite of the dire gravity of the conversation, I was intrigued. 'What do you mean, crazy?'

He hesitated, and the smile returned. 'She talks to dead people,' he said, chuckling.

'Andrew, this is serious—' I began.

He interrupted me, saying, 'I'm serious, too. She's a spiritualist, you know? In contact with the *other side*.'

He wasn't joking.

Stop, I thought, rewind. This has gone too far. It was time for me to lay my card (singular) on the table.

'Andrew,' I said, 'I've got something to show you.'

The world had been turned upside down. My ex-lover and Scottish poet-in-residence was actually a redundant marketing executive with terminal cancer, and my teenage apprentice was really a thieving, twenty-something confidence trickster. The whisky was a welcome relief. I gave Archie's postcard to Andrew and showed him the tickets. We drank and talked, returning repeatedly to certain events: Aimée's appearance and the cruel charade that forced us apart, her return to Fontloube and her subsequent dramatic departure.

She had come to Libourne to find Andrew, but grander

ambitions soon overtook her initial plans. Her acting talents won her a comfortable home, a source of income and plenty of free time. Realising that Andrew and I were a couple, she'd plotted successfully to split us up, and all the while she knew that she could lie her way back into my life, whenever she wanted to. The next time I saw her, she was certainly upset. She'd been beaten up, and she'd just found out about Andrew's illness. The role of the abused and betrayed victim was an easy one for her to play. How could I have refused to help her? When I thought she was attending classes, she was with her associates in Bordeaux. She must have known that her days at Fontloube were numbered, and she would surely have prepared a ready-made excuse for lying to me. But, with a fat envelope of cash in front of her, there was no need to continue a farce that had already begun to bore her. Oddly, I felt no animosity, just a weary melancholia – for myself, for Andrew, maybe even for Aimée, too. Perhaps we were all victims, in one way or another, of our various crimes.

The shadows lengthened on the grass, spawning shapes of elongated, crooked cars and flattened caravans that crept, imperceptibly slowly, across the campsite. Our cyclical conversation could go no further. It was time to leave. We stepped out into the warm, saturated glow of the early evening sun. The whisky, the cool breeze that blew across the plateau, and a sudden rush of oxygen to my brain made me feel dizzy. I steadied myself by gripping the handlebars of my bicycle. I felt hungry.

'Remember when you invited me to dinner and I turned you down?' I said, squeezing and releasing the bike's brake handles distractedly.

Andrew looked at me, squinting into the lowering sun. 'Of course I do,' he said, 'don't tell me you want to accept the invitation now?'

'Well,' I replied, still fidgeting with the brakes, 'if you're not doing anything . . .'

'I'll have to consult my social diary, Jean. Just hang on

a tick.'

He disappeared back inside the camper and returned a few seconds later carrying a dusty bottle. 'If I take you to Saint-Emilion's best restaurant, d'you think they'd mind if I brought my own wine?'

I looked at the bottle's label, completely astonished. 'I'm sure the sommelier could be convinced to open *that*, Andrew. Where the hell did you get it?'

'Oh, it's part of what's left of my fortune. I've got another couple of bottles in the van, too.'

I re-read the label: *Château Pétrus 1990.* 'I hope the lock on that door is a strong one, Andrew,' I said, *sotto voce*. 'Have you got any idea how much this stuff is worth?'

'More than the camper van,' he said, laughing, 'that's for sure.'

I left Turk with his master, and cycled home to shower and change.

Andrew showed up, shortly before eight o'clock, wearing his best, least crumpled suit, an exclusive tie and an idiotic smile. Clémentine was still refusing to budge, so we went back to town in the camper van. I'd only just managed to get a table for two at the town's top restaurant (the sommelier there buys a modest quantity of Valeix wine every year), and the *maître d'hôtel* apologised for putting us by the door. But Andrew didn't complain; he was delighted. He could show off his fabulously expensive wine label to all the wealthy tourists and well-to-do business people as they came through the door, greeting them all with a cheery *'Bonsoir, M'sieurs Dames!'*.

I'd eaten there once before, as a guest of the hallowed Saint-Emilion brotherhood, *la Jurade*, but the menu had been a simple three-course affair, and I hadn't seen the bill. When our waiter handed me the menu I almost gawped at the stratospheric prices. Andrew was unfazed. He ordered the *Menu Découverte* for both of us, reasoning that, since we weren't paying for the wine, we might as well splash out on the food. All the same, I wondered who was going to pay the bill. I sneaked a quick look at the wine list and discovered that the house was charging more for a bottle of Pétrus than Aimée had stolen from me (the cash *and* the cheques). I needed a drink to calm my jittery nerves. When the waiter brought us two flutes of chilled champagne, I could have kissed him. Andrew and I brought our glasses together, and, winking at me, he said, 'Chin-chin.'

'Good health,' I replied.

Tactful, Jean, very tactful, I thought, closing my eyes in shame and muttering, 'I'm sorry, Andrew – here's to you!'

'Here's to us, Jean,' he countered.

'Okay then,' I conceded, glad not to have upset him with my thoughtless toast. 'Here's to us.'

We sipped our fizz, and nibbled the dainty *amuse-bouches* that came with the drinks. My curiosity broke the easy silence. 'So,' I began cautiously, 'don't keep me in suspense. Are you going to tell me about your real job?'

'Och, it's very tedious,' he said, flourishing a napkin. 'I don't want to bore you with it now. Can't it wait until after dinner?'

I narrowed my eyes and held up a salmon-and-caviar-laden spoon, taking aim. '*Talk!*' I ordered.

'Alright, alright!' he said, holding up his hands in mock surrender. Our high jinks had caught the attention of the waiter, whose haughtiness had surely been honed in some Latin Quarter brasserie. Andrew smiled at him placatingly then looked at me. 'I'll tell you,' he said, 'Just put the fish eggs down, okay?'

I popped the cold canapé into my mouth and grinned back at him.

Two tables away, a cheery, florid-faced American summoned the waiter, and Andrew began his résumé.

'I used to be the marketing director of a large UK drinks company.'

I eyed him questioningly.

'It doesn't matter which one, and anyway they fired me

after their most recent merger.'

'Ah, so this is one of the mementoes you told me about,' I said, stroking the wine bottle's label.

'Aye, but that was paid for with a bonus from a previous company take-over, about ten years earlier. I did rather better out of that one . . .'

'Three bottles of Pétrus! Must have been a tidy bonus.'

'Well, prices weren't so exorbitant back then. Not so many Chinese and Russian billionaires about.'

'So, how did you end up in the drinks industry?'

'After I graduated, I went to work at one of the big distilleries in Perthshire. My degree, and my . . .' he paused, '. . . natural loquaciousness, steered me towards sales and marketing.'

'You do surprise me!'

His smiling eyes narrowed. 'What are you saying? Anyway, branding was the big thing in the late '70s, you know. The company launched a new Scotch whisky for the international market called *Bonnie Prince Charlie*, and my creative talents produced the slogan. Can you imagine it? I built my career on two words on a label – *"God Speed!"* – printed on millions of whisky bottles all over the world from Acapulco to Zurich . . . no, not Zurich – the Swiss would never drink it – Zagreb perhaps?'

'Why, wasn't it any good?'

'Terrible! Even worse than the tagline. Still, it made the company a fortune and gave me a kick up the career ladder. Then, in the '80s I got into the wine side of the business, buying cabernet sauvignon in bulk from Bulgaria and selling it to our eager British buyers who'd just discovered a taste for red wine.'

Andrew emptied his champagne flute and leaned forward conspiratorially. 'Funny thing about Bulgarian wine,' he said in a low whisper. 'After the end of Apartheid, when the trade embargoes with South Africa were lifted, it all mysteriously dried up. . .'

I was flabbergasted. 'You mean they were selling South African wine and calling it Bulgarian?'

'Don't tell me that shenanigans like that don't go on here in France.'

'Not in my winery they don't.'

'No, of course. Anyway, after flogging Eastern European wines, I ended up in the fine wines business, discovered France and fell in love with Saint-Emilion – the drink *and* the place.'

'Ah, hence your pilgrimage here in the van.'

'Yes, like Steinbeck and his poodle!'

'Well, I'm glad you did, Andrew. I could do with some help selling my wine.'

'I will help you, Jean. I might not be in the trade any more, but I know a lot of people who are. Your wines should sell very well indeed across the Channel. You'll see.'

Andrew ordered two glasses of white Pessac to drink with the first of the *entrées*: spiced langoustine tails served on a bed of stir-fried *nouilles thailandaise*. 'You know,' I said, fiddling with my white linen napkin, 'there's one thing that still puzzles me.'

'Go on,' he mumbled, covering his mouth as he ate.

I tasted the seafood; it was excellent.

'How did she get hold of the postcard?'

Andrew swallowed and took a sip from his glass. 'She knows where Archie goes to school. I'll bet she chatted him up in some West London coffee shop somewhere and stole the card from him. She's a born confidence trickster. She had old Wendy eating out of the palm of her hand. She can talk for hours about art, French literature, poetry – but with very little real knowledge. Like a hangman, she can weigh somebody up with a handshake.'

'You mean she can empathise?'

He looked at me incredulously. 'She's certainly never showed any empathy towards me, Jean,' he said.

'No, I suppose not. You'll contact him, then – Archie, I mean – to find out?'

'Aye, I'll see him soon enough, anyway,' he said,

adding vaguely, 'I hope.'

'You don't sound too sure, Andrew. Why are things so bad between you two?'

He took the postcard from his inside pocket and stared at it like a nervous best man who'd forgotten the words of his speech. 'Archie,' he began, 'like a few people in my family, is a bit of a special case.'

'What do you mean?'

He beamed joyfully, as though recalling some happy memory of his son. He said, 'He's a bit ... loopy, you know? But he's great, don't get me wrong. I love him to bits, and his sister, too. It's just that, for Archie, everything's got to be ordered and predictable. He can't abide change. My split-up with his mum devastated him. Then, when I told him I was leaving the country, he just sort of clammed up, wouldn't speak to me. It's just his way.'

I pictured a truculent adolescent, spurning his father for having destroyed his small, self-centred world.

'Perhaps, when he's older, he'll take a more intelligent view of the situation,' I ventured.

'Och no, he doesn't lack intelligence. He's the most intelligent person I know. I don't know where he gets it from, though – certainly not from my lot. He can learn languages, do incredible sums in his head, remember everyone's birthdays, car registration numbers, you name it. He's a bloody miracle.'

'You mean,' I said cautiously, 'that he suffers from autism?'

'Yes,' he nodded, 'although he wouldn't say he *suffers*. He doesn't consider it a handicap. He says everyone's somewhere along what they call "the spectrum". He's got mild Asperger's Syndrome and a very rare form of synaesthesia. He sees smells.'

I misunderstood. 'He sees, smells and *what*?' I asked.

'No, I mean, when he smells the odour of something, he associates it with a particular colour or texture. Olfactory Synaesthesia is what they call it. He's a marvel to modern science.'

I was fascinated by Andrew's description of his son's heightened sensory powers and extraordinary mental abilities. Archie's behaviour, too, interested me. I learned that, like many people with his condition, he needed structure and predictability in his life. His father had to slice his morning toast in a particular way, had to butter it and spread it with just the right brand of strawberry jam. Andrew's work meant that he returned home late in the evenings, but he would always be there at bedtime to read stories or recite poetry to his son. This rite continued well into Archie's teens, and woe betide the family if Dad wasn't there to do his duty. His parents' divorce devastated Archie's life, and he had never forgiven his father. Andrew's daughter, Poppy, blamed him for everything that had happened, too. She wasn't speaking to him either.

We chatted throughout the meal, but our conversation – however fascinating and revealing – could not overshadow the superlative food: a feast of fresh market ingredients, expertly prepared, fastidiously matched, and all presented and served with great reverence and impeccable style. I wondered what kind of shimmering polychromatic flashes this food would reveal to Archie's mind's eye. Apparently, though, he was a fussy eater and wouldn't like this 'fancy cooking'.

If the food was exceptional, then the Pétrus was divine. A wine to be explored rather than tasted, it lured me, like an exquisite bird of paradise, through a lush jungle of many-layered, complex flavours. I brought the great bowl of the crystal glass to my nose and inhaled deeply. I could smell ripe black fruits and evening violets, white truffles, cinnamon, liquorice, musk and, on the finish, something elusive, smoky and dark. The powerful aromas carried me on a journey, an olfactory voyage to summer orchards, cottage gardens and misty autumn forests, through Zanzibar's spice markets, past Byzantine coffee houses and backstreet Patagonian chocolatiers. I knew, from my studies, the names of the volatile compounds that created these nuances – the aldehydes and terpenes, esters and polyphenols, that constitute a wine's smell – but the bouquet exploding from my glass wasn't chemistry, it was sorcery, alchemist's gold; and I was holding the Holy Grail.

Andrew stared at me, grinning like an imbecile. I sipped, slurped – as quietly and discretely as I could – and let the wine sit on my tongue for a moment before swallowing.

'My God, that's good,' I whispered, observing Andrew's reaction as he, too, enjoyed his first mouthful. What was that look on his suntanned, wrinkled face? Beatific? Post-orgasmic? He certainly looked very, very happy. I tried a morsel of my tournedos of Bazadaise beef, topped with foie gras and Perigord truffle, and took another sip. When food writers and wine journalists talk of symphonies of flavour, describe their tasty discoveries as rhapsodies, or sonatas, or any other musical metaphor, I tend to drift off. Nevertheless, if I'd heard the Hallelujah Chorus, as I tasted the Pétrus with the chef's heavenly concoction, I would not have been in the least surprised.

We finished the red wine with the cheese, and ordered a half bottle of sticky, sweet Sainte-Croix-du-Mont to go with the dessert.

I still had questions.

'Why do you think she kept it? The postcard, I mean.'

Andrew, who had drained his glass, accepted a refill from our waiter. 'Currency,' he said, taking another sip before continuing. 'She knew how valuable Archie's card would be to me. It proves that she found her own way here, that *I* didn't tell her my whereabouts. For her it was something else to bribe, bargain or blackmail with, at some point in the future. Like the thing with the railway ticket, she was always planning several moves ahead. She's a bloody Grand Master!'

The dessert wine was delicious. I took another sip and

moved the conversation away from Aimée. 'Speaking of finding people,' I said, 'how do you suppose Turk found his way back to Fontloube?'

'Ha! Old Turk?' Andrew laughed, his voice turning as sweet as the wine. 'That's easy. He could always find his way home. The kids used to say he was a homing terrier. He likes to round people up, too. I sometimes wonder if he's got a bit of border collie in him. He'd have had no trouble finding his way back to Fontloube after he left me. And he didn't waste any time either. Abandoned me as soon as I pitched camp, he did, the wee tyke. I was pretty sure he'd gone back to you, though. I knew where he'd be when I needed him.'

I thought about Andrew's imminent departure, and asked, 'Would you have come looking for him then? I mean, before going back to Scotland.'

'Of course. And anyway, I couldn't leave without saying goodbye to that glorious vineyard of yours, could I? But, like a lot of things I do, I was kind of leaving it to the last minute.'

The last minute.

I thought: isn't it funny how circumstances can give an otherwise simple and mundane expression such depth, such palpable weight. Despite not wanting to spoil the evening with tears, I started to cry. My date produced a silk handkerchief from his top pocket. 'Don't, Jean,' he implored, 'this was supposed to be a happy night. Come on, here—' He reached across the table and dabbed my teary face gently with the hanky. He furrowed his brow and eyed me earnestly. 'Come on,' he said again, 'I know you've lost your car, your money, your staff, maybe even your dog but—'

'Are you trying to cheer me up?' I asked, laughing, in spite of my tears, at his sarcasm. 'Oh God, I've missed you, Maconie. I don't know what it is about you – it must be your overwhelming concern.'

'That's better,' he said cheerfully. 'Now, just let me settle the bill. Your chariot awaits you, Miss Jean!'

We walked arm in arm back to the car park near the church. Turk was waiting patiently in the van, sitting on the driver's seat, panting and grinning, clearly happy to see his friends return. When we climbed into the cab, the dog hopped down between the two front seats and sat there worshipping his master.

'Hey, Turk,' I said, 'you've forsaken me now, is that it?'

Andrew took a small, paper-wrapped parcel from his jacket pocket and carefully revealed its contents on his lap. 'That's not favouritism; that's cupboard love,' he said. 'Here you go, Turk, this is your treat for looking after the van.' He placed the little smorgasbord of leftovers on the floor and encouraged the dog to tuck in. 'That's a Michelin-starred doggie bag that is, Turk. I hope you appreciate it.'

'Are you spoiling him, or bribing him?' I asked suspiciously.

He turned to me, poker-faced, and said, 'I am shocked by the accusation, Miss Jean, I have only his happiness and well-being in mind, thank you.'

He slipped the clutch and steered the van past the church. I glanced at the stained and weatherworn features of the great west door and the tympanum's mutilated depiction of the Last Judgement. Any painful associations I felt with the place, however, quickly dissolved as I giggled at Andrew's mock-pompous, supercilious expression.

'Just drive carefully, Andrew,' I said, '*very* carefully. You've had far too much to drink.'

'Yes, Miss!' he said.

When we arrived back at the château, we agreed not to say goodbye. Andrew promised to come back at Christmas, and said that he would try to convince Archie to come, too. We kissed, but not the way lovers do. I got out of the van and encouraged Turk to follow me, but – I'm sure it was the doggy bag that did it – he decided to stay with his master. An orange harvest moon – a great glazed croissant, sinking over my western slopes in the starry night – marked the end of a prefect evening, but also, too cruelly, closed a chapter in our lives. The camper van made its way slowly up the *côte*. I listened to the sound of the engine as it faded gradually into the stillness of the night.

I was having the nightmare about the accident when a distant barking released me from its spell and brought me back to the utter darkness of my room. I padded over to the open window and peered out into the cool, black night. The moon had set, and a veil of cloud shrouded the stars. I listened. A tawny owl's screech echoed over the valley, prompting her mate to respond: *hulule, hulule.* I heard the barking again – not a dog's bark, but the savage cry of a red fox, calling from the woods on the high ridge of the *côte*. The cold air chilled me, so I returned to the warmth of the bed, listening to the wild noises beyond the window and the faraway-sounding tick-tock of the grandfather clock in the kitchen below. I couldn't get back to sleep. Many of my dilemmas had been resolved, but I was still anxious about my future, still picking at the sores of my past. My life had been a series of disasters – I could count them, in multiples of three – but why did I have to accumulate so many regrets? Andrew was going to die, completing a tragic trinity of deaths. All I would have left, apart from a few fond memories of the man, would be yet another regret. Despite his promises, I knew that he would never return to Fontloube. If he left me now, I'd never see him again, never meet his family – his extraordinary son, his beautiful daughter, his fey sister – never again laugh at his predictable jokes or feel his touch. Unless, unless . . . A confusing set of scenarios – some possible, some implausible – presented themselves to me, like the branching pathways of a maze. I considered my options and tried to foresee their outcomes, following the dark alleyways of a labyrinth of possibilities, arriving at dead ends or at confusing junctions, retracing my steps and searching, searching ... When, finally, I had made up my mind, a pale light announcing the dawn began to glimmer at the curtain. I knew what I had to do next and promptly fell into a deep, dreamless sleep.

Wine

There is no other medicine for misery.
- Euripides, *The Bacchae*

I woke up late. The room was full of sunshine and the colourful noise of birdsong. Daylight had chased away the creatures of the night, but not my resolve. I jumped out of bed and washed and dressed hurriedly, desperate to get to the campsite before Andrew set off on his journey home. I tied up my hair and flew downstairs, taking a bitter-tasting swig of orange juice from the carton in the fridge before leaving. This time, sans Jack Russell terrier, my ride up the hill was easier, and I reached the campsite before ten o'clock. Coasting through the gates, I crossed my index and middle fingers and said to myself, please be there, please . . .

I brought the bike to a halt in front of what remained of Andrew's camp: a worn patch of sparse, parched lawn next to a light-deprived rectangle of grass where his van had stood. My evil gremlin said nothing; he didn't need to. I looked up at the billowy white clouds, scudding across another perfect blue sky, and cursed. A voice, some way off behind me, made me jump.

'Are you looking for Andrew?'

I craned my neck to see who had addressed me and saw a tall, elderly woman dressed in a pair of Ali Baba trousers and a garish, baggy tee shirt. She put on a pair of spectacles and waved to me, calling, 'Halloo! Are you Jean?'

I turned the bicycle round, pedalled over to her and dismounted. 'Yes,' I said breathlessly, hoping that she hadn't overheard my expletive, 'I'm Jeanne, er, Jean

Valeix. I was hoping to catch Mr. Maconie before he left.'

'I thought it was you,' she said lispingly, covering a toothless grin with her hand. 'Oh, my,' she mumbled, 'I've forgotten to put my teeth in. Wait here.'

She disappeared into a small caravan. I waited, as instructed, leaning on my bike. Presently, her head appeared over the half door of the trailer. 'The power of speech is restored to me!' she called. 'Better to be silent and be thought a fool, than to speak and remove all doubt! Don't you agree?'

I couldn't help but agree. 'Yes,' I said.

'You look thirsty. Would you like a drink?' she asked, still talking to me from the doorway.

'Er, thank you, yes. That would be nice.'

'How about a cold glass of Rivesaltes? It's closest thing to sherry that I can find at the shop in the village.' She went back indoors.

'Isn't it a bit early?' I said, hoping to be heard through the caravan's thin plastic skin.

She opened the door and stepped down holding two glasses of amber-coloured liquid.

'Don't be ridiculous,' she said, 'I've taken a mid-morning pick-me-up all my adult life, and I'm seventy-five years old. You wouldn't believe that now, would you?'

'What,' I couldn't stop myself saying, 'do you mean your age or your sherry habit?'

She gave a hearty guffaw and said, wheezing, 'I can tell I'm going to like you. Andrew said you were a clever one. It's lovely to meet you, Jean.' She passed me my glass and offered her hand. 'Wendy Snook,' she said.

We shook hands. 'Hello, Wendy,' I said, 'I've heard a lot about you – most of it completely untrue, I think.'

I could tell that she was intrigued. 'Ooh, that does sound interesting – tell me all.'

As pleased as I was to meet Andrew's friend (and relieved, too, when I considered that their relationship was unlikely to have been a physical one), I didn't have time to chat. I needed to know if there was any chance of catching up with my man. 'I don't mean to be rude, Wendy, but I really do need to speak to Andrew. Do you know what time he left?'

'Well, yes dear.' She sounded concerned. 'He left about half an hour ago. If you wanted to see him, I'm afraid you're too late. He was supposed to set off at nine, but he left all his packing until the last minute – he went in such a rush.'

Wendy's words recalled something to me. *The last minute*. It was the phrase that had struck me so poignantly the previous evening. What had Andrew said? He was putting off saying goodbye to my vineyards until the last minute . . .

'Thank you, Wendy,' I said, downing my drink in one and passing her the empty glass. 'I think I know where he might be,' I called to her, over my shoulder, pedalling hard towards the exit.

'Go, go!' I heard her shout. 'Whilst we delay, life speeds by!'

I have never, before or since, ridden a bike so fast. Keeping a lookout for kamikaze tractors, I sped along the straight road that follows the ridge of the *côte* from the campsite. When I reached Saint-Emilion, the narrow streets were clogged with weekend traffic. Undeterred, I cycled on at speed, overtaking the queues of cars and vans. Pedestrian tourists scattered before me, cursing the manic, middle-aged speed freak whose ringing bell and shouts of '*Allez*! Get out of the way!' echoed down the cobbled lanes. Once out of the town, I pedalled harder, taking the shortcut across my western vineyards, skidding through the courtyard, and down into the lower field. I stopped at the place where I'd first spotted Andrew's van on that distant, sunny April day.

There, on the other side of the low trees, was the white camper. A little way off, half submerged in the fruit-laden vines, stood Andrew. Turk, on hearing my approach, turned towards me, barking. When he recognised his mistress, he trotted round the hedge, bounded up to me and sat down beside the bike, panting. He let out an excited yap to announce my arrival to Andrew who wheeled round and removed his hat, waving it theatrically. 'Hello, Jean,' he shouted, 'I couldn't go without one last look at the vines!'

I dropped the bike on the ground and went quickly to join him.

As I approached, he said, 'You look like you've run a marathon.'

'No, just a marathon cycle ride,' I beamed, so happy to have caught up with him, 'with a glass of wine at the half-way mark. Which way did you come? I can't believe we missed each other.'

'I came via Castillon, to fill her up with diesel.' He nodded towards his home on wheels, then opened his arms in welcome.

We embraced. I pressed the side of my face against his chest, listening to the beating of his heart, and hugged him so tightly that he pulled away from me, coughing.

'Are you trying to kill me?' he said, laughing, clearly surprised by my behaviour.

I took his hands in mine. 'Andrew, please don't go,' I blurted, my tears coming quickly like a summer rainstorm. 'I don't want you to go. Please. Please!'

He eyed me suspiciously. We were not, it seemed, sharing the same emotional state. His voice was dispassionate yet tender. 'Jean,' he began, drying my tears with his handkerchief for the second time in twenty-four hours. 'I thought I'd made all that clear. I can't put you through any more grief. You have to get on with the rest of your life now and forget about me.'

I was distraught. 'That's just it,' I sobbed, 'without you I don't have a life. If you leave me now I'll . . . we'll *both* regret it. You can stay here at the château and get all the treatment you need. I'll care for you even when—' I stopped myself, and looked at the fat, ripe bunches of grapes and the vine's broad leaves that had begun, recently, to take on their autumn colours. 'When, and if, the time comes,' I continued, 'I'm prepared to do everything to look after you. I've thought it all through, Andrew. Don't you see? I can't say goodbye to you now, for ever. This story's not finished, and I still want to be part of it.'

Andrew took a step backwards, removed his glasses and wiped his eyes. 'Jean, this is torture for me, you know that. If I could wave a magic wand – be the kind of fit, healthy person I should be – then I'd love to stay. There'd be so much I could offer you. But now? Now I'm buggered, Jean. I'd only be a burden to you, and that's the last thing I want to be.'

I closed my eyes, inhaling the sappy, earthy smell of the vines, preparing my case. 'Andrew,' I began, 'we met in this vineyard. We made love in that camper van, there. We worked together in *these* vines. We lived together in *that* house. Only one thing has changed since then, and I don't mean Aimée and her little games. The only thing that's changed is your illness, and the only *burden* that bothers me is the burden of guilt I'll feel if you clear off out of my life now.'

'Oh Jesus,' he sighed, 'Jean, you are a very difficult and stubborn woman.'

'You have to be, in my business,' I countered. 'Well, are you going to stay or what?' I put my hand on my hip and starred at him. For a moment, I saw him as I had that first time, eyeing me up, weighing his options, planning his next move.

'Okay, I'll stay, at least for the harvest, if . . .' he paused, 'that's what you want.'

I nodded. 'And you'll let me register you properly as living and working here?' I asked.

'Aye,' he said cautiously, 'I mean, if you're sure?'

'Are you sure, Andrew?'

'Sure as I'll ever be . . .'

I don't know why, but I put out my hand and said, 'Shake on it,' and we closed the deal with a handshake and a smile. Leaving the bike at the end of a vine row, we strolled up to the house, hand in hand, with Turk chasing at our heels.

'Och, I get it,' he announced, 'You only want me to stay because you know I've got another couple of bottles of that wine.'

'That's not true, Andrew,' I replied, adding, 'although the thought had occurred to me. It is very, very good wine.'

He gave my shoulder a gentle shove that threw me off balance. 'Oops, sorry, Jean,' he said.

Both laughing, I said, 'Oh, I nearly fell for you then!'

We continued to walk up the slope.

'Anyway,' he said, 'I was planning to give you a bottle as a parting gift. I'd have said goodbye with a kiss and a bottle of the world's most expensive wine.'

We neared the top of the slope and turned to admire the view of the fruitful, verdant valley. I nodded thoughtfully and said, 'I wouldn't have accepted.'

'What the wine, or the kiss?'

'Oh, I'd have accepted a kiss . . .' I answered, sidling closer, acting the coquette.

'Would you accept one now?' he asked softly.

'Why don't you try your luck?'

I felt his arm slip round my waist, drawing us together, facing each other.

'My luck's been running a bit thin lately,' he said.

'That's the thing about luck,' I said, 'you never know when it's going to change.'

We kissed, sensitively and cautiously at first, but soon with a rediscovered passion that prompted our swift return to my bedroom and the lovers' rite that deceit had denied us for far too long.

Exhausted by the morning's exercise and sated by our lovemaking, I slept until Andrew's gentle snoring woke me. I lay on the bed searching for the source of an unfamiliar emotion that had crept in, unseen, through the curtained half-light of the room. What *was* this new feeling that our coupling had revealed to me? A déjà vu recollection of adolescent thrills and sensual discoveries perhaps? Or a deeper, more mature sense of spiritual love? Or was it just a wild, abandoned, reckless fist shake at time's irrepressible creep? I couldn't see it then, but now I realise that it was something far more mundane. Our act of love was an affirmation, like the handshake in the vines, of a mutual commitment – an unspoken oath, a tacit agreement, an understanding. It satisfied a yearning for some predictability in my chaotic life. My love for Andrew had altered, but it remained undiminished, and I would never be parted from him again; at least not for the time being.

The next day, Andrew's belongings made their way back into the house. A Trumper shaving brush and bowl appeared under the mirror in the bathroom. I found his Panama hat hooked on the back of the kitchen door. Colourful silk ties and cotton shirts hung in my bedroom closet, permeating my clothes with a whiff of his cologne. The reappearance of these familiar things made me realise how much I'd missed their owner. Unfamiliar to me then, though, were his medicines and pain killers which I helped him to organise, and together we transformed the random jumble of pharmaceuticals into an ordered personal infirmary.

I called the *hôtel de police* to give them Andrew's new description of Aimée. We received a return visit from Captain Lefèvre. He brought with him my jeep's keys (apparently, the vehicle had been found abandoned in Bordeaux, scratched and dented but otherwise in working order) and the manila envelope which still contained my cheques – but not the cash. Andrew described my fugitive apprentice, as she had been before coming to Fontloube. He also gave the policeman a photograph, taken a year earlier, which showed a professional young woman (older looking than the Aimée I knew) with long, luscious chestnut hair. I recognised the penetrating gaze – the same challenging look, the same animal cunning – in those dark, familiar eyes. Lefèvre told us that this new description might reveal Aimée's true identity and possible whereabouts. But many days would go by before we received any news.

I seldom thought of Aimée, and apart from one sunny Saturday, when I noticed her saint's day on the calendar, we never discussed her. At the end of September the preparations for the harvest preoccupied us. The weather remained warm and dry, and the fruit that had survived nature's perils earlier in the year, was ripe and sweet. Barring heavy rains during the picking, we would be making wine from good grapes this year. My grape pickers arrived, during the first weekend of October, and moved into their lodgings in the cottages adjoining the winery. The prospect of several sunny days of tractor driving thrilled Andrew. Turk was delighted, too, to have so many new people to bark at or adore depending on his mood. My mood, as always just before the harvest, swung unpredictably between bouts of manic jubilation and desperate anxiety. The rest of the crew seemed content to believe that this year's harvest would be a success, and the atmosphere of excitement and bonhomie was usually enough to cheer me up during moments of distress. But after Captain Lefèvre's phone call on the Sunday afternoon, my already frayed nerves would be left in tatters. I was in the office when the telephone rang.

'*Allo?*' I answered cheerily.

The captain introduced himself in the usual formal way. 'I'm sorry to call you on a Sunday, madame, but we have made a positive identification of your apprentice, Miss Loroux, aka Gonzalès.'

'Oh, I see,' I said, 'thank you for calling me.'

'Yes, well, under the circumstances, I thought it was better to let you know.'

I had a bad feeling about this. 'Okay, please tell me,' I prompted.

'Did I mention to you that I have a contact in London?'

He had told me, on his first visit, of a seminar he'd attended at Scotland Yard.

'Yes,' I said. 'What have you found out?'

'Well, after your friend told me that Aimée had worked in London, I sent her description and photo to my English colleague. Okay?' he paused, but I didn't say anything. 'He has identified her for us,' he continued. 'Aimée Loroux was born in Lisle to French and Russian parents. She was an exceptional student. At convent school she had a gift for foreign languages, her talents as a dancer won a scholarship to the Conservatoire . . . Then, it seems, things started to go wrong. She absconded from school, got into trouble with the police . . . Eventually her parents lost touch with her, and she was registered as a missing person over ten years ago. Now we know that she ended up in London, which is where my counterpart there comes in.'

'Go on.'

'Her details match the description of someone wanted by the CID.'

'What do you mean *wanted?*'

He cleared his throat. 'It's in connection with the shooting and killing of a young man in . . .' – I could hear him shuffling some papers – 'Chelsea.'

Silence. My mind raced back and forth like a confused sniffer dog, trying to recall where Andrew's son went to school.

'Are you still there, Madame Valeix?'

'Yes, sorry,' I said, exhaling an exasperated sigh. 'You . . . you think that she's connected with the boy's death?'

'From the information we have so far from the undercover people, she's the main suspect.'

Undercover? 'So, is this related to a drugs investigation?'

'Yes . . .' He hesitated. 'You'll understand that I can't reveal too much about the case—'

I cut him short. 'Just tell me one thing,' I begged. 'The boy's name – it's not Archie, is it?'

'Archie?' he said, nonplussed. 'No, madame, that's not the victim's name.'

I thought: what's in a name? 'Well,' I went on, 'he's not at school in London is he? A student? About sixteen?'

'No, no,' he said, 'he was a known drug dealer, supplying cocaine to wealthy Russians in the West End. He was ...' – more paper shuffling – 'twenty-nine years of age.'

'Oh, thank God,' I babbled, 'I thought for a moment it was Andrew's son, Archie. We think that Aimée might have been in contact with him. I'm sorry, you must think I'm mad. After all, how many millions of people are there in London?'

Lefèvre took my rhetorical question at face value and said, 'About seven million, I think, madame.' His tone turned inquisitive. 'But not many of them have a connection with Miss Loroux. I would be very grateful if Mr. Maconie would give me his son's details. Let me give you my number . . .'

'Yes, of course,' I said, writing Lefèvre's direct line down as he dictated it. I repeated the numbers back to him, before asking my next question. 'Do you think Archie is in danger?'

'It's unlikely, but just to be on the safe side I would like to send his details to London.'

I was curious to know more. 'Was the victim a bad man?'

'Yes, madame, we believe he was a very bad man. But now he is a very dead man. And now, we are no longer looking for a car thief but for a killer. Please be vigilant and call me if anything out of the ordinary occurs. Meanwhile, I'll send someone over to the château to change the locks. Don't worry. I don't expect that Mademoiselle Loroux, or anyone connected with her, will bother you now. Please, don't worry.'

We said goodbye just as the first drops of misty rain adhered to the windowpane. I put the phone down slowly, worrying.

I found Andrew in the hangar, tinkering with the tractor. Before I could finish relating Lefèvre's disturbing news, he put down his tools and rushed to the office to telephone his son. I felt anxious, but Andrew looked terrified. He picked up the phone and dialled the number from memory. When I heard him say 'Oh, thank God you're alright, Son' I left him alone to his cross-channel conversation and shut the study door discretely behind me.

When Andrew returned to the kitchen, I'd brewed some tea. His face showed no signs of concern. Apparently, Archie knew almost nothing about Aimée, except for having met her briefly in a café near his school in April. She'd chatted to him about France, and he'd shown her the postcard. When he came back from a visit to the loo, the girl had gone, taking the postcard and leaving the bill. Hearing Archie's voice had assuaged Andrew's anxieties. Talking to his son, for the first time in nearly eight months, seemed to have reinvigorated him. During their conversation, he'd told Archie about moving in with me at Fontloube, but not about his illness – he wanted to deliver that unsettling announcement in person.

He finished his tea, put the empty mug in the sink and went back to work, whistling an unfamiliar tune as he crossed the courtyard.

Sunrise brought a lavender-pink dawn and only the wispiest of clouds to the eastern sky. We started picking the merlot at seven a.m. Andrew took the harvester and worked the young vines in the lower fields while I, with my motley band, picked the older vines on the slopes. By lunchtime, we had brought in a good third of the crop. We rested, massaging our aching lower backs and shoulders with purple-stained hands. The weather was fine and warm; the fruit was near perfect. I enjoyed a brief moment of self-congratulation before bringing myself, abruptly, to task. There remained nearly three hectares of vines to pick.

After lunch, I supervised the arrival of the fruit at the

winery. Andrew had finished the mechanical harvest and was busy to-ing and fro-ing with the tractor, bringing crates of hand-picked bunches in from the fields. As daylight faded, we finished sorting and de-stemming the last load of fruit. I estimated the day's yield at just over six thousand litres from two and a half hectares of vines.

The weather stayed kind to us: fine, dry and not too hot. Paul and Valentin arrived on Friday afternoon and stayed for the weekend, helping to bring in the cabernet franc grapes.

Having Andrew with me was a real blessing. In spite of his condition (or, perhaps, because of it), his phone conversation with Archie had given him a renewed source of energy that surprised and inspired us all. Whenever my morale flagged, I drew strength from his new-found enthusiasm. His jocular charm set the tone of the harvest and, of course, everyone fell for it, especially the cousins who became willing acolytes to this exotic and mysterious foreigner. Andrew and the boys had little by way of a shared vocabulary, so I was surprised when they hit it off so quickly. I came to understand the innate strength of paternal friendships – Valentin and Paul adored Andrew, to whom they became substitute sons. It saddened me to think about the future and the inevitable brevity of these relationships. I decided, even then, to cherish what each day brought, not dwell on the difficult, painful times that lay ahead.

By the end of the third week of October, the vines were bare and the harvest was over for another year. My vats contained barely ten thousand litres of macerating grapes, but I was hopeful that the wine's quality would compensate for this lack of quantity.

My migrant grape pickers left as suddenly as they had arrived. Replacing them, a peacefulness settled on the rooms of the house and winery which, only hours before, had been full of chatter and laughter. Now, only our tired, hoarse voices and the grandfather clock's ticking penetrated the silence.

I relaxed on the sofa next to Andrew, relishing the weight and warmth of his arm as I shimmied my shoulders in its crook. 'Thank you,' I murmured.

'Whatever for?' he asked.

I opened my eyes and looked into his. 'You were a real help.'

'Och, I just drove the tractor.'

'No, Andrew, I mean it. You gave me the strength to make this harvest a success, in spite of all that's happened – especially with your illness ... I just wanted you to know how grateful I am, that's all.'

'I'm sure you can think of some way of rewarding me,' he said, stroking the soft hair on the back of my neck.

Surprised, I said, 'Aren't you tired?'

'I'm always tired but never *too* tired.'

'Well,' I suggested, 'an afternoon nap might be in order. The grapes are busy macerating and we'll need to get busy soon, too. You'll need to recharge your batteries for what comes next.'

'What do you mean?'

'Well, up to now you've really only done a bit of gardening and winery management. I wonder if you've got what it takes to be a winemaker.'

'You call all that hard work gardening!' he said indignantly.

'Don't pout, Andrew,' I said, getting up from the sofa and taking his hand. 'Come to bed.'

That weekend, the cousins and Valentin's father came to dinner to celebrate the end of the harvest. Andrew asked if he could invite Wendy; of course, I agreed. Our brief meeting at the campsite had convinced me that she would make an entertaining dinner guest. I invited Isabelle Lavergne. Although Stéphane would be sweating away in his kitchen that Saturday night, she would certainly come and, in true French style, bring the kids, too.

Ten for dinner made a jolly party round the great oval

table in the dining room. Andrew had offered to cook. When Isabelle went into the kitchen to offer some professional advice on a salad dressing, I knew she was really giving him a covert character assessment. Thankfully, when the two of them came back to the table, after serving the *entrée*, they seemed to get on fine. I sat next to Wendy and listened, enthralled, to her fascinating experiences – her travels in the Holy Land, her love of classical history, and a romantic adventure with (of all people) the Dean of Saint Paul's. Andrew sat between the cousins and Isabelle, working his charm on both parties. Michel played a blusteringly avuncular role to the three Laverne children, who giggled at his jokes, ate hardly anything, then went off to watch television in the salon before falling soundly asleep. I can't remember what Andrew cooked for us that night or even which wine I served. But I do remember my conversations with Wendy which were as profound as they were funny.

'. . . so it was my research into the minor medieval saints that first brought me here,' Wendy concluded, explaining why a retired academic was staying on a caravan site in Saint-Emilion.

'You have such a passion for the history of religion,' I said. 'Are you at all religious yourself?'

'Not whatsoever,' she said, raising her glass and looking up at the ceiling. 'God strike me down if I'm wrong!'

I couldn't suppress a wry smile. 'What do you believe in then, Wendy?'

She paused, took a swig of red wine, and said, 'It's the word *believe* that I struggle with, Jean. It's one that we historians rely on rather too much, I'm afraid. It's a psychological concept. Its meaning is at best vague, and at worst misleading. Phrases like "I believe in Father Christmas" or "Elvis believed in aliens" mean nothing to me at all. Others, like "we now believe that Agincourt's rout was due to thick mud churned up by the French cavalry" or "the Cathars believed that the God of the old testament was really the devil" seem more credible, but are no less tricksy. The fact is we just don't know. I am sure only of what I know, and old age is systematically plundering what little of that remains.'

I waited for Andrew to go and fetch the cheeseboard before putting my next question. 'What do you think about Andrew – about his illness I mean?' I asked, feeling like a small child seeking comfort and reassurance from an all-knowing mother.

'I think Andrew is a charming, funny, intelligent man who, like so many others like him, wasn't destined to die in toothless old age. Unlike me, eh?' She paused and adjusted her dental plate for effect.

'You know he's not a real poet, don't you?'

'Oh, I worked that out the first day I met him. I've known a few poets and Andrew's not like them – too cheerful and not nearly sexually repressed enough.'

'And what did you make of Aimée?' I asked, curious.

'From what little I saw of her I thought she was a nasty piece of work,' Wendy said, then, returning to our previous theme, asked, 'Anyway, what about you, Jean – what do you believe in?'

'Fate,' I said, without hesitation.

I paused to read her expression, but she continued struggling noisily with her dentures, forcing me to look away and expand my reply without eye contact. 'I suppose I've come to understand that everything happens for a reason, that our lives have a pattern. That they're . . . mapped out?' I risked a glance back at her, relieved to see that the gurning had stopped.

She fixed me with a pair of fiendish eyes. 'What nonsense,' she said, her tone condescending but kindly. 'If you experience, with the benefit of hindsight (and, let's face it, how else do we experience things?), that life is a pattern of extraordinary coincidences, it just means that you are an extraordinary person, that life is – well, extraordinary. Don't call it fate or destiny—'

I interjected. 'Ah, but you do,' I said, lowering my voice as Andrew appeared with the cheese. 'You mentioned

Andrew's destiny.'

She took a piece of baguette and spread it with some gooey Camembert. 'Mmm?' she mumbled, swallowing. 'A figure of speech, that's all. Accepting destiny removes any possibility of free will. And then where would we be, eh? Imagine that! It would be like listening to Radio 4 Long Wave during an everlasting test match.'

'You don't like cricket then?' I chuckled.

'Can't stand the game. I prefer Rugby.'

'Why's that?'

'Bigger balls.'

It seemed hilarious to me that our conversation, which had started with an 8th-century monk, had ended in puerile sexual innuendo. I couldn't help but laugh. Wendy's sporting preference was translated into French as it went round the table. Soon we were all in hysterics.

Our revelry continued in this joyous, celebratory way for the rest of the night. When, finally, I went to the kitchen to make the coffee, I noticed how late it was and immediately felt very tired. The clock said two a.m.

Michel and the boys stayed the night, and Isabelle dropped Wendy off at the campsite on her way back to Bordeaux. Andrew and I cleared the last of the coffee cups and finished the washing-up. I wanted to know his plans and whether, as he'd implied, he still intended to visit Archie.

'Will you go to England before Christmas?' I asked.

Drying the last of the pots with a damp tea towel, he said, 'I have to, Jean. What I've got to tell Archie can't be said on the phone.' I assumed by this he meant his illness, but his tone implied there was something more.

'Of course.' I paused, trying to find the right words. 'You will come back, won't you?'

'Oh, believe me, Jean, I'll be back.'

'Wendy says the word *believe* is misleading.'

'Okay, how about this: I'll come back alright, and when I do, you'll meet my son, too.'

'Archie?' I questioned. 'But you're barely allowed to

see him, let alone take him out of the country. What about the terms of the custody order?'

He grinned at me. 'Aye, that's why I'm going to kidnap him.'

'Are you crazy?'

'Blissfully.'

'You love him, don't you?'

'More than life,' he said. 'And if I can speak to him, face to face, I know everything will be alright between us.'

'How will you tell Poppy about, your . . . you know.'

'If I get chance, I'll tell her while I'm in England. Otherwise I'll call her once Archie knows. I can't let her know just yet, or she'll tell Archie and their mother, and all Hell'll break loose.'

'You do still . . . love Poppy don't you?' I asked.

His look was both hurt and confused. 'She is – or was – my universe.'

The moment's emotion tipped and fell. As we embraced, his cold tears soaked my shoulder, prompting my own to flow. 'I'm scared that I'll never see those stars shine again,' he sobbed.

'Don't be mawkish, you sentimental old fool,' I said, hugging him.

'But I think I've lost her for ever, Jean,' he said. Composing himself, he added, 'And less of the old, eh?'

Instead of dispensing the customary hollow platitudes – *don't worry . . . she'll forgive you . . . there, there* – I resolved to be practical. 'Just go to her, Andrew,' I said. 'Speak to her – it's all you can do.'

'What if words aren't enough,' he said, dabbing his eyes with the towel.

'Words are all we have,' I said. 'Come on, there's work to do tomorrow.'

That autumn, every day was another tomorrow. Like the time we climbed Europe's biggest sand dune, frozen by the Atlantic wind and burned by the early November sun; or our lunch at Chez Stéphane and the afternoon of sightseeing in Bordeaux; or when we started the malolactic fermentation, got tipsy on the new wine and went to bed for the rest of the day.

But not all our tomorrows were so pleasant. Like the ones with the scary prospect of medical examinations with oncologists or appointments with bureaucrats and home-visiting nurses. Andrew dreaded most his consultations with the radiotherapists and chemotherapists whom he referred to sardonically as 'the rapists'. I don't know if he discussed his prognosis with these people, ever posed the question – the classic Hollywood cliché – *how long have I got, Doc?* If he did, he never told me, so we lived in the moment, enjoying today, planning for tomorrow and trying not to think about the future.

Winemaking preoccupied us as the days shortened. Andrew was a pragmatic student. He distilled my lectures and demonstrations – on the maceration, extraction and fermentation of grape juice – into a simple analogy: 'it's just like making a cup of tea'. The longer the brew, the more colour and flavour are extracted; but stewing the leaves too long makes the tea taste, well – stewed. To complete his analogy, I pointed out that the quality of the tea leaves and the temperature of the water were also crucial factors. I wondered what Professor Vérac, at the Libourne School of Oenology, would make of such a typically British comparison. Armed with his newly acquired knowledge, Andrew took to winemaking as avidly as a foie gras goose takes to its feeder. Through November and into December our tomorrows in the winery came and went quickly. Soon Christmas was only a couple of weeks away, and then the worst tomorrow of all was upon us – the one when Andrew had to go back to England.

Goodbyes

...and when night
Darkens the streets, then wander forth the sons
Of Belial, flown with insolence and wine.
  - John Milton, Paradise Lost, Book I

I hate goodbyes. Long ones sadden me; short ones make me nervous. Saying goodbye to Andrew though, on that cold December Wednesday, was not the heart-wrenching farewell I'd anticipated. I knew he was coming back. I just knew it.

In the morning, we packed the camper van with everything Andrew needed for his journey back to England. He'd booked a Channel crossing on the overnight ferry from Caen to Portsmouth, so he didn't need to set off until after lunch. For our last meal together before his trip I cooked a spicy Moroccan tajine. Lunch passed so quickly. It seemed that one minute we were discussing French colonial food legacies, and the next we were finishing our coffees and kissing each other goodbye. Before the coffeepot was cold, I was alone again. This would be the last time I'd watch the camper van burbling up the lane to the top of the *côte*, because Andrew had found a buyer for his vehicle in Hampshire.

I was asleep on the sofa when the phone rang. I looked at the clock and thought: nine-fifteen; Andrew must have arrived at the port.

The line was terrible, but his voice was calm and confident. 'Hello, Jean!' he said.

'How are you? How was the journey?' I responded.

'What? I can hardly hear you.'

I repeated the questions.

'I'm fine, but it's pouring down here in Normandy. I got soaked just running from the van to the phone box.'

'You should buy a mobile phone,' I said.

'What? Yes, I suppose it's time I joined the 21st century. How are you?'

Yawning, I said, 'Fine. You just woke me up.'

'Oh, sorry. Well, I said I'd call from the ferry port. My boat sails at ten-thirty – it's on time but I think it'll be a rough crossing.'

'Get yourself a cabin,' I said, fussing, 'and don't spend all night in the bar.'

'Righto. I've got to go now – no more coins. I'll call you from the other side, okay?'

The other side. I thought about Andrew's clairvoyant sister but resisted (thankfully) the urge to make a joke about his remark. 'Okay, I'll see you at the weekend anyway.'

'You will, Jean. I promise.'

'Bye then.'

'B—'

The line went dead with a click followed by a continuous, high-pitched tone.

The next time we spoke was on Friday morning.

'Hi, Jean. I've bought myself a mobile telephone. It's *intelligent.*'

'That must be a bit demeaning,' I said, chuckling, 'having a phone that's cleverer than you are.'

He laughed. 'Thanks a lot! That's what I told the guy in the shop, but he was a talented salesman. It cost me a small fortune.'

He gave me his number which I scribbled on the writing pad next to the phone. 'So, is everything alright?' I asked.

'Aye. I've sold the van, got all my paperwork, been to see my lawyer . . . and a few other things.'

'Have you seen the children yet?'

'I'm seeing Archie this afternoon. I'm picking him up

147

from school – it's the last day of term.' He paused. 'Ask me a question, Jean – go on, anything you like – like, "what's the capital of Romania?" Go on.'

'Okay, what's the capital of Roma—'

'Not that,' he interrupted. 'Another country.'

'Okay . . . Venezuela?'

'Hold on . . .' – another pause – 'Caracas!'

'That's amazing, Andrew,' I conceded sarcastically.

'I know – it's a bloody marvel this thing.'

'So, what about Archie,' I asked, hearing a crackle on the line.

'I'm losing the signal, Jean. I—'

Bucharest, I thought, as we were cut off. Who needs an intelligent phone?

That night, I went to bed early intending to read my book but fell asleep before my eyes reached the bottom of the first page. I slept dreamlessly, untroubled by nightmares of fiendish intruders or roadside accidents, until a noise woke me. Isn't it strange how the little noises, the barely audible sounds, tug at the sleeve of the unconscious mind? I can sleep through thunderstorms, the klaxon howl of a midnight freight train, early-morning alarms . . . But that night, a near-imperceptible creak on the stair dragged me back to consciousness with a start. I sat up in bed. I heard the rush of my breath and my heart's beating. Then something else: the faint click of a door's latch. Someone was in the house – *upstairs*.

My heart raced faster. I had no weapon, except for Henri's ancient shotgun (which was never loaded) in the cupboard in the salon. The phone, too, was downstairs in the study. My door had no lock. I didn't even have Turk there to protect me. Thinking about the twenty-or-so vertical feet between my bedroom window and the gravel courtyard made me reluctant to jump – and where would I go from there if I did? I listened again. Now the noises sounded more distant, muted perhaps by the walls which separated the burglar and me. Next, the sound of somebody carefully moving furniture came from what I guessed was the spare room – Aimée's room. A drawer was opened and then closed, carefully. Whoever was in my home was clearly trying hard not to wake me. Let the intruder know that you're awake, I said to myself. Let them think you're not alone. What I did next took, for me, a great deal of courage.

'Wake up, Edward!' I called theatrically, using, for my ploy, the first given name that came to mind (my father's, incidentally). 'There's someone in the house. Quick, phone the police!'

I hopped out of bed and stomped to the door. My bravery stopped short of opening it, and cowardice compelled me to wedge a chair under the handle, but this subterfuge seemed to work. I heard the loud crash of a body trip and fall and a young woman cursing. A door at the opposite end of the corridor opened and shut noisily. Hurried footsteps came towards my room, but then began to descend the stairs. I risked removing my barricade, stepped onto the landing and peered over the balustrade at my intruder's retreating form. In the half-light emanating from my room, I recognised her.

'Aimée!' I cried.

The body continued to flee, down through the hallway and into the kitchen, replying, 'No, it's not her; it's . . . someone else.'

A strange response, I thought.

She may have denied her identity, but the voice was unmistakably Aimée's. I heard the side door bang shut, then, after a few seconds, the growl of a powerful engine roaring off into the night.

My third meeting with Captain Lefèvre proved to be the most disconcerting – all the more so because of my state of fatigue. I'd had a bad night. Following Aimée's uninvited visit I hadn't slept, nor had I been willing, despite my curiosity, to go downstairs to discover how she'd gained entry to the house. Instead I'd lain beneath the covers like a terrified child, frightened by imaginary monsters under the bed, drifting in and out of semi-consciousness, waiting for the dawn.

When, at last, I dared to go downstairs, I heard a door banging and felt a cool breeze emanating from the study. Someone had forced open a window, but only a person of Aimée's slim build could have passed through its narrow frame. That confirms my intruder's identity, I thought.

Forty minutes after telephoning Lefèvre, I heard his car skidding to a stop on the gravel outside. Two doors thudded shut. I went outside to greet the captain and, as it turned out, his lieutenant.

We shook hands.

Lefèvre's expression – that of a troubled, overworked man who nonetheless still cared about his work – concerned me. I invited the two men into the house, but the younger officer was told to wait outside and search the grounds. Curiouser and curiouser, I thought.

I showed Lefèvre the forced window and gave him an account of the previous night's intrusion. He looked shocked when I told him that I'd almost confronted Aimée on the landing.

'Did she appear to be aggressive in any way?' he asked, adding, 'May I?' and pointing to one of the two office chairs in front of my desk.

'Of course,' I said. 'I mean, please do sit down.'

We both sat, each leaning forward slightly.

'No, she wasn't aggressive,' I continued. 'In fact, she flew out of the house when she realised that I was awake.'

He nodded, slowly. 'Good,' he said. 'That's good.'

There was clearly something he wasn't telling me. 'What is it?' I asked. 'Why should Aimée have been aggressive towards me?'

Lefèvre carried on nodding distractedly then looked at me. 'I did not expect Mademoiselle Loroux to bother you again, madame, but now that she has, there are some things about her that you should know.'

'Go on,' I said.

'Well, according to my London colleague, the CID are now fairly sure that it was Aimée Loroux who shot a young man called Peter . . . Staniszewski,' Lefèvre said, struggling with the surname, 'in April of this year. It's not, I think, what you call an open and shut case, but the night the boy went missing, he was seen arguing in a nightclub with a girl fitting Aimée's description. Later that evening they were witnessed entering the boy's apartment by a taxi driver who had taken them home. No fingerprints, other than his own, were found on the deceased's pistol, but nearly a quarter of a kilo of cocaine – that the CID's informants say was in the man's possession – was missing from the flat. No money was found at the crime scene either, even though the taxi driver claims that the man paid his fare in cash from a well-stocked wallet.'

Lefèvre's lieutenant appeared at the open window, examining the frame and the glass.

'As yet, they have no *proof,* but it would seem that Miss Loroux – or someone who looks just like her – shot her boyfriend and took his drugs and cash. It's possible that she smuggled the drugs into France, in order to use them as an entrée into the Bordeaux underworld—'

'The tickets,' I whispered.

'I'm sorry?'

'I . . . I found some tickets in Aimée's room,' I explained. 'A ferry ticket, from Dover to Calais and a railway ticket to Libourne.'

Lefèvre's eyes shone. 'Do you still have them, madame?'

'Yes, er, they're in my safe,' I said, rising from my seat. I retrieved the small cardboard wallet and passed it to the policeman.

'Thank you, madame,' he said, opening the envelope and reading its contents at arm's length. 'These are dated the day after Staniszewski was last seen. Now we have some very compelling evidence for our friends in London and, perhaps, a motive for last night's break-in. When did you find them?'

My gaze shifted, guiltily, to the open window, then down to the floor. 'A couple of months ago, I suppose,' I said vaguely.

'I'll keep these, if I may, Madame Valeix. You should have told us sooner, you know. I hope you realize that now.'

I returned to my chair, feeling like a guilty schoolgirl in front of the headmaster. 'Yes, I'm sorry, but I didn't think it was important,' I lied.

Lefèvre stared at me. He looked cross. 'You say you discovered some cocaine in her room, too, no?'

'Yes,' I answered meekly. 'Well, at least I think it was cocaine.'

The man continued to stare at me, as though he was about to reveal my punishment. 'Trafficking is a risky endeavour, but not an uncharacteristic one for a person in her mental state.'

'What do you mean her *mental state*?' I asked.

'We have received Miss Loroux's medical, psychological and criminal reports from Lisle. As well as suffering from anorexia nervosa and kleptomania, she was diagnosed with antisocial personality disorder with psychopathic tendencies. She had a record of petty crime – mainly theft and a few drug-related offenses.'

I was relieved to be sitting down; had I been standing up I would have fainted. 'My God,' I said quietly, 'How did such a bright kid fall so far?'

'I'm an averagely competent policeman, Madame Valeix, not a psychologist,' Lefèvre sighed, staring at the ferry ticket.

'But she's so young.'

'We deal with young people with far more elaborate résumés, madame. Like, for instance, the young man that we believe she is currently . . . attached to.'

'You know her boyfriend?' I asked.

'Yes, we think so, but we're finding it rather difficult to locate him. All we know about him is that he arrived in

Bordeaux a few months ago from, we believe, Romania, and that he's known to our contacts as Le Balafré.'

The word sounded familiar, but the blank look on my face told the captain that my French vocabulary was still far from comprehensive.

'Scarface,' he said, translating the nickname for me.

Scarface. The driver of the black BMW. His grimacing, disfigured visage came back to me, and I shuddered.

A polite tap at the half-open door of the study dragged my thoughts away from Le Balafré.

'Ah, my lieutenant has completed his search,' Lefèvre said to me, his tone changing instantly from stern to amiable. '*Entrez,* Dauzac.'

Lieutenant Dauzac entered the room and nodded to me.

Lefèvre resumed his description of Aimée's scary-sounding friend. 'He was, until recently, a small-time drug dealer, but we have reason to believe that he was planning something more ... adventurous. Recently, large quantities of heroin have been arriving in Bordeaux and Libourne. We believe that Le Balafré may be the local contact for the organisation responsible. The problem is that, since Aimée's disappearance, we have lost touch with him.'

The Lieutenant addressed his superior officer: 'Excuse me, *Capitaine*. There's nothing to identify the car I'm afraid, but I'm sure we'll find plenty of prints on the window and on the furniture upstairs.'

'Very well, Dauzac,' Lefèvre said, rising from his seat, 'do the necessary would you, and please put in a request for the surveillance boys to install some cameras. Oh, and make the arrangements for a couple of uniformed officers to keep an eye on Madame Valeix's property for the next few nights, okay?'

He turned round to face me, smiling. 'You should sleep easier in your bed tonight, madame.' Did I look *that* tired? 'Don't worry, I don't think that Aimée will try *this* again.' He indicated the open window with its damaged frame. 'But if you see – or hear from – either of these characters again you must phone me immediately. We need to find Aimée before she does something to hurt herself or others. Here, take my card – my cell phone number is written on the back.'

He handed me a white business card and showed me his personal number, scrawled in biro on the blank side.

'Just call me,' he said, 'any time.'

We walked over to the police car. As the officers climbed in and closed the doors I remembered something and gestured to the captain to lower his window. 'She called him Gregory,' I said, 'if that's any use to you. She pronounced it the English way, you know, but he could be Grégoire, or Gregor, I suppose.'

'Thank you, Madame Valeix,' the policeman said, then repeated those two anxiety-inducing words: 'Don't worry.'

I got on the phone as soon as the police had gone. After several rings, Andrew answered. His relaxed tone was a comfort to me, despite the hundreds of miles between us.

After I'd related my account of the previous night and my conversation with the police, Andrew said, 'Look, Jean, we're catching the ferry tonight. I'll be with you tomorrow, anyway. I'm sure that Lefèvre will keep you safe till then. Don't worry.'

Those bloody words again.

'Don't worry?' I almost shouted into the mouthpiece of the phone. 'Andrew, the house was broken into last night. I'm being stalked by a . . . psychopath . . .' I struggled to say the word, and hearing the melodrama in my voice, I hesitated, giving Andrew a chance to interrupt my flow.

'Jean, you're overreacting—' he began.

'*Overreacting?*' I cut in. 'Can you imagine—' I stopped myself. 'Er, what do you mean, *we?*'

'Like I said, Jean, I'm bringing Archie with me to spend a few days at Fontloube.'

Andrew's impetuosity was, perhaps, understandable, but to abduct a minor and bring him here, where a couple of fugitives seemed bent on God-knows-what, seemed like complete madness. 'Oh, come on,' I remonstrated. 'Surely you don't intend to bring him with you *now*.'

There was a pause. 'It's now or never, Jean,' he said calmly.

I knew that trying to reason with him was futile but couldn't help using a little emotional blackmail. 'Look, Andrew, if anything happens to Archie I will never be able to forgive myself, *or you*.'

'Jean, listen – bugger, this thing's beeping at me. I think it's the battery. I don't think I charged it properly when—'

A silence, followed by a distant, whispery white noise, replaced Andrew's voice. I sighed, put the phone on the hook and decided to make a cup of tea. I would, of course, get another call from him later that day, letting me know the arrival time of his ferry, assuring me that everything would be alright and telling me to drive carefully. But if he tells me not to worry again, I thought, he can find his own bloody way back to Fontloube.

I was more than usually anxious about leaving the house, especially in the dead of night, but I looked forward to seeing Andrew and meeting his son. As I pulled out into the dark lane, I spotted a police car, its interior light casting a pale glow on the faces of two officers, in a lay-by a few hundred metres from the end of my drive. Unlikely to get any intruders tonight, I mused. I turned right on the D670 and accelerated towards Libourne, trying not to think about the four hundred miles of tarmac between me and the English Channel.

I put a Billy Holiday cassette on the jeep's stereo and tried to clear my mind of anxieties and frustrations. I joined the empty Aquitaine highway at Saint-André-de-Cubzac and headed north. As I passed the exit for Blaye, the soothing notes of a sax played the intro to *God Bless the Child*. My thoughts turned to Aimée Loroux and, inevitably, to her sinister-looking friend, Le Balafré.

Clearly, someone had been watching the house and had noticed that Andrew's van was missing – why else would

Aimée have waited until this week to break in? I imagined her and Scarface watching us, perhaps from the road that climbs the *côte* (from where they would have had a clear view of the camper van), waiting, to be sure that I was alone . . . Yet again, I shuddered at the thought of Aimée's boyfriend and of the time we nearly collided with each other in the lane.

Had she told him what it was she was searching for in my house? I was willing to believe, knowing how she lies, that he was unaware of her real intentions. She'd killed her previous boyfriend; could her current one be complicit in helping her to recover the evidence? I thought not, but the possibility was appalling. He'd probably been told that there were more drugs or money hidden the house. I hoped that now, with a visible police presence, the couple would leave me and my property alone.

Bizarrely though, despite what I knew about Aimée and what I'd learned of her exploits, I retained an emotional connection with her that wouldn't go away. Not for the first time, I found myself fantasising about how different our situations could have been, if only I'd been more sympathetic. I imagined what might have happened if, instead of scaring her off into the night, I had called to her, asked her to stay, talked things through . . . I pictured her, frozen on the stair, turning slowly to look up at me, her eyes welling with tears. I saw the embrace of reconciliation with the girl who yearned for forgiveness and knew it would be granted.

Who was I kidding? Aimée was a calculating, cold-hearted liar and thief. Of course, I knew it. Even so . . .

My mixed feelings weren't only concerned with Aimée Loroux. I looked forward to meeting Andrew's son, but since the break-in I had terrible misgivings about inviting a vulnerable young man to my home. Had Andrew told Archie about Aimée's antics? Somehow, I doubted it.

Nor did I know if Andrew had talked to his son about his cancer. I wondered how a child with autism would take such devastating news.

The final track faded. I ejected the tape and tuned the radio to an all-night classical music programme. After half an hour or so, I began to feel drowsy, so I turned off the motorway into a small service area, relieved that there were no black BMWs in the car park. I applied the handbrake and raked the seat back. Sleep came quickly. When I opened my eyes, the clock showed that over an hour had passed. A sudden, adrenal rush shocked me awake: I was now running late. I drove back onto the deserted carriageway, sipping warm black coffee from a thermos, and sped on, a little faster than before, into the long night.

Synaesthesia

Of colours of Wine be four manners, white, black, citron and red.
- Herbert West Seager,
Natural History in Shakespeare's Time

I arrived at the port shortly after seven a.m. A passenger information board, spanning the car lane to the dock, announced that high winds had delayed the ferry from Portsmouth by an hour.

I sat in the car and waited. When the first trucks began to roll off the boat, I got out, locked the doors and walked over to the terminal building. A couple of rows of plastic benches in the centre of the hall were occupied by sleepy (and some sleeping) travellers, waiting for the late departure to England. Some were reading English newspapers. I read the headlines – *Another Black Friday* ... *Pound Slumps to Record Low* ... *Credit Crunch Christmas* – trying not to think about my own money problems. Then I went over to a drinks dispenser near the customs point from where I'd be able to see Andrew and Archie coming through passport control.

First a trickle then a flow of disembarking passengers exited the customs hall. Soon the exodus slowed and stopped. A couple of customs guards, who'd been monitoring the gate, walked past me into the concourse and headed towards the cafeteria. I felt a sudden pang of despair. Had Andrew missed the ferry and been unable to contact me? Just as I was about to go and look for a public phone booth, I spotted them, ambling through the gate, laden with heavy bags. It was like seeing two Andrews. The boy had clearly inherited his father's physique:

medium height and build, strong – you might say stocky – in the chest, with a confident swagger. What had I expected? A feeble, cowering youth? A shuffling, eye-rolling idiot? It certainly surprised me to see such a fit young man, and I chastised myself for my prejudices. As they approached, I could see that Archie was anxious though, perhaps at the prospect of meeting a stranger.

Andrew and I embraced. 'Good to see you, Jean,' he said, 'Sorry to keep you waiting. They took ages checking the dog's papers.' I detected a whiff of whisky on his breath.

'Great to see you, too,' I replied, 'I've missed you, you old devil.'

Turk appeared, on a leash, from behind Archie's back. 'And you, too, Turk,' I cooed, stooping down to stroke the dog. 'I've missed you so much. I could have done with a guard dog the other night.'

Andrew and I exchanged glances.

I asked, 'How are you feeling?'

'A bit hung-over actually,' he said sheepishly. 'We had a few bevvies in the bar last night, eh Archie?'

I turned to the boy and put out my hand, saying, 'I'm so pleased to meet you, Archie.'

He shook my hand limply, avoiding my gaze.

'Are you okay?' I asked.

'Yes, thank you,' he said quietly. 'I'm just a bit nervous about driving on French roads. You see—'

'Let's not bother Jean with all that now, Archie,' his father interrupted. 'He gets anxious on long journeys.'

'Well,' I said, 'do you want to take a break here or hit the road?'

'Let's get moving, eh?' said Andrew. 'I think Turk needs some fresh air.'

The four of us hastened to the exit – Andrew, smiling, already recounting the highlights of their journey; Archie, silent, still looking worried; and Turk scampering ahead, pulling at the lead.

The sky was still dark when we walked out of the brightly lit arrivals hall and into the ferry port's car park. In the sodium glow of the street lamps, the jeep's roof could be seen above the rows of Peugeots, Renaults and Citroëns. When Archie spotted the vehicle's number plate, his nervous, introspective mood changed, and a smile appeared on his face. 'Now that's what I call a lucky car!' he exclaimed, quickening his pace.

Andrew slipped his arm round my waist and said, 'He likes the registration number.'

Archie opened the front passenger-side door, climbed in and encouraged Turk to jump up next to him. I looked at the jeep's number plate, perhaps for the first time.

1314 AM 33

'Do you know, I've never noticed your initials there,' I said to Andrew.

'And mine, too,' called Archie excitedly through the open door. '*And* the year of the battle of Bannockburn *and* a double lucky number – this car will never crash!'

I thought: he clearly hasn't seen the deep scratches on the driver's side. 'Don't speak too soon, Archie,' I said, opening my door, 'you haven't seen me drive yet.'

Andrew loaded the boot with their luggage and duty-free goods. 'Archie prefers to ride in front,' he called from behind the car. Then, moving round to my side, he whispered, 'I haven't told him about our intruder . . .'

We left the ferry port. While Andrew struggled with his seat belt, Archie pulled out a paperback from his rucksack and started to read. 'I was a bit worried about driving in France,' the boy said, while seemingly engrossed in his book. 'There were fifty-seven percent more road deaths in France last year than in the United Kingdom. Four thousand six hundred and twenty compared to two thousand nine hundred and forty-six—'

'Okay, Archie,' Andrew interrupted, 'that's enough statistics, eh?'

His eyes left the page. Looking at me disinterestedly, he asked, 'Did I say something wrong?'

Andrew patted his son, ever so gently, on the shoulder. 'Archie has many talents,' he said, 'but tact isn't one of them. Don't you remember, Son, I told you that Jean's husband died in a car accident?'

'Yes, of course I remember.'

He went back to his book, and I caught a glimpse of the title: *The Wasp Factory*.

I was keen to change the subject. 'That looks interesting,' I said light-heartedly. 'I could do with someone who knows about wasps. My vines were full of them this year. I got stung twice.'

Still staring at the page, Archie said, 'It's not about wasps.'

Silence.

'It's about someone who thinks they're one thing, but eventually they discover that they're something else entirely.'

'Sounds fascinating, Archie. Do you like reading?' I asked.

He stared at the dual carriageway ahead and said, 'I like this kind of book, but the characters in most stories I've read are always pretending to be something that they're not. In this book, the main character is desperately trying to find out who he really is.'

More silence.

'It's like my Asperger's. Everyone tells me what my condition is, but no one can tell me who I am. I'm hoping that one day, like the person in the book, I'll find out.'

The straight road in front was clear of traffic, so I risked a look at my passenger. Smiling, I said, 'I'm sure you will, Archie. And you're no different from any other sixteen-year-old. It's called being an adolescent – I was just the same.'

On our left, as we joined the Caen ring road, the eastern horizon was brightening, but when we reached the autoroute the clouds had darkened the sky. It started to rain. The familiar sound of Andrew's snoring told me that at least one of my passengers was now fast asleep.

Listening to the hypnotic rhythm of the windscreen wipers made me feel drowsy, too. I needed conversation to keep me alert. Assuming I didn't fall asleep at the wheel, the six-hour drive would give me plenty of opportunity to learn more about Andrew's remarkable son.

'So tell me, Archie, why is three a lucky number then?'

'Well, it's the first lucky prime, of course.'

The timbre of his voice was monotone, but not unusually so for a boy of his age. 'It represents the three primary colours; as a denominator of any even integer it results in an infinitely recurring decimal; it's my favourite colour: iridescent blue—'

'Iridescent blue?' I queried, stopping him.

A pair of blue eyes flashed me a look. 'Yes, like the morpho butterfly, a peacock's neck, the kingfisher's back, a damselfly's thorax, a cicindella's wing case, blue tetra fish, dragonflies' eyes, the—'

'And your eyes, too, Archie,' I interrupted again.

'What? Are they? I never really look at my eyes much.'

'You should,' I said, 'They're very nice eyes.'

I sneaked another look at him. A broad smile – Andrew's smile – had spread across his blushing face.

His father shifted position on the back seat, waking up. 'I can see you two are getting on fine,' he said, yawning.

'How do you pronounce that?' Archie asked, pointing at a road sign.

'Lisieux,' I said, 'It sounds like *lizzy-uh*.'

He mouthed the place name slowly, silently.

Later, I learned how Archie associated smells, as well as numbers, with colours. As we approached the bay of Le Mont Saint Michel, a brief interlude of winter sunshine illuminated the hilltop abbey in the distance and turned the grey English Channel into a horizontal ribbon of blue. 'Look how beautiful the bay looks today,' I said. 'You can almost smell the sea air.'

'Yes. Magenta,' Archie said, inhaling deeply.

Ah, I thought, the other facet of Archie's synaesthesia.

When I asked him if smells had colours, too, he said nothing, but nodded slowly. I suggested that it might be confusing being surrounded by colours all the time. He told me that he could mask the everyday things, ignore the familiar smells – rush-hour traffic, classrooms, the school canteen, deodorant – in the same way that people who live on a flight path no longer hear the aeroplanes, or how city dwellers eventually stop noticing police sirens. New or long-remembered smells shone most vividly in his mind's vision. So far this trip, he had re-encountered the dark orange hue of the ship's fuel, the pale grey-blue of the harbour at Portsmouth, Turk's own colour: bright pea-green ... I enjoyed testing him. What about mint? – *turquoise*; coffee? – *battleship grey*; furniture polish? – *olive drab*. I footled in the glove box, found the small scent bottle I was looking for and sprayed a little of the perfume in his direction. To Archie it was a bewildering cocktail of smells, camouflaged amongst the colours of a multitude of aromas. He said he could pick out the bright yellow of musk and the deep crimson of cinnamon, but that was all. Too many smells together, he told me, like too many paints mixed together, just produce a brown mess. He identified one other aroma – the slate grey of alcohol – and I joked that what he could smell was his dad's breath. No, he told me, all perfume houses use ethanol as a base for their perfumes.

I thought, this boy could make a formidable wine taster.

Misty green meadows and mistletoe-choked orchards gave way to the arable flatlands of the Loire Atlantique. We stopped at a service station after crossing the broad river at Nantes. Good, strong, black coffee revived me. Andrew was relieved to stretch his legs. Archie seemed delighted with the comic-strip books on sale in the kiosk. Even Turk enjoyed himself, exploring the lawns and shrubs that flanked the car park. Everyone was happy. I bought three baguettes, filled with pallid *jambon blanc* and wafer-thin slices of rubbery Swiss cheese, then filled the jeep's tank with diesel.

Andrew offered to drive the rest of the way. I judged that, by now, his blood would be practically alcohol-free, so I passed him the keys and climbed into the back.

We rejoined the motorway and ate our lunch en route, saving the crusts for the ever-grateful dog. Archie asked me to pronounce the names of all the small towns that we passed – Montaigu, Saint Fugent, Sainte Hermine, Fontenay le Comte – repeating each word to himself almost inaudibly.

I tried to make myself comfortable on the bench seat and enjoyed eavesdropping on the conversation between the two men in the front, watching their profiles as they turned to each other to pose a question, seeing their smiles, listening to them laugh at impenetrable in-jokes. There was something comforting, reassuring about their easy interaction. It was, well – nice.

I dozed. When I opened my eyes again the two of them were still chatting away.

'So have you thought about what you want to do when you leave school?'

'I don't know, Dad.'

'Well, you've got to think about what the future will bring, you know.'

'The future doesn't bring anything, Dad.'

Something about Archie's response intrigued me, so I leaned forward to join in the conversation. I asked, 'What do you mean, Archie?'

'Oh, hello, Jean. Did you have a nice sleep?'

'Yes, thank you. What do you mean "the future doesn't bring anything"?'

Archie shifted forward a little and craned his neck to talk to me. 'My best friend Jonathan explained it all to me in Physics last week,' he said. 'Time doesn't flow. The future doesn't arrive. Everything that has happened – and everything that will happen – is just there, like the chapters in a book.'

Andrew interjected. 'Och, come on now, Archie, don't start boring Jean with your theories.'

'No, not at all,' I insisted, 'Please go on, Archie.'

He smiled and took a deep breath.

'Well, you only *perceive* the flow of time, but really time stands still. Life is like reading a book – the ending's already been written. But, since the cosmos has recreated itself an almost infinite number of times, occasionally you can bump into a parallel universe, almost exactly the same as the one you're in now.'

Another big breath.

He continued. 'At that point, you can cross over into the new universe and experience a totally different future from the one you were destined to have in the old one. Of course, you don't make a conscious decision to jump – it just happens at a quantum level in the synapses when you make a choice.'

Strangely, Archie's fantastic theory sounded far from implausible. I wanted to know more. 'So, when I make a choice between two alternatives, say, shall I go to the bakery now or wait until it stops raining, I'm between two parallel universes? At a crossroads?'

'Erm, more like a motorway junction. You imagine two possible futures and follow the one that you choose. You stay on the main carriageway or take the slip road that runs parallel with the motorway for a while, then branches off to a completely different destination.'

The idea that the imagination could change the future amazed me. 'So, can I imagine that I'm going to win the lottery and become a millionaire?'

'No,' Archie said. I wondered if he'd found my question facetious, but after a pause, he continued. 'Not consciously. There will be a millionaire Jean out there somewhere, but you have to get there one quantum step at a time. Buying a lottery ticket is the first step, I would say. After that, whether you jump into a future where you win or one where you lose is completely random.'

'Oh, well,' I said, leaning back, 'it's back to grape

picking, I suppose.'

'Two hundred kilometres to Bordeaux,' Archie muttered tangentially.

'So, would you like to be a cosmologist then?' I asked.

'Maybe, but most of them go to America and I wouldn't want to live there – too many guns. I'd really like to be an astronaut, but I'm not dextrous enough,' he said, glancing discomfitedly at his father.

'No problem, son,' said Andrew. He moved his right hand from the gear lever and held it just above, but not quite touching, Archie's knee. 'Don't worry – I never expected to see you scoring tries at Murrayfield.'

I felt sorry for the boy.

'We'll have to take you to Toulouse,' I suggested, 'to the European space centre?'

Archie's smile returned. 'Is that near Saint-Emilion?'

'Not too far – only a couple of hundred kilometres further south.'

'Are there vineyards there, too, Jean?'

'Yes,' I said, recalling a winemaking friend of Olivier's who owned vines in nearby Fronton, 'I think so.'

Archie looked thoughtful. 'Do you think I could be a winemaker who does space research?' he said.

'Why not, Archie,' I said. 'But whatever future you choose, choose it wisely. I don't suppose that theory of yours lets you travel back in time?'

'No, nothing can travel beyond its light cone because that's a physical impossibility.'

'Quite,' said Andrew, giving me a bewildered look. We passed a huge road sign that read:

BORDEAUX 198

'Ha! Archie, you're losing your touch. You were out by two kilometres.'

'No, Dad, that was two kilometres ago.'

'How *do* you do that, Archie?' I asked.

Archie stared straight ahead at the road and shrugged. In the rear-view mirror, I could see the smile of a proud and loving father.

Near Royan, we stopped again to change drivers. A few kilometres later, the first vine-strewn fields began to appear. We cruised southwards, through the cognac vineyards of the Charente and the northernmost hillsides of the Côtes de Blaye. The familiar sight of the vine rows made me glad to be returning home. When we arrived at Fontloube, at just before three o'clock, Archie stared in awe at the château's decorative façade, its honey-yellow stonework glowing in the December sunshine. He was clearly impressed with his dad's new lodgings.

I applied the handbrake. 'Here we are,' I said.

Archie turned to me and said, with near-perfect intonation, '*Merci beaucoup, Madame Valeix, vous conduisez très prudemment.*'

'Well, thank *you* for being such a good driving companion, Archie,' I replied. 'I'm glad you think I'm a careful driver. And I must say you're French accent is excellent.'

'Thanks,' he said nonchalantly. 'My French teacher, Mrs Clarke, is always telling me to improve my pronunciation.'

'Ah, that's why you were asking Jean to repeat all those place names,' Andrew cut in. 'He'll be talking French like a local from now on, Jean, you'll see.'

'Well, I'm impressed, Archie,' I enthused, thinking: let's test him with something more colloquial. '*Depuis quand tu suis des cours de français?*'

With neither hesitation nor even a blink, he replied, '*Depuis cinq ans,*' adding, 'I've studied French for five years.'

'I wish I'd been as good at French when I was your age,' I said. 'I flunked O-level. Come on, I'll show you the house.'

After we'd unloaded the car, Andrew showed Archie to his room on the first floor, and I went to the kitchen to make some tea. The house felt cold. When the kettle boiled, it produced great billows of steam. I watched the cloud rise to the ceiling then fall slowly down, covering the window like a translucent blind. I rubbed the misted pane with my sleeve and peered up at the black, flapping shapes of the rooks, high in the horse chestnut's bare branches. It was already going dark. I shivered.

The tea was ready when I heard Andrew's familiar footsteps descending the stairs.

'Someone's happy,' he said, raising his eyes to the ceiling. He walked to the counter and put his hand on the teapot. 'Is this brewed?'

'He's happy with his digs then?' I asked, adding, 'Yes, go on, pour. I could murder a cup.'

He filled two mugs from the pot and added a little milk to each.

'Archie's more adaptable than people give him credit for,' Andrew said, stirring the tea. 'Especially when his new environment is so . . . comfortable.'

'Not too cold for him, I hope,' I suggested.

'Nah, Archie's got Scots blood in his veins. We're made of strong stuff.' He winced slightly, dropped the teaspoon on the countertop, and rubbed his side and lower back with the heel of his hand.

'Are you okay,' I said, getting up.

'Oh, it's nothing,' he answered, gesturing at me to sit down. 'It's just the long journey.'

'You've been taking all your medicines?' I fussed.

'Aye,' he said noncommittally.

He joined me at the table and we sipped our hot tea, listening to the quarrelsome rooks outside.

I broke the silence. 'He's not what I expected, you know.'

'Who? Archie?'

'Yes. I mean, he's so . . . normal.'

'What did you expect: Quasimodo?'

I flushed, so easily shamed. 'No,' I said, 'but, well, you know. He doesn't seem to be, in any way . . . disabled by his condition.'

'No, he'd argue that his Asperger's and his synaesthesia are gifts, not handicaps. He's pretty much the same as most people except that he rambles a bit, he's easily distracted and he doesn't like holding hands.'

I sipped my tea noisily. 'So, like most of the men I know then?'

Andrew gave me one of his looks. 'Miss Jean,' he said, 'I *do* enjoy holding hands!' He took another swig from his mug. 'No, seriously,' he continued, 'he doesn't like physical contact. And he hates loud noises and any change to his routine. If you say something like "I could murder a cup of tea" to him, he'll take it literally – depending on the context he'll be either horrified or amused, but either way he won't get the message. If you ask him to do something, don't be ambiguous – tell him exactly what to do. When you've shown him something once, though, he'll never forget. He's a good little worker.'

'Well, I'm sure I can find some jobs for him to do in the winery, to earn his keep.'

'You should, Jean. You should. He's nearly seventeen, you know. He's old enough to be helping out – not that his mother would agree with me.'

'Ah, yes.' I said, eyeing him. 'Just what did you say to her about Archie's little holiday?'

He looked at the window. 'Nothing,' he said quietly. 'She doesn't know – yet.'

'Oh God, Andrew, you've got to let her know.'

'Aye, I know.'

After tea, Andrew went to see how his son was settling in, but he came back immediately to report that the boy was sleeping soundly. He produced a bottle of malt whisky from one of his bags and poured out two small glasses. When we returned to our previous conversation, Andrew was keen to know what action his ex-wife could take when she discovered that her son had been abducted. I told him not to rely on my limited (and mostly outdated) knowledge of the law, but I assured him of one thing: even though a cross-border infringement of a custody decree was a criminal act, it would take Deborah several weeks to obtain a return order. And as Archie was planning to go home within a week or so, there was very little, legally, that his mother could do. Though whether she'd ever let Andrew see their son again was another matter. I did, however, insist that Andrew contact her immediately. I could only imagine how distraught she'd be feeling about her son's disappearance. At first he procrastinated, but when I threatened to call her myself he gave in.

While the child abductor went to the study to phone his ex-wife, I poured myself another glass of malt and wondered how he would phrase his confession. When he returned, looking a tad abashed, I consoled him with another dram. I'd already told him on the phone about the break-in, but I went over it all again, including Captain Lefèvre's latest visit and the security cameras and round-the-clock surveillance that he'd arranged.

Andrew seemed more content than I was to believe that Aimée's intrusion would be the last we'd ever hear of her. In his view, Aimée must have realised that the incriminating tickets were now in police hands. She'd be unlikely to return, especially with the extra security and – at least for the moment – the police presence at Fontloube. Andrew's reasoning (and the whisky) eased my doubts, but I was still concerned for Archie's safety. However, now that I'd seen what a capable young man he was, I was more than happy to let him stay for Christmas. Returning him to England, though, for the start of the winter term, was a tricky issue that would need to be dealt with later.

From upstairs came the sound of shuffling feet; Archie had woken up. I still didn't know what, if anything, he had learned about his father's illness.

'So,' I said.

'So?' Andrew echoed, smiling.

'How much does he know about . . . you know?'

His smile faded. 'I told him everything – last night, in

the bar.'

'Ah, that explains the hangover,' I said, taking his hand. 'Dutch courage, eh?'

'Aye, I kept putting it off, you know. And in the end, it was a lot more difficult for me to say than it was for him to hear.'

'What do you mean?'

A door banged shut upstairs followed by the noise of the château's noisy plumbing.

'Well,' Andrew continued, 'he took it very calmly – too calmly, you might say. He said that he'd been coping quite well without me for months, so he'd already got used to living without his dad.'

'Andrew, that sounds terrible, but isn't it because—'

He cut me short, 'Yes, yes. His Asperger's makes it difficult for him to empathise with people – he finds it hard to express his feelings. Still, it's bloody hard when your own son . . .'

I covered his fidgety hands with mine. 'Don't take it to heart. He loves you, anyone can see that. What he's got – his *condition* – only masks his emotions. I'm sure of it.'

'Aye,' Andrew began, just as his son came into the kitchen.

'Hello, Jean,' Archie said, 'is there anything to eat, please?'

Andrew and I looked at each other, our sincere frowns curling into smiles.

'You're a typical teenager, Archie,' I said, pushing my chair back. 'Let's see what we've got in the fridge, eh?'

'Thank you, Jean,' he said, adding a third smile to the group.

After dinner, the phone rang while we were clearing away the dishes. It was Captain Lefèvre. For a panicky second, I thought he was phoning about Archie's abduction, but his cheerful tone suggested otherwise. He was calling to update me on Aimée's whereabouts. According to a reliable police informer, a man named Grigor Popescu – a

Romanian with a prominent facial scar – had just arrived, by plane, in Bucharest, accompanied by a beautiful, blond French girl. The captain's counterparts in Romania would liaise, through Interpol in Lyon, with the London CID in order to apprehend Loroux. They would also be keeping a close eye on Scarface's activities. His words concurred with Andrew's prediction: 'I don't think Aimée is likely to return to Bordeaux for the foreseeable future.'

Andrew was right, of course. We didn't see or hear from Aimée again that year. However, we did get a visit from our other mutual acquaintance, and her arrival was a joyous surprise. Like *Père Noël*, Wendy arrived bearing gifts on Christmas Eve. We were sitting in the salon reading, the evening sky had darkened following a dramatic mid-winter sunset, and Andrew had lit a fire of old vines that glowed and crackled in the *cheminée*. A loud knock on the door made us all start. Turk trotted off into the kitchen, panting and wagging his stumpy tail.

The side door clicked open, and Wendy's sing-song voice resounded in the corridor, 'It's only me, my dears! Halloo? Is anyone at home?'

Andrew and I jumped up and went to welcome our guest, leaving Archie to his book.

'Wendy!' we said in unison, shaking hands all round and exchanging kisses. She was freezing.

While Andrew helped her off with her thick fur-trimmed coat, I relieved her of a number of grocery-filled plastic supermarket bags.

'It's lovely to see you, Wendy,' I said.

'Oh, my gorgeous girl, it's lovely to see you, too!'

'We thought you'd left after the harvest, along with the swallows,' Andrew said.

'Well, yes I did, but I returned to Bordeaux this weekend to speak at a symposium on the Gallo-Roman poet Ausonius. Most of these events are very dry affairs, but this one was quite a piss-up – incidentally, that's the contemporary English translation of the word *symposium*, you know: *piss-up* – or *drinks party*, I suppose, if you prefer.'

She paused and took a deep breath before continuing. 'Where was I? Ah, yes . . . A couple of my fellow speakers and I stayed on an extra day to enjoy the city's fine food and wine. Anyway, I'd hoped to catch a plane back to London on Tuesday, but all the flights were full – some sort of religious festival going on apparently – so I'm stuck in Bordeaux until Friday. But what joy! I've heard tell of unfortunate souls getting stuck in places like Raleigh Durham, or Brisbane, or the third circle of Hell . . . but imagine being forced to stay in a wonderful place like Bordeaux over the Christmas holiday!'

At last, I managed to interject. 'Wendy,' I said, 'you should come and sit down by the fire before you fall down – you look as though you've walked all the way from Bordeaux.'

She took out a handkerchief and blew her nose loudly. 'No, only from the station, my dear,' she said merrily, 'it's only half a mile or so.'

I put Wendy's shopping on the kitchen table and went to close the door, noting the wintry squall of sleet through which our septuagenarian visitor had just hiked.

'Come through, Wendy,' Andrew insisted, taking her arm. 'Come and warm yourself.'

'Don't mind if I do,' she said, walking arm in arm with Andrew into the corridor. 'A small cognac should do the trick . . .'

'Do you believe all that stuff about her missing her flight?'

Andrew and I had escaped to the kitchen to pour some drinks. Wendy was in the salon chatting affably with Archie.

'I don't know,' I answered, in a whisper. 'But we can't send her away. She'll be good company. We should invite her to stay here tonight and have Christmas dinner with us tomorrow.'

'Aye, the poor old thing,' Andrew said. 'I don't think

she's got anyone else to spend Christmas with. She's no kids, you know.'

'Well, she's very welcome. It'll be nice.'

'If any of us can get a word in edgewise.'

'Oh God, yes!' I giggled. We looked at each other and both started to laugh. Andrew popped the cork from a bottle of champagne and poured four frothy glasses. He passed me a glass and said, 'Happy Christmas, Jean.'

'Aye, Happy Christmas,' I said, aping his Scots burr. 'I love you, Andrew Maconie.'

He pulled me to him and planted a slow, sensitive kiss on my lips. 'I love you, too, Jean. Here's to our first Christmas, eh?'

Our embrace was interrupted by Wendy who appeared, twinkling, in the kitchen doorway. 'Now then,' she said, 'whilst you two love birds are cooing in your nest, young Archie and I are dying of thirst in there.'

'Oh, *pardonnez-moi, madame!*' Andrew exclaimed with an exaggerated Gallic accent. 'Here, have a wee glass of champagne.'

'*Ah, merci, monsieur,*' she said, accepting two glasses then turning to leave. She tottered slowly down the corridor, singing: 'I get no kick from champagne; mere alcohol doesn't thrill me at all; so tell me why should it be true, that I get a kick out of you?'

That evening, we'd intended to eat a cold supper as a sort of semi-fast before the following day's feasting, but Wendy wanted to prepare us a hot meal with the groceries that she'd brought. Confited duck legs, precooked white beans, Toulouse sausage and fatty strips of *poitrine fumée* provided the main ingredients for a winter-warming cassoulet. Between hot, salty mouthfuls of the hearty stew, we swapped our news and sipped my wine. This was Archie's first taste of Château Fontloube, so I was understandably keen to hear his judgement of it. His descriptions were both fascinating and highly unusual. He described the colours in the wine's bouquet: the green-gold of ripe blackcurrants, the steely hue of toasted oak, the vanilla on the finish like a pink sunset . . . When he'd finished his analysis, Wendy stared at him, spellbound (her sense of smell, she told us, had all but disappeared in 1979). Archie, who was studying the wine's label, asked me to explain how our village wines were classified. He was intrigued to learn that there were several classes of Saint-Emilion, and surprised that most of them were superior to mine.

'So,' he said thoughtfully, after listening to my long-winded explanation, 'there's lots of ordinary Saint-Emilion wine, then there's the *grand crus*, like Fontloube. Next come the *grand crus classés*, which are supposed to be better; then the *premiers grands crus classés*; then, right at the top of the heap, two wines, called Ausone and Cheval Blanc, which are known as *premiers grands crus classés "A"*. Is that right?'

'In a nutshell,' I said, 'that's it.'

Wendy chipped in: 'One named after my Latin poet, of course; the other, referring to the French King's white horse.'

'Well done, Wendy,' I said, 'There you are, Archie – as clear as mud, eh?'

'I don't know about that,' Archie said, looking terribly earnest. 'It seems logical to me. And you say that it hasn't changed for fifty years?'

'Not much changes very quickly round here, Archie. But that's nothing compared to my neighbours over the river in the Médoc. They classified their wines in 1855!'

'Wow,' Archie said. He paused, composing his next line. 'I still don't understand how these other wines could be any better than yours, though, Jean.'

'Flattery will get you everywhere, Archie.' I said, raising my glass to him.

Andrew gave me a top-up. 'See, Jean,' he said, 'Archie agrees with me. Your wines are undervalued.' He poured a splash into Archie's glass. 'You know, Son, some wines are worth hundreds – even thousands – of pounds a bottle.'

'Wow,' he said again. 'I wonder what a thousand pound wine tastes like.'

'Well, Archie,' he said, winking at Wendy and me. 'Wait till tomorrow – who knows what Father Christmas might bring.'

Christmas

Poetry is devil's wine.
- St. Augustine

The third sense woke me on Christmas Day morning. A trio of breakfast smells – toast, bacon and fresh black coffee – dragged me away from some transitory predawn dream. Andrew, bless him, had brought me my breakfast in bed. I switched on the lamp, yawned, and gazed with sleepy indulgence at the silver tray before me. Along with the bacon and eggs, the rack of hot toast, and my customary coffee, steaming in a china mug, there was a small box tied with a bow of red ribbon.

'*Bon appétit*,' he said, getting back into bed next to me and planting a kiss on my cheek.

The temptation to open the box was even stronger that the urge to tuck in to the food. Inside was a ring. For a moment, I feared that Andrew was going to propose.

'Don't panic,' he said softly, registering the sudden look of confusion on my face. 'It was my mother's wedding ring. I just wanted you to have it.'

I held my present in the palm of my hand and admired it. Into the ring's gold channel were set two groups of diamonds, and two of emeralds, with three stones in each cluster.

'Oh, it's beautiful, Andrew,' I whispered. 'But, it's an eternity ring isn't it?'

'Aye, that was my dad's fault – he was half cut when he bought it and he didn't speak much English in those days. I'll tell you the story behind it later, if you like. Go on, try it on.'

I slipped the band on the ring finger of my right hand. It

fitted perfectly.

'Happy Christmas,' he said, gazing at me and smiling.

I was uncomfortable about accepting a family heirloom and suggested to Andrew that, rightfully, the ring belonged to his daughter, or his sister's family. He argued that his mother had wanted him, not Mary, to have the ring. If ever I wanted to pass it on to Poppy then, of course, I was free to do so.

I ate my toast and bacon as Andrew unwrapped his present – an early illustrated edition of Robert Burns' poetry I'd found in an antiquarian bookshop on the Rue Emil Kraepelin. I could tell he was pleased with his gift, although apparently he'd have appreciated some new socks, too.

Once everyone had congregated in the kitchen and the day's first glasses of champagne were poured, we were faced with an awkward situation. As Wendy's arrival was both unplanned and unannounced, we hadn't bought her a Christmas present. Adding to our shame, she gave each of us a beautifully wrapped gift – a Macsween's haggis for Andrew (goodness knows where she'd managed to find it) and a Tuareg necklace in silver and amber for me. Archie carefully and methodically unwrapped his presents, and while Wendy helped Turk to tear the brown paper wrapping from a large ruminant's shinbone, Andrew and I gave each other guilty sidelong glances.

I thanked her for the thoughtful gifts and asked, 'Wendy, when was your first visit to the region?'

'Now, let me see,' she said, surrendering her game of tug-of-war with Turk and his bone. 'That was the year I finished my book on Eleanor of Aquitaine – I was here to visit the cathedral in Bordeaux – so it was in 1988, in the autumn. Lovely weather.'

'Just excuse me for a moment, will you?' I said, putting on my wax jacket.

'Where are you off to, love?' asked Andrew.

'Just getting something from the cellar,' I called and

closed the door behind me.

Wendy was delighted with her gift of a magnum of Château Fontloube 1988 in a presentation box. She offered to share it with us over lunch but, of course, I insisted that she save it for a rainy day. Anyway, I had Christmas dinner all planned, and Andrew had selected the wines.

Years ago, I'd grown accustomed to celebrating Christmas the French way, but since living alone I'd barely celebrated it at all. This year, however, I was going to enjoy a thoroughly British Christmas feast. Dinner would be served after the Queen's address, which we would listen to on the radio. Andrew and Archie groaned when they calculated that this meant waiting until after four o'clock before eating, but I placated them with promises of hot sausage rolls and aperitifs before the broadcast. Andrew, in turn, said that he'd prepare and cook a first course of pan-fried scallops flambéed in whisky, and Wendy offered to make her special cranberry sauce – a secret recipe, revealed to her apparently by a famous cookery writer. This delicacy would, she assured us, go perfectly with the Gascon goose that was, by then, hissing and spitting in a hot oven. Along with the haggis, Wendy had procured a Christmas pudding, thus sparing us from Andrew's threatened clootie dumpling. I had no idea what wines he had chosen, but I had a suspicion that his selection might include a bottle of Pétrus.

Outside, the misty calm weather had preserved the previous night's frost. The valley scene looked like a greetings card cliché. Andrew was in the kitchen, preparing his starter, Archie was busy stoking the fire in the salon, so Wendy and I decided to take Turk for a walk round the vineyard.

Leaving the men to their tasks, we strolled through the bare vines, arm in arm, down the shallow slope of the lower *côte*. Somewhere, out of sight, above and ahead of us, the sun was trying to burn through a dense mist that clung to the dormant valley like a shroud. The fog diffused the dim sunlight, creating an eerie, mustard-yellow haze that surrounded us as we walked.

For once, Wendy seemed content not to talk, but as we skirted the trees and began our return journey along the western side of the vine rows, she stopped and said, 'What will you do when he's gone?'

For many weeks I hadn't dared ask myself the same question. Hearing the words aloud stunned me.

'I—' I stammered, 'I haven't thought about it much . . . I mean, I've tried not to think about it, I suppose.'

'Well it's about time you did, Jean,' Wendy said calmly, slipping her arm from mine and resting her hand on my shoulder. 'Who's going to look after you . . . afterwards?'

Look after *me*? Surely, *I* was the one doing the looking after. I felt slightly irritated, but not wanting to hurt my friend's feelings, I said, 'Oh, I'll be alright on my own – I've managed well enough all these years.'

Wendy looked at me. A sympathetic smile replaced her usual mischievous grin. 'No, that's just it, Jean: you haven't. I know this place is struggling and I know that you struggle, too. You need someone here with you.'

We walked on at a slower pace than before. I wanted to lighten the seriousness of the conversation.

'Well, I've got wee Turk, haven't I boy,' I said, addressing the dog who was peeing unselfconsciously at the end of a vine row. Looking at my friend, I added, 'And you know that there'll always be a place for you here, Wendy.'

'Oh, no, no,' she said, shaking her head, 'I'm sure I'd be no use at all – and anyway, I'll be dead and buried pretty soon, too.'

She looked away, towards the river. 'Oh, bugger,' she said. 'I'm sorry to be such a clot – it's just the way I am.'

When she turned back to face me, her damp eyes shone with their former playfulness.

'No, you're right,' I conceded. 'I'm hoping that the Valeix boys will come back to work here, after they've finished their exams. And I'm thinking about taking on an apprentice from the wine school.'

'That's more like it, Jean! Get some young life in the place. That's what you need – someone with ambition and energy and enthusiasm.' She stopped, to catch her breath. 'Don't dwell on the past; think of the future.'

The word was as bitter as unripe grapes. 'The future is the place I most dread,' I said, the chill of the air catching my throat. 'Come on, Turk, let's head back.'

We reached the gable end of the house. I glanced at the eroded façade, choked with the naked, sinewy branches of the ancient wisteria. Wendy gazed at the skeletal climber, then, perhaps to change the subject of our conversation before going back indoors, she said, 'Gosh, what a wonderful *glycine* you have. It must give a splendid show of flowers in May.'

I sighed.

'I'm thinking of cutting it down. I can't stand the way it looks in winter. It's bad enough being surrounded by all these bare, lifeless vines for four months of the year—'

'Oh, that would be such a shame,' Wendy interrupted, still staring up at the house. 'Just think about the gorgeous display of blooms you get in the spring, eh?'

'Only for about a week,' I countered, 'until the first Atlantic storm blows them all away.'

It was Wendy's turn to sigh. 'Yes,' she said, 'but what a week! There's beauty in the ephemeral, my dear. Without it, how are we to appreciate the eternal?'

We made our way to the side door. From inside I could hear the sound of Andrew chopping shallots and singing *In the Bleak Midwinter*, badly. Wendy put her hand on the door handle, but hesitated before going in.

'The most beautiful thing I ever saw,' she said, lowering her voice to a confidential whisper, 'was a flower clasped in the hand of a mummified boy – a delicate bloom, whose colours had faded only days after the child's burial, but whose message had reached me three thousand years later.'

She released her grip on the doorknob and held my

hands in hers. 'What will survive of us is love, as the poet said,' she said softly. 'Don't resent the drabness of winter – spring is coming!'

As we crossed the threshold into the warm, food-scented kitchen, she added, 'And don't go cutting down that wisteria, either, gorgeous girl. Otherwise, I shall be terribly cross. Now then, my gorgeous, let's see if Andrew has left us some of that excellent champagne shall we?'

After a couple of hours' work in the kitchen, the preparation for dinner was done, and we collapsed on the sofas in the salon to listen to the Queen. I passed round a platter of *amuse-bouches* while Andrew poured everyone a glass of malt. Archie tuned the radio. As the strains of the national anthem filled the room, his father (no royalist he) stood to attention and gave a facetious salute. When the music faded, we heard the sound of a car pulling up on the drive.

Seconds later, Valentin and Paul came strutting through the door delivering gifts and good wishes. They'd driven from Corrèze to surprise us, assuming that we, too, had finished our lunch. When I told them we wouldn't be eating until after four, they looked at me incredulously. My leg-pull, that British citizens have to wait until they've heard their Queen's message, seemed to them quite logical, and they joined us, listening in respectful silence to the speech.

Her Majesty began by saying that this year would be a sombre occasion for many (well, I thought, I'm not going to let that happen). She went on to say that there were many things that we take for granted that suddenly seem less certain (I couldn't have agreed more). In closing, she reminded us of how fortunate we were to have family around us (true, I thought), but when she added that Christmas was a time to reflect on the memories of those who were no longer with us, I had to disappear to the kitchen on the pretext of rescuing the Brussels sprouts.

Notwithstanding the day's lazy indulgences, I had a good appetite. I wondered if the cousins were hungry, too. When I enquired, Valentin's look of baffled incomprehension told me that I'd be setting two more places at table. There would be six of us for dinner.

Before tucking in to the pan-fried scallops, Andrew insisted on saying the Selkirk Grace (the cousins were as confused by its meaning as they were relieved by its brevity) then served us all a glass of old and (I imagine) extremely expensive white burgundy. A prune and Armagnac sorbet, dowsed with a shot of the fiery liquor, followed the seafood. By the time the goose arrived, my entourage was in jubilant mood, but a reverent hush descended when Andrew brought the red wine to the table. Valentin and Paul looked at each other, amazed; Archie seemed fascinated by the wine's label; and, sensing the sudden absence of noise, Turk let out a shrill woof, before going back under the table to gnaw on his bone. Even Wendy was shocked into silence as she received a glassful of the precious Pétrus.

'I have a toast or three to give,' Andrew announced, standing and raising his glass. 'To you three bachelors, I'd like to say: may you have nicer legs than yours under the table before the next harvest is in.'

We cheered and applauded as Archie attempted to translate for the cousins. 'To my dear friend, Wendy,' Andrew continued. 'May you be in heaven – as my mother always used to say – a full half hour before the devil knows you're dead.'

Far from being affronted, Wendy seemed delighted, saying, 'Quite so, Maconie. Quite so. But I doubt I will!'

'And to our host, the lovely Madame Valeix: I have known many, and liked not a few, but loved only one, so this toast's for you.'

Wendy groaned, I told Andrew that he was an old fool, and, for a moment, all was silent as we sipped the hallowed wine.

'Now, don't let the food get cold,' I said, '*Mangez!*'

There was so much to celebrate that night. As well as the festive occasion, with all its trappings (the cousins were enthralled by the notion of Christmas crackers), Valentin had passed his driving test and Wendy's lecture at the symposium had earned her an interview on French television in the New Year.

Andrew's Pétrus was a celebration in itself. We all agreed that it was a superlative, unforgettable, monumental wine. Archie sat silently sniffing his glass, scrutinising the bottle.

'Why isn't it a *grand cru classé*, Jean?'

'Ah, Archie, that's another Bordeaux quirk. Pétrus is from the next village, Pomerol. They don't have the same system there.'

'Why not?'

'Oh, they probably think they don't need to,' I replied.

'*Vino vendibili hedera non opus est*, gorgeous boy,' said Wendy, adjusting her paper hat. 'Good wine needs no bush.'

'I don't understand,' said Archie.

Wendy explained. 'In classical times, Archie, an ivy bush, representing the wine god Bacchus, was the sign of an inn or tavern. The expression means that the best things don't need to be advertised.'

'Oh, I see,' he said, turning to me, 'in that case, your wines need no bush, either, Jean.'

'I wish that was the case, Archie,' I said, adding, 'Anyway, that's enough of your flannel. Just enjoy the wine. But I want to hear what you think of it later.'

There were more toasts to be given, songs to be sung, pledges and promises to be made and forgotten, bets to be won and lost. In short, a good time was had by all. Andrew gave us a rendition (almost completely by heart) of Burns' *Now Westlin' Winds*, but Wendy upstaged him. She came through from the kitchen, clutching a flaming Christmas pudding on a worryingly wobbly tray, and, placing the burning centrepiece on the table, began her own short recitation:

'My candle burns at both ends,' she warbled, 'it may not last the night. But, oh my foes, and oh my friends, it gives a lovely light!'

We were still cheering as the brandy's blue flame flickered and died. I don't think I've ever enjoyed Christmas pudding so much. Nor have I laughed as loud as I did when Valentin swallowed the silver coin that Wendy had secreted in his serving. His feigned choking made us laugh all the more. After he stopped coughing and spluttering, and our mirth had abated, I explained this peculiar British custom to him. When I'd finished, Paul said, *'T'inquiète pas, Valentin, plaie d'argent n'est pas mortelle!'* and the French speakers round the table fell back into hysterics.

After the boys had cleared the dessert dishes, Archie and I started the washing-up. I asked him what he thought about his dad's wine. He told me that he'd enjoyed the aromas of black fruit, flowers and spice (green-gold, mauve and crimson – in his mind's olfactory eye), but there was something else that he couldn't identify: a very nice smell (as he put it) which he described as a shimmering purple-silver. I was intrigued to hear that he remembered tasting it, the previous evening, in my own wine.

Very interesting, I thought.

'Archie,' I said, taking the damp tea towel from him, 'it's time we went to see how things are getting on in the cellar.'

A subjective, professional judgement it was not to be. Waving my pipette like a baton, I led the tipsy party across the frozen courtyard and into the winery. We started in the vat room, with the current vintage – made from the grapes that Andrew and the cousins had helped to harvest. Hardly wine at all yet, the nascent 2008 was raspingly tannic, piqued with harsh malic acid that would, given time, soften and mellow with age. It promised, with its power and concentration, to be a great wine. Despite its rough edges, those of us who'd had a hand in making it felt proud of 'our wine'. I wanted Archie to taste the 2007, so we took our glasses through to the barrel cellar. The room felt warm compared to the icy chill outside. I showed Archie how to remove the bung from the cask and how to thumb the pipette, drawing a little wine and releasing a splash into the tasting glasses. We watched him as he tasted, inhaling from the glass, sipping and slurping to release the wine's aromas. He spat into the grid on the cellar floor and contemplated the length of the flavour.

'So, I said expectantly, 'what colours are you getting?'

'Greenish gold and crimson,' was his verdict.

'Nothing else,' I asked.

'Nope.'

I tasted it. He was right. The wine was still dominated by fruit flavours and the oakiness from the *barrique* in which it was maturing. Everyone agreed, though, that it was very, very tasty – not that, by that stage of the evening, our palates were at their most acute.

'Okay, Archie,' I suggested, 'try that barrel over there.'

My novice tasted from another batch, drawn from new barrels of Tronçais oak. He detected the 'pink' of vanilla. Spot on, I thought.

The other guests were losing interest in the tasting. Andrew had given each of the cousins a cigar and the three of them were sitting on a bench in the corner of the cellar, smoking, and listening to Wendy's reminiscences (in French and English) of Cuba during the mid-'70s. I did not allow smoking in the winery, but I thought, what the hell, it's Christmas.

Archie wandered off to sample another barrel as Wendy approached the end of her tale.

'. . . of course I'd never even *met* the President,' she said, 'but his wife was awfully understanding about it all . . .'

Archie's expression caught my attention. I missed the

conclusion of Wendy's story.

'What is it, Archie?' I asked.

'It's that shimmering purple-silver I was telling you about,' he said.

He'd just sampled a batch made from the cabernets that grow on a parcel of heavy soil at the bottom end of the vineyard – vines that Oliver had planted just after we were married.

'Is that the same flavour you tasted in the Pétrus?' I asked.

'Yes,' he said excitedly. 'So, does that mean that you could make a wine from this barrel that would be as good as Pétrus? You could become millionaire!'

'It's not that simple, I'm afraid,' I said, taking his glass and sniffing deeply. 'But it does mean that you have a very good palate, Archie, and I might just use a little more of this batch when I'm blending the wines in March. Maybe you could come and help me.'

'That would be great,' he said.

After the tasting, we went back indoors and finished what was left of the cheese and biscuits. I wasn't going to let Valentin anywhere near his car, so I insisted that he and his cousin stayed the night. Wendy was the first to retire, but the boys would continue the merrymaking until the early hours of Boxing Day morning. Andrew and I left them to it and staggered upstairs to bed.

I finished in the bathroom then got into the cold bed. Instead of picking up my book, I lay quietly focussing on Andrew's gift, turning the ring slowly on my finger and watching the light glinting green and white in the stones' facets. *See*, my gremlin whispered, *even gemstones come in groups of three, just like your many sad misfortunes – miscarriages, illnesses, bad harvests, deaths* . . . Well, I thought, watching Andrew as he loosened his tie and turned up the collar of his shirt, this man's not dead yet. I pushed all dark thoughts aside, thinking instead of Archie's rare skills, the cousins' dawning careers and

Wendy's fabulous tales. I thought, too, about Aimée, and hoped that, wherever she was spending Christmas, she had found the one thing that she so desperately needed: the comfort and contentment of unconditional love.

Andrew came to bed and asked me what I was thinking.

'Oh, nothing,' I lied.

He took my right hand and examined the ring with a critical eye.

'It suits you,' he said, propping himself up on a couple of pillows and opening his Burns.

'Thanks,' I replied distractedly, adding, 'I mean, really – thank you. It's a lovely present. I'll keep it safe forever.'

'You'd better. I promised my mother I'd look after it when she gave it to me. If it wasn't for that ring . . . Well, that's the story I mentioned earlier.'

Ah, I thought, here comes another Maconie family anecdote. 'Oh, I love bedtime stories – do tell.'

'Well, just after the war, my dad and my uncle Tony – well, he wasn't really my uncle; he and Dad were best mates, you know. They were internees together—'

Andrew glanced at me to see if I was paying attention.

'Yes,' I said, sidling closer to him and putting my left foot on his warm calf, 'go on.'

'Ouch! You've got cold feet, woman.'

'Sorry.'

'Can I continue?'

'Please do.'

'Okay. It was V-J Day, I think, and Dad goes up to Glasgow with Uncle Tony. They visit a couple of pubs on Argyle Street and then go in search of a bookie's. Dad puts five quid on a horse called Campanelli. He chooses the only runner with an Italian name, even though it's a rank outsider. But the horse wins! Tony's probably a bit miffed at losing his stake, so he teases my dad, saying, "That's a sign from God, Gianni. He wants you to marry that beautiful Irish girl from the co-op, *come si chiama?*" So, Dad says, "Rose, you mean? How do you work that out?" "Well," says my uncle, "you know, *campanelli* . . .

wedding bells?" Anyway, they collect Dad's winnings, go straight back to the pub, order a couple of pints, and Tony asks him what he's going to do with the money. "Well," says my dad, "I think you're right Antonio. I'm going to get a ring for Rose and ask her to marry me." "That's great," says Tony, "let's go over the road to that jeweller's shop now." But then Dad says, "Hold on, just let me finish my beer," and so Tony says, "If you finish that beer, *stupido*, another one will follow it and we won't get out of here till your pockets are empty!"'

Andrew looked up at the heavy oak beams above us and smiled. 'My mother always joked that if Uncle Antonio hadn't dragged my dad away from his pint, she'd have ended up with a curtain ring for a wedding band.'

I looked again at the ring. 'You loved them, didn't you?'

'Aye,' he sighed. 'They were great – really wonderful parents. I miss 'em.'

He continued to stare at the ceiling, but the focus of his gaze was miles away.

'Penny for your thoughts,' I asked.

'Och, I'm just thinking about where they are now.'

I hesitated. Was he talking about the afterlife? 'You mean—'

He stopped me.

'I mean the cemetery in Kirkcudbright.'

'Oh, I thought—'

'You should see it, Jean,' he continued, ignoring my misunderstanding. 'It's not far from the town. There are these woods behind it, and in front you look right down the valley to the Dee estuary below. You can see the sunlight glinting on the river, the church steeples, all the wee farms on the hills over on the other side . . . Promise me something, Jean? There's a place for me there – with them, I mean. It's all paid for. Will you make sure they put me there, with Mum and Dad? Will you make sure I . . . go back?'

I wasn't prepared for this.

'Stop being so maudlin Andrew,' I said, 'it's Christmas.'

'Well, promise.'

'Okay, I promise.'

He sighed. Then, adopting a business-like tone, he said, 'There'll be lots to do. I've put a copy of my will in the drawer in the study. Everything's left to Archie and Poppy, of course. You'll have to call my lawyer in London when . . .' He looked at me over his reading glasses, '. . . you know. The phone number and everything's in the envelope.'

When he went back to his poetry, I shut my eyes and recalled his impromptu recital at dinner. I remembered the soothing, lilting sound of his voice, the gold-toothed smile and the wink that he'd given me when we all applauded and he took a bow. The last lines of the poem had stayed with me: *not vernal showers to budding flowers; not autumn to the farmer; so dear can be, as thou to me; my fair, my lovely charmer.*

He put down his book, removed his glasses and turned to me. 'Now you've warmed your feet, if you're not too tired . . .'

'Andrew,' I said prudishly, 'Don't go burning your candle at both ends.'

He smiled. 'Don't worry about that, Jean. There's nothing wrong with my candle.'

I looked at him. You're the charmer, I thought, you handsome devil; you wonderful, sensitive, perfectly flawed man.

I switched off the light.

January 2010

Death

Over the wine-dark sea.
- Homer, *The Iliad*

Had only a year gone by? It seemed far longer. That
Christmas and its joyous, drunken celebrations of life and
love, was a distant memory. But a memory, like the
diamond and emerald ring, that I horded, treasured, kept
safe; because the following year, despite being an
excellent vintage, would always be remembered as the
year when Christmas never came. Andrew passed away,
eighteen months after his diagnosis, on Tuesday the 22nd
of December 2009.

I grieve, but I know how to cope. When, many years
ago, I decided once and for all to stop taking my
medication, I learned the techniques and routines that help
me to survive. But it doesn't get any easier; it still hurts.
The pain of loss never fades. It sticks in the head like a
tumour, neither growing nor shrinking, until it becomes
part of you. Fortunately for me, good memories are just as
stubborn – as long as I nurture them. Being stuck on a
snow-clogged autoroute in northern France, in a column of
stationary, dispirited traffic, was giving me plenty of time
to do just that – recalling, over and over, happier times.

Last January arrived like a hangover, but Andrew was my
cure. When he was fit enough, and the days – though
short, dark and cold – were dry enough, we enjoyed our
work outside, pruning the vines. We became quite
competitive; we'd start a vine row at opposite ends and try
to beat each other to the middle. At dusk, the one with the
most winning rows received, as a prize, a shoulder

massage from the loser (who also had to clean the dishes after supper). More often than not, Andrew won.

I finished the pruning in February. After Andrew's first chemo treatment we drove down to Sète, on the warm Mediterranean coast, to spend a weekend in a converted fisherman's shack. When we weren't eating grilled sardines or drinking chilled Costières de Nîmes, we played Scrabble or made love listening to George Brassens songs and the distant, suserrating sound of the waves caressing the shore.

In March we blended and bottled the 2007, sadly without Archie whose mother had forbidden him to return to Fontloube. Much to my surprise – but not in the least to Andrew's – the wine won a gold medal in Paris. I received the news on my birthday. The summer was glorious. When we found the time we returned more than once to Arcachon, to picnic on the towering dunes and watch the crimson evening sun sink into the Atlantic Ocean.

There was, as yet, no sign of movement ahead – just a long, winding snake of tail lights stretching to the horizon. I tried to focus on the time before Andrew's third round of treatments when the days grew longer and the vines just grew.

Everyone came. We'd convinced his specialist to allow Andrew to be treated at home, and the château's courtyard became a busy car park. Every day brought a stream of visiting nurses, doctors and, of course, our friends. The Lavergnes and their cherubic children paid us a call during the school holidays. The cousins came back to work until the harvest, which was when Wendy returned. Even Captain Lefèvre dropped by one October morning (ostensibly to buy some wine; but after he'd gone, Andrew looked at me slyly and said, 'You'll be alright there, Jean. He's got his eye on you.'). Sadly, the one visitor who Andrew yearned to see more than any other never made it back to Fontloube; but Archie phoned every Sunday afternoon at three o'clock sharp. Andrew's son was one of many people he would talk to on the phone, propped up comfortably on the cushioned sun lounger in the shade of the chestnuts. Following my wine's success in Paris, he convinced an ex-colleague of his to buy a sizeable consignment of my 2007. Château Fontloube would, at last, be sold in England.

It was a perfectly beautiful summer. Perhaps we should have expected the hard winter that followed.

God, it's cold, I thought; cold as the— Well, bloody cold anyway.

I fiddled with the heater controls. There was a dull mechanical sound from inside the dashboard, then a gust of dusty, warm air blew into my face. I blinked, but a tiny piece of grit had lodged itself under my eyelid. My reflection in the sun visor's mirror looked at me through red, travel-tired eyes. I still hadn't cried yet – not properly. I removed the smut with a moistened fingertip, blinked again, and stared back at my reflection. My memories fast-forwarded to the recent past.

One afternoon (was it only two weeks ago?) I was reading by the fireside in the salon, when I heard a creak on the stairs. The visiting nurse wasn't due for another hour or so, and Turk, who lifted his head briefly before settling back to sleep, was curled up at my feet. Andrew startled me. I saw him in the corridor, dressed in his towelling robe and slippers, holding a bottle of wine and two glasses.

'What are you doing up?' I said, trying to sound cheerful. I stood up and went over to help him into the room.

'I just fancied a drink,' he said, showing me the bottle. It was his last Pétrus. 'It won't keep forever. It would be a shame to let it spoil.'

I almost remonstrated with him, but instead I said only, 'Of course, what a lovely idea.'

I took the bottle and glasses and put them on the low

table. He shuffled slowly into the room with me supporting him, then we sat together on the sofa near the fire. His PCA morphine pump made its soft, sad little clicking noise. He sighed.

'Can you open it, Jean?' he asked, rummaging in his pocket and producing a corkscrew.

Turk moved over to sit at his master's feet. I removed the cork and poured two glasses.

'Here's to you,' he said.

'Here's to us,' I replied, cuddling up next to him.

He took a tiny sip of the divine liquor.

'It's been quite a year hasn't it?'

'Yep,' was all I could say in reply.

I sipped, and tried to recall the ecstasy of flavour I'd experienced the last time we tasted this wine together. Another year had not diminished it, but I detected a slight bitterness that had escaped me before.

'Do you still love me?' I whispered.

'No, I adore you.'

'Will you love me tomorrow?'

'No, I'll love you forever.'

'Do you feel frightened?'

'No, just . . . cheated.'

The following day he woke up only twice.

'Sell the wine,' he mumbled, staring at me fixedly.

'What?' I said, rising from my chair next to the bed and putting my ear to his dry, pale lips.

'Sell the wine . . .' he repeated, '. . . the Pétrus. You'll need the money.'

I caught the words but not their meaning. 'We drank it yesterday, silly,' I said softly.

'Wha? Oh, yeah.'

I was there with him. We were together at the end.

'I can see it!' he said. 'I can see . . .'

And then Andrew had gone and there was only me.

A blaring car horn wrenched me from my thoughts. Evidently the vehicles in front had begun to move. I put Clémentine into gear and crawled on through the snowstorm, towards Calais. My passenger, who was perched next to me on the bench seat, stared through the windscreen, transfixed by the unfamiliar snowscape outside. It would be a long journey – five hundred miles in a blizzard with the car's heater struggling to do its job. But at least I had Turk to keep me company and, hopefully, some happy memories to keep me sane until we reached our destination. All the same, Scotland, and the seaport town of Kirkcudbright, seemed a long, long way away.

The girl in the ticket booth at the ferry terminal handed me a numbered card, and asked me to hang it from the mirror. She flashed me a sympathetic smile, then wished me a good day. I attached the card and caught a glimpse of my reflection. Black, teary streaks of mascara had dried on my pallid face.

Once on British soil, the novelty of driving on the left held my attention and kept the tears at bay. I allowed myself three stops on the way north – at Canterbury, Rugby and Kendal. Feelings of nostalgia replaced my sombre mood, and in spite of the harsh winter chill, the appalling road conditions and the tacky festive music on the radio, it felt comforting to be back in England at Christmastime.

It was after nine p.m. when I joined the A75. The blizzard and the weight of holiday traffic on the single carriageway road made the going terribly slow. It was nearly midnight when I arrived at Andrew's sister's farm. I was relieved to have reached my destination but nervous about meeting my hosts, unsure as I was about their reasons for inviting me. Why had they been so keen to let me stay with them? Was the invitation motivated by Mary's sense of duty, or by a superstitious respect for her brother's wishes (it's what he would have wanted . . .)? Or was it simply a generous, compassionate gesture – a genuine expression of Scottish hospitality?

I was about to knock on the front door when Mary opened it. She greeted me on the step, embraced my cold, tired body, then ushered me inside. We exchanged polite condolences, while Turk, who had trotted in behind me, stared up at the two of us, panting. Mary held me at arm's length, looking me up and down from my woolly hat to my snow-covered boots, simultaneously beaming and weeping silently. She pulled a paper handkerchief from the sleeve of her cardigan and blew her nose.

'It's so good to see you, Jean,' she said, taking a deep breath and closing the creaky door. She had Andrew's eye colour, his dark, sensitive brows, and his warm, caring voice. Her accent, though, was much stronger; unlike her brother, she had never left Kirkcudbright. 'Andrew told us so much about you. I'm really glad you came. Thank you so much.'

'No, Mary, I should thank you. For putting me up, I mean.'

'Och, it's a pleasure to have you here, hen. You just make yourself at home.'

Mary took my canvas holdall and led me through the hallway into the warmth and light of the kitchen. I was invited to take a seat at the table while she stoked the kitchen range with a shovelful of shiny black coal. My host lifted a huge teapot from the hob, brought it to the table and fetched two cups and saucers from a cupboard. Finally, she retrieved a blackened stewpot from the oven and poured a steaming hot ladleful of its contents into a china bowl.

'Here you go,' she said, serving my supper, the tea and a huge chunk of homemade bread. 'I saved you some broth. I thought you'd be wanting something good and hot after your long journey, especially on such a snell night as this.'

Clouds of steam rose from the pot and drifted up between the oak beams in the ceiling. Any anxieties I had about meeting Mary drifted away, too, as the sense memory of well-seasoned mutton, slow-cooked root vegetables and pearl barley wafted back to me across four decades. I was a thousand miles from Fontloube and right back at home. Relishing the moment, I hesitated with my spoon poised over the bowl.

Mary noticed my hesitation. 'Oh, dear, I hope this is okay for you? I mean, it's only simple home cooking, I'm afraid.'

I looked up distractedly and said, 'What? No, it's better than anything I've eaten for weeks.' It was the truth. I put a spoonful of the stew into my mouth. 'Mmm,' I mumbled, 'it tastes as good as it smells, as well. Mary, you are clearly a great cook.'

She sat down opposite me and smiled. 'Oh, no, Jean,' she giggled, 'I can't cook for toffee. It's Robbie who does all the cooking now, since the bairns left home.'

Mary glanced up at the chimney breast. On the oak bressumer above the range, next to a potted poinsettia, was a faded colour photograph in a silver frame. The picture showed a proud father surrounded by four smiling children, all perched on a shiny, blue tractor.

'The flowers have lasted well this year,' she said, sighing.

I took another couple of mouthfuls of stew.

'My grandmother was Scottish, you know. Her broth was almost as good as this.'

'Och, Andrew never told me you were part Scots.'

'I never told him,' I said, adding, 'I don't talk about my family.'

'Oh, but Jean, family is all we have in this world.'

'Well, in that case, I don't have much then.'

'Och no, not at all, Jean,' Mary said, wagging her finger and rising from her chair. She went over to a large Welsh dresser in the corner of the room. 'From now on you'll always be part of this family.'

She opened the cupboard door and brought out a couple of tumblers and a bottle of single malt. 'Now then, tomorrow's going to be a long, hard day, so how about a wee dram to help us sleep, eh?'

    'Mary,' I said, 'you read my mind.'

    We had already become friends.

Spiritualism

The wine of life is drawn, and the mere lees
Is left this vault to brag of.
  - William Shakespeare, *Macbeth*

We left the house and walked across the yard to where the
cars were parked. The previous night's snowstorm had left
a fresh fall of powdery snow that muted the noises of the
farm. The lowing cows, the milking parlour's machinery,
the feuding rooks that wheeled above the barn, all sounded
as distant and subdued as my mood. Only my footsteps,
crunching through the pristine snow, came to my hearing
with any clarity. Even Mary's words, as she chatted to me
from a few paces ahead, were remote, separate. When we
climbed aboard Mary's Land Rover, I apologised for being
so sullen and withdrawn.

'Don't be daft,' she said. 'You just collect your
thoughts.'

She turned the key, put the car into gear and moved
forward a few feet. I'd just managed to fasten the seatbelt
when Mary applied the brake and cut the engine.

She looked at me and said, 'Jean, are you sure you want
to do this? I mean, if you don't want to go, well, it's okay,
you know.'

I exhaled a cloud of breath. 'It's fine, Mary,' I said. 'I
want to see him. Really, it's fine.'

'Of course, hen. I just wanted to make sure,' she said,
restarting the engine and then skidding off into the lane in
the direction of the town.

We parked in the little car park behind the chapel of rest. I
asked Mary if she wanted to come with me, but she said

that she'd already said her goodbyes and would rather, if I didn't mind, wait in the car.

I entered the chapel alone.

Andrew looked peaceful in his padded crib, illuminated by a random palette of colours that shone from a stained-glass window in the east wall. He was dressed in his best tweed suit and a collar and tie. The Panama hat had been placed on his chest, his hands were clasped at his belt, and his face looked so unusually placid that the smile I saw could almost have been described as smug. I smiled, too, lifting his hands to place the book of Burns' poetry underneath them. Then I slipped a cut poinsettia stem between his fingers. I would always remember him like this, clutching his Burns and a tiny flower that would fade and wither, while my memory of it would continue forever. I kissed his cold brow, whispered my last goodbye and went out into the light.

The church of Saint Andrew's and Saint Cuthbert's was crammed. More than three hundred people came. Of course, I knew hardly anyone. Apart from Mary and her husband Robbie, I didn't know any of Andrew's family. And I'd never met any of his ex-colleagues or old friends (well, except one that is, and I wasn't expecting to see *her*). But I did recognise one face in the crowd. Wendy Snook had flown up from London ('any funeral that's not mine is a bonus these days,' she'd quipped, before gathering me to her ample bosom and bawling like a baby). I'd hoped to see Stéphane Lavergne, too. He was staying with an ex-sous-chef of his, who was now the owner of Glasgow's chicest restaurant. He arrived just as the priest began the service. Everyone turned and stared at this late arrival, who tiptoed sheepishly into the nave, genuflected like a good Catholic and took a seat at the back.

I was still hoping that Archie might appear.

As funerals go, I suppose it was a good one. Mary had been reluctant to organise the order of service, so I'd offered to arrange the music and so forth. Albinoni's *Adagio* on the way in and *The Wild Rover* on the way out had been Andrew's choices. The priest, Father Thomas, had suggested *Abide With Me* for the middle. It was a brief, sensitive, but unsentimental sermon.

Later, during the interment, just as I was about to throw a handful of pale, stony Saint-Emilion soil onto the coffin, I noticed a lone figure loitering by the entrance to the graveyard. For a split second, Andrew, who had been foremost in my thoughts throughout the sad, cold day, was there, physically, standing a few hundred yards away. My barely suppressed gasp and the look of shocked surprise on my face made the other mourners look round.

'Archie,' I heard Robbie say. He and his brothers went quickly to fetch the boy. When they returned to the graveside, Archie shuffled forward and positioned himself between Mary and me. I sprinkled a little of the earth into his gloved hand. It slipped through our fingers and into the grave like dust.

After the service, Archie's aunt and uncle suggested we might go for a little stroll while they waited for us in the car park. I was pleased to see Archie and grateful for the opportunity to talk to him alone.

We climbed to the top of the southwest-facing slope of the graveyard. When I looked down at the glittering bay in the valley below, I couldn't help imagining what a fine vineyard this hillside would make – if only it was ten degrees of latitude further south. But no vines adorn the slopes that overlook the Dee estuary and the church-steepled town of Kirkcudbright, just rows and rows of pale grey and pink granite headstones. Andrew was right though. It was beautiful. The view across the river to the forests and fields of the Galloway hills, with the snow-covered horizon shimmering in monochrome black-and-white in the lowering sun, was absolutely stunning.

'I'm glad you came, Archie,' I said. 'But, my goodness,

you did give me a fright.'

His eyes tracked the flight of a lone cormorant as it made its way over the estuary towards the Solway Firth and the Irish Sea.

He smiled and asked, 'Why is that, Jean?'

'Well, you look so much like your dad now. For a moment there I thought it was him watching us from the gate.'

'Why did you think that? My dad's dead, Jean.'

'Oh, you know, the mind plays tricks.'

'For some people, maybe,' he said. 'Not for me though. There's no such thing as ghosts and all that stuff – despite what Aunty Mary might say.'

He began to tell me how much more likely it would be to bump into a space alien than the ghost of a dead person, but I put my finger to my lips to stop him.

'Oh, I know,' he said. 'That means shut up, doesn't it?'

His gaze went back to the horizon.

'Archie,' I said. 'Would you . . .?'

'What?'

'Would you . . . hold me?'

His eyelids fluttered like startled moths, but he turned towards me, shivering slightly, and said, 'Okay.'

We hugged each other gently, tentatively. The moments passed and I began to shiver, too. It was time to go.

'Come on,' I said, separating from the embrace. 'It's getting cold. Let's go back to Mary and Robbie's house and get warm, eh?'

'Okay,' he said again.

We strolled back down the hillside.

'Thanks for the hug, Archie.'

'That's no problem, Jean. I like you.'

'I like you, too, Archie.'

'. . . so I studied the map and the train timetables, took Mum's credit card, got on the District Line to Edgware Road, then the Circle Line to King's Cross and bought an Intercity student saver return to—'

'Oh, Archie,' I said, putting my whisky tumbler down on the mantelpiece, 'you did tell your mum you were coming didn't you?'

'I left her a note saying sorry for nicking her card. I've never taken anything before, but I knew it was the only way to get here. She wouldn't have allowed me to come otherwise.'

'Well, I'm glad you did,' said Mary, arriving to refill my glass and kissing Archie on the cheek. 'We're so proud of you my boy! You were ever so brave to come all that way on your own.'

Archie, who had flinched away from his auntie's kiss, rubbed his cheek with his sleeve and muttered something about fetching another coke.

'Come on, Jean,' Mary said, 'let's sit down by the fire and have a wee chat.'

Mary and I sat opposite each other on a pair of battered leather armchairs in front of the glowing inglenook. We sipped our scotch in silence for a few moments, staring at the flickering flames that danced and curled among the burning logs.

'I know what you were thinking today,' Mary began.

'What?' I said, looking up from the fireplace.

'At the grave. You thought it was him didn't you? You thought you saw Andrew.'

'Oh, that,' I replied. 'Well, Archie's grown so much since the last time I saw him – he certainly takes after his dad.'

Mary sat forward in her seat, so I followed suit. She put her hand on my knee and stared searchingly into my eyes.

'Well, in a way, he is still with us, Jean,' she said, lowering her voice so as not to be heard by the other guests in the parlour.

I was uncomfortable with this. 'Oh, I know you believe that, Mary, but—'

She cut me short. 'Aye, Jean, I do. But more than that – I've *heard* from him.'

'Mary—' I began, but again she interrupted me.

'No, listen, Jean. I went to see a friend – oh, I suppose you'd call her a medium—'

This time I stopped her. My patience was running out as fast as my whisky.

'You mean you've had a . . . séance or something?'

'Och, we don't like to call them séances in my branch of the movement.'

'Movement?' I said, raising my voice. 'You make it sound like a chapter of the Hell's Angels!'

She registered my irritation, leaned back and smiled at me. I regretted reacting so judgmentally. 'I'm sorry, Mary,' I sighed.

'Don't mention it, hen – and some of us are much scarier than the Hell's Angels, believe you me.'

She laughed, drained her glass and reached over to take mine. 'Anyway, I just call it having a cup of tea with my friend when, you know, we communicate with the other world. Another drink?'

She shifted forward on the chair, then reached up to the mantelpiece for the bottle and topped-up our glasses.

Curiosity had replaced my annoyance.

'What did he . . . say?' I whispered as we chinked glasses.

She relaxed into the armchair, took a sip.

'Well, we don't like to talk too much about our communications. There are those who would like to stop us doing what we do.'

'You mean atheists like me?'

'No, not at all, Jean. You non-believers are no trouble at all.' She paused, throwing a quick, sidelong glance at Father Thomas who, at that moment, was chatting with Wendy by the door. 'No, I mean the Catholic Church and the Church of Scotland . . . Even the Jehovah's Witnesses have got it in for us.'

'Why would they want to stop you?'

'Oh, they say that the spirit world is a deception.'

'I don't know about that, Mary,' I said, 'but sometimes I think that this one is.'

She chuckled. 'You're right there, hen,' she said, sighing. 'But I believe what I see with my own two eyes and what I hear with my own two ears. What do you believe in, Jean?'

'Oh, I suppose I believe that there are many things in the world that we can't explain or understand – and perhaps we never shall.'

'I'll drink to that,' Mary said, and we brought our glasses together again.

'You don't read fortunes as well do you, Mary?' I asked. 'I could do with something to look forward to.'

'No, Jean, I don't. But something tells me that you're troubles are over now. From here on in you'll be fine.'

'Thank you, Mary, but I doubt it,' I said, adding, 'So, what did you . . . hear? From Andrew, I mean.'

'He said goodbye, Jean,' she replied. 'But the way he said it touched me very deeply. Would you like me to tell you why?'

'Yes,' I admitted.

'Well, when Andrew and me were bairns, Mum bought him some blue-and-white striped pyjamas, and Dad used to tease him, calling him Andy Pandy.'

She stared at the fire, smiling, as she recalled her childhood memory.

'One day Andrew made a mask out of an old cardboard box and dressed me up as Muffin the Mule. Mum and Dad were in stitches when we put on a daft wee puppet show for them, dancing round the front room like a pair of eejits. Anyway, all that winter Andrew's pet name for me was Muffin. That was over fifty years ago. I haven't thought about it much since. I've certainly never told a soul, until now.'

I waited, without prompting, for her to continue.

She left her memories in the grate, blinked and looked directly at me.

'Three days ago, my medium gave me Andrew's message. It was . . .'

She tossed her head back and swallowed the last of the

whisky.

'. . . goodbye, Muffin.'

The drinking continued into the late evening, when the singing began. Robbie, we discovered, was a talented singer. His deep baritone gave an appropriately mournful tone to the Scottish ballads that soon had the men folk sobbing into their glasses. It was quite a relief to me that, after the songs, his son Tony took up a fiddle, and a few of the guests, encouraged by Wendy, led a Highland dance. The dancing was much appreciated, except by a handful of Presbyterians – cousins of Robbie's – who decided that that was the time to leave. Not long after, Stéphane said goodbye, thanked us all – in perfect English – and promised to visit Fontloube in the springtime and Scotland in the summer.

After Wendy and Archie had retired and all the other guests had gone home, I said goodnight to Mary and Robbie. We embraced at the foot of the stairs, thanking each other again and promising to keep in touch. Robbie went to see to the fire in the parlour, leaving Mary and me together in the hallway.

Just as I was about to climb the stairs, Mary said, 'The spirit will always try to contact us, Jean. Especially if they've been taken too soon and have something to pass on . . . a message, you know.'

'I don't think I'll be hearing anything, Mary,' I said, 'I'm just not tuned in like you are.'

'Well, that's as maybe. Not many people are. But don't be surprised if you get something – a small message from the other side. And don't be alarmed. They're in a better place there.'

'Okay, Mary,' I said, touching her hand. 'Goodnight.'

I went to bed thinking about Mary's words, far from convinced that I would ever receive a message from beyond the grave, little knowing that over the coming weeks I'd effectively get two.

Pruning

Wine is bottled poetry.
- Robert Louis Stevenson

For the first stage of our journey home the dog was
relegated to the 2CV's back seat. Wendy had asked me for
a lift and, of course, I'd agreed. Turk was a good travelling
companion, but he wasn't a great conversationalist, so I
was pleased that Wendy was coming along with us. She
would keep me entertained (and hopefully awake) at least
as far as London.

We'd planned to set off before sunrise, expecting the
roads to be busy with holiday traffic, but we had a slow
start. After saying farewell to Mary and Robbie, we took
Archie to the railway station (he'd insisted on travelling
back to London by train), and so we didn't get on the road
until after ten o'clock.

For the first hour or so, we were both content to sit
silently, listening to the radio, each of us nursing a whisky
hangover, both tired for the lack of a good night's sleep.
We were nearly at Gretna Green before Wendy broke the
silence. She began with a complicated anecdote about a
friend of hers (a society debutante) who'd eloped in the
'50s with a Glaswegian stevedore. But, as though
prompted by the pips on the radio announcing midday, she
said, 'Ah! Helios drives his golden chariot to the zenith
. . .'

'What?' I said, looking across at my passenger who was
staring at her wristwatch.

'Oh, I see,' I said, making sense of Wendy's non
sequitur. Peering through the windscreen at the heavy
skies ahead of us, I added, 'Not that you'd know it in this

God-awful weather.'

'No, dear, but I make it twelve o'clock, and I fancy a drink.'

'Okay . . .' I said, hesitating. 'But I've still got to drive to France, remember?'

'Oh, you can have a coffee or something, my gorgeous girl, but I want a schooner of sherry. Look! There's a sign for a pub.'

I slammed on the brakes and steered Clémentine off the carriageway and onto a slip road that led us to a small town. Following the roadside directions, we arrived in the car park of a faux half-timbered coaching inn.

I never did hear the end of Wendy's story.

I've never really liked pubs. When I was young, they seemed to me to be smelly, soggy-carpeted places, full of cigarette smoke and overweight men. In the lounge bar of The Crossroads Inn, the smell of strongly perfumed disinfectant had replaced the smoky atmosphere of my memory, and the clientele included as many women as men (most of whom seemed to be Americans). But the damp carpet, and the beer bellies round the bar, had prevailed.

I sat at a small table between a flashing gambling machine and the gents' lavatory and waited for Wendy to bring our drinks. I caught the sound of her raucous laughter over the noise of the jukebox – clearly she had made friends at the bar. A couple of minutes later she tottered over and delivered our refreshments: a grey-looking café au lait for me and a glass of sherry for her. We toasted each other's good health, but in spite of Wendy's assertion that we'd found a friendly little spot, we didn't linger. When I tasted the tepid coffee, I realised how much I missed my adopted home.

After struggling with her seatbelt, Wendy finally clicked it into place and looked at me questioningly.

'So, my dear, you never did tell me the whole story

about that girl who stole your car.'

I slipped the clutch and turned right out of the car park, initially on the wrong side of the road. An oncoming vehicle's headlights flashed, and I swerved back into the left-hand lane, waving feebly and apologetically at the driver as he sped past us.

When Wendy's laughter – and my adrenalin rush – had subsided, we rejoined the trunk road in the direction of the motorway.

'Sorry, Wendy – what were you saying?' I asked.

'That young girl, you know, Amy something . . .'

I hadn't thought about Aimée Gonzalèz (or Aimée *Loroux*) since the previous winter. It had been over a year since I'd last seen her. It surprised me, when I tried to bring her face to mind, that I'd almost completely forgotten what she looked like. It was as though the painful events of 2008 – the theft of my money and car, the discovery of her drugs cache, and her supposed betrayal – were insignificant details, mere footnotes to the story of my time with Andrew. There were, however, many details that still puzzled me, and I was reluctant to return to them.

'Aimée Gonzalèz, you mean,' I replied. 'I'd rather not talk about her if you don't mind, Wendy.'

'Oh, go on, Jean. Why not?'

'Well, it was all so complicated – there's still so much I don't understand about what happened that summer. I'd really rather forget the whole sordid business.'

'Suit yourself,' she said, leaning back and relaxing, as much as possible, on the 2CV's bench seat. 'It might help you though.'

'Why do I get the impression that you think you can explain it all to me, Wendy?'

'What, me? Do I look like Miss Marple?'

I turned to look at her, trying not to laugh.

'Well, yes, actually,' I said, grinning.

Her eyes narrowed. 'Which one?' she asked.

I reflected, then replied, 'Angela Lansbury?'

She considered my response, staring at the motorway that stretched ahead of us. 'Oh,' she said, 'that's alright then, I suppose. I thought you were going to say, oh, you know . . . Margaret Rutherford.'

Despite myself I said, 'Well, come to think of it – yes, you're very like her, too.'

She reached over to my right knee and squeezed hard on the joint. My leg flexed, the car slowed suddenly and I let out an involuntary scream that quelled my laughter. 'Ow! That hurt,' I said, giggling.

'Serves you right, Valeix. Anyway, if I'm Margaret Rutherford then you're . . .'

She fell silent for a moment, frowned and finally shrugged her shoulders. 'Oh, I don't know, I can't think of anyone.'

'Oh, come on, Wendy, I must look like someone.'

Again she hesitated.

'Well,' she said, turning away from me to admire the view on her side of the road. 'I suppose you're a sort of young Jacqueline Bisset.'

I instantly felt guilty about teasing her. 'Wow,' I said, watching the traffic up ahead. 'Thanks for the compliment. I'm happy with that!'

'Well, it's true, Jean, you're a gorgeous girl.'

She sighed, put on her reading glasses and began to examine the road atlas.

'Okay, okay,' I said. 'You're flattery has worked. I'll tell you how it all happened.'

She removed her glasses. 'Including all the juicy bits?' she said, looking at me eagerly.

'I don't know about that, Wendy. There were no juicy bits. Well, perhaps one or two . . .'

'Oh, goody – do tell!'

The M6 rumbled on under Clémentine's skinny tyres. Trucks and coaches appeared in my mirror, then roared past us as we clung to the inside lane at a stately seventy kilometres per hour.

I began at the beginning, relating the events as they

211

occurred, but also including the information that I'd learned later from Andrew and Captain Lefèvre. I told Wendy how Aimée had come to France following the shooting of her boyfriend in London, how she knew of Andrew's whereabouts only from a scribbled address on a postcard she'd stolen from his son, and how she'd changed her appearance and assumed a false identity. When she asked me why Andrew had been so willing to support the girl's story, I told her about the ferry and rail tickets that I'd discovered, along with the postcard, hidden in the girl's room.

'The proof of a lie and the proof of a truth,' she said.

'What?' I asked. 'Oh, the tickets and the postcard, you mean.'

'Yes. My goodness, she was clever. She finds a place to live and work, far away from her troubles. If Andrew won't cooperate, then she only has to show you the tickets, blame him for setting the whole thing up, and appeal to your good conscience. But if she falls out with you, she knows that Andrew will do anything to prove that he was innocent of colluding with her – and the postcard does just that. Am I on the right lines so far?'

Wendy was right. Aimée could blackmail Andrew or bribe him, depending on the circumstances. The proof of a lie and the proof of a truth. But also the evidence for a murder.

'You've got it, Wendy,' I said. 'But she wasn't *that* clever.'

'What do you mean?'

'She's still wanted for questioning about her boyfriend's death. The postcard proves that she was in London before it happened; the tickets prove that she left for France the day after.'

'Oh, my gosh, Jean. Did you tell the police?'

'Yes, but it didn't stop her breaking into my house last December.'

'You . . . you don't think she did it, do you? I mean, shot the young man?'

212

'Wendy, do you remember last Christmas when I asked you what you thought about her?'

'Yes . . . I think so.'

'You said that the first time you met her, you thought she was a nasty piece of work.'

'Yes, I suppose I did. Oh, Jean, do they know where she is now?'

'The policeman investigating the case told me that she'd left the country – somewhere in Eastern Europe, apparently.'

'Thank goodness. Let's hope she never comes back, eh?'

'Yes. Let's hope.'

We stopped at a motorway service station in Cumbria, filled up with petrol, and bought some sandwiches and a couple of scalding-hot coffees. After we had rejoined the flow of southbound traffic, I resumed the story, moving forward to my houseguests' departure, Aimée's deceitful reappearance and her final exit when she took off with my jeep and my money.

When I'd finished, I said, 'There's still one thing I don't really understand. According to Andrew, Aimée left him almost as soon as he'd made camp in Saint-Emilion. Surely, with her out of the way, he could have explained everything to me. I'm sure I'd have believed him. I just don't know why he continued to deceive me.'

'He never deceived you, Jean. He didn't deceive anyone – except perhaps himself, that is.'

'What do you mean?'

'Oh, I'm not sure – just something he said when I first met him . . .'

'Go on.'

'I don't know, but I think he knew he was ill even before you threw him out.'

An articulated lorry whooshed past us, forcing my little car over the rumble strip.

'Jesus—' I cursed. 'Sorry, Wendy. What? What makes

you think that?'

'Well, of course I can't be sure, but when he first arrived at the campsite, and the girl went off with those young people from Bordeaux, we had a few drinks and, you know, talked. He told me what had happened between you, and how awful he felt. I advised him to tell you the truth, but he said he couldn't. He said he didn't want to hurt you . . . I didn't think anything of it at the time, but after his diagnosis, I did wonder if he knew all along that there was something wrong.'

'So this was before his diagnosis?'

'Oh, yes. We'd only just met, really. It was about a week later when he fell quite ill, and a couple of weeks after that when we went for his test results. I helped him with the translation, you know.'

As we crossed the River Lune, a half-forgotten memory returned to me: a warm midsummer's night; a low, gibbous moon in a starry sky; and the sound of a gipsy guitar.

'Oh, I see,' I said.

We stopped again, near Birmingham, as the daylight began to fade. Wendy ordered a double espresso in the cafeteria, and I had a surprisingly decent cup of tea. She was in a forthright mood.

We began by chatting about Fontloube. She suggested that it would be difficult for me now, to live alone in such a big house, coping with the vineyards and the winery. She was right. I'd been thinking about it a lot. In one way, being a winemaker is quite simple – you grow grapes, you make wine and you sell the stuff. It sounds simple, but it's hard work, and I'd begun to realise that I couldn't do it all on my own.

'Do you mind if I ask you a personal question?' I said.

'Not at all, Jean, fire away.'

'Why did you never have children?'

Wendy hesitated, but not for long.

'Oh, I don't know. I never wanted them, I suppose –

horrible, noisy little things mostly. No, I had my students and my nephews and nieces. They were enough for me.'

'You know, once upon a time, starting a family was the most important thing in my life. For nearly ten years we tried to have children. Olivier and I tried everything: HRT, vitamins, diets, IVF ... Henri, bless him, prayed for us every Sunday at Mass. He even convinced me to sit on the Saint's magical stone seat – you know, in the monk's cell above the monolithic church. All I got from that was piles. Getting pregnant was difficult enough, but carrying a baby to term was – well, it wasn't to be.'

I slurped my hot tea noisily.

'When he died, I experienced this terrible yearning. The older I got, the more I wanted to have children of my own – even though, with the passing of each year, the possibility of it ever happening became less and less likely. Now, I'm coming round to your way of thinking. There are more than enough children in the world, so I've decided to help the young people who can most benefit from what I can give. I'm going to offer an apprenticeship to each of the cousins – after all, Fontloube has always been a Valeix business. Paul is already a competent *viticulteur*, and Valentin has the makings of a great winemaker. So, what do you think?'

'Oh, my dear, I think it's an excellent idea. Have you told the boys yet?'

'No, not yet. I'll call them when I get home.'

Thinking about the boys, and praising their talents, brought to mind that other member of our little team – the girl who'd tricked us all.

I said, 'Even after everything that's happened I can't help feeling sorry for Aimée. I mean, how can such a talented, beautiful young woman, with every opportunity in the world open to her, become so cruel, so deceitful.'

Wendy stared out of the window at the darkening skies. '... in Sicily,' she said, in a low, sonorous voice, 'the black, black snakes are innocent, the gold are venomous.'

'Lawrence's *Snake*?'

'Well done, Jean! He was right, too. I was in Sicily once – walking in the footsteps of Saint Paul, you know – when a young archaeology student caught a yellow-brown snake. When the owner of the property saw the boy dangling the coiled serpent on the end of a stick, he became hysterical. He was convinced that it had killed one of his neighbours the previous week.'

'Oh, don't! I hate snakes. What did they do with it?'

'They shot it, Jean.'

She downed the dregs of her black coffee and pushed back her chair.

'Now then, my dear,' she said, 'are you going to tell me the juicy bits, or what?'

'Nothing to tell really,' I said.

'Don't give me that, my girl, I know you. Go on, tell.'

'Well, there was the time, after a terrible hailstorm, when I tried to seduce Andrew in his camper van. That's all really, apart from the time when Aimée tried to seduce me after a thunderstorm . . . What is it, d'you think, about severe climatic events—?'

'Never mind about the weather! What happened?'

I finished my tea and put the cup down gently on its saucer.

'He succeeded; she didn't,' I said.

'Oh, good. *Tant mieux pour lui; tant pis pour elle.*'

I got home in the early hours of Friday morning, New Year's Eve, and slept until noon. Stéphane had left a message on the ansaphone, inviting me to dine at his restaurant. And then, just before lunch, Michel Valeix phoned, asking me to celebrate the festival of *Saint Sylvestre* with his family in the Corrèze. But in the end I decided to spend New Year alone. I didn't feel much like celebrating. In fact I was so shattered that I was in bed by nine o'clock. The next morning, my book and my nightcap glass of Armagnac were still there on the bedside table – the one unread, the other untouched.

The weather was relatively mild, but with more snow on

the way and not much else to do, I chose to spend the bank holiday working in the vineyard. I received a call from Mary at lunchtime, wishing me a happy New Year, and another from Wendy shortly afterwards. It seemed as though everyone was concerned about me. Funnily enough, I felt okay and threw myself at the job of pruning the vines with uncharacteristic verve. When my enthusiasm flagged, or when the penetrating, icy air made me want to run back to the warmth and comfort of the hearth, or whenever the secateurs fell from my fumbling, frozen fingers, I'd hear Andrew's voice in my head as I'd heard him a year before at the opposite end of the vine row: *come on, Jean, last one to the middle does the washing-up* . . . I'd smile, carry on and lose myself in the work.

I pruned fifty rows that New Year's Day.

By Monday the 4th, I'd finished the lower field, beyond the line of trees and down to the southern boundary. At twelve o'clock the yellow post van arrived, bearing its usual handful of bad tidings. The post lady passed me the mail through the open window of her van before skittering off down the drive to deliver more post-Christmas bills to the residents of Saint-Emilion. I stood there in the courtyard and opened the most ominous-looking item of mail. Apparently the bank was about to institute a legal procedure to recover my unauthorized debts.

Bankrupt, I thought, then: oh, bugger, if the bank takes the property, it's the cousins' loss, not just mine. But I also felt a curious sense of release, as though Fontloube and its crumbling buildings, its glorious vineyards and its cellar full of wine, were weights that had been lifted from my back. For the first time in days I felt as though I needed a drink.

I decided to go indoors and take the cork out of my lunch.

I'd just poured myself an over-generous glass of wine when the phone rang. A couple of minutes later, everything had changed.

Poetry

A sight of the label is worth 50 years' experience.
- Michael Broadbent

Although I'd never been curious enough to buy a ticket,
I'd often wondered how it felt to win the lottery. After
talking on the phone to the quietly spoken lawyer – a Mr.
Stirling of Bright, Macintyre and Stirling – I had some
idea of what it must be like. I felt a constriction in my
chest, as though my torso had been strapped into a tightly
fitting corset. I realised that for several seconds I'd
forgotten to breathe. I took a deep breath of cool air and
exhaled slowly and loudly.

I was rich. Andrew had left me a quantity of fine wines,
currently lying in bond with a London wine merchant,
valued at over a hundred thousand pounds. *Something tells
me that you're troubles are over* ... Mary's optimistic
prediction made sense to me now; of course, she must
have known. Again I inhaled deeply, then held my glass
up to the silvery light coming from the small window and
took a swig. My God, Andrew, I thought, you always were
full of surprises. I glanced at the writing pad by the phone
and read the notes I'd just made. Scribbled there was a
phone number and the name of the company whose cellars
contained Andrew's wine: Parry Bros., Saint James's,
London SW1. Of course, anyone in the wine trade would
recognise the name, but to me Parry Brothers were also
good clients – last year we'd managed to sell them a batch
of the 2007 vintage.

I picked up the receiver, once again feeling the tightness
of anxiety in my chest, and dialled.

The young woman who answered told me that Mr. Parry

was expecting my call and asked me to hold. I looked through the window at Turk who was under the horse chestnuts barking at a red squirrel.

The line clicked.

'Hello, Madame Valeix.' The voice was deep and confident, old-school bourgeois. 'This is George Parry speaking. Thank you for calling us.'

I was impressed, though still a little nervous. 'Not at all,' I said, 'I was given your number by . . .' I hesitated; do I say *our* solicitor?

'Indeed, madame. Mr. Stirling was kind enough to let me know. Please accept my condolences. I knew Andrew very well, you know.'

'Oh, I see. Thank you.'

'Yes, Mr. Stirling asked me to inform you of your wine's value, should you wish to sell at auction. The market has recovered well since last year's fall. You might be well advised to sell now if you wished to realise the full potential of your investment . . .' He made the statement sound like a question.

'Oh, yes,' I said, remembering Andrew's whispered instructions – *sell the wine* . . . 'I suppose that would be the right thing to do.'

I was curious to discover what precious bottles Andrew's 'investment' consisted of. 'What exactly is there – I mean, in the collection?'

'One second, Madame Valeix.' I could hear the sound of pages turning. 'Here we are . . . Mr. Maconie's cellar includes several cases of first- and second-growth Pauillac, Saint Estèphe and Margaux from the '89 and '90 vintages . . . five cases of Château Cheval Blanc 1990 and a case of Pétrus from the same year—' He interrupted himself. 'No, wait a minute – nine bottles of Pétrus. He took three bottles out of bond the year before last.'

My God, I thought, and nearly said it.

'I think, at auction, the wines could realise a figure of between a hundred, and a hundred and fifty thousand pounds – less fees and taxes, of course.'

'Goodness,' I said. 'Thank you, Mr. Parry.'

'So, I'll fax you all the relevant paperwork. There's an auction at Christie's coming up next month – why don't you come to London for the sale? Then, if our buyers want some more of that tasty Saint-Emilion of yours, you could bring us a delivery at the same time.'

Tasty? Well, it's a start, I thought. Not bad from the man who buys and sells (and, presumably, samples) the world's most expensive and exclusive wines.

'I'd be delighted, Mr. Parry,' I said and thanked him again before hanging up.

Yes, I was rich. And it felt good, this fizzy feeling of elation mixed with the sweetness of relief. But there was something else, some other ingredient that had slipped into the peculiar cocktail of emotions sloshing around inside me, a dash of something bitter in the mix: guilt.

Perhaps Archie should have the money. After all, here in France it was illegal to disinherit one's children. But Archie wasn't French, and his inheritance – from Andrew's savings, investments and property – would surely be enough to pay his college fees and help him through the challenges of leading an independent life. The bank's letter lay on the desk, next to the notepad. My own financial needs seemed more immediate, more tangible than Archie's. I heard Andrew's words again: *sell the wine, sell the Pétrus . . .*

I decided to keep the money.

At Christmas, I could barely afford the fuel for my journey across the Channel. This time, when I filled up my gas-guzzling 4x4 at the petrol station in Castillon, I didn't even look at the price. Parry's had ordered a gross of Fontloube 2007, and Andrew's wines were going to be sold at auction the following day. Well, not all Andrew's wines. I'd be keeping three bottles of Pétrus – three hugely expensive, square-shouldered, red-topped bottles of pure liquid ecstasy – to remind me that sometimes even good things come in threes.

I joined the autoroute at Saint-André-de-Cubzac and headed north. Turk sat on the passenger seat gazing at the crystalline skies ahead of us. There were twelve cases of paid-for wine in the back of the jeep, and there would soon be money in the bank. I was happy – almost.

*

I'd chosen the hotel, not for its reputation for good quality and service, but because the proprietor allowed dogs. In its favour was its proximity to Saint James's, the offices of George Parry and the auction rooms. But the stale aroma of fried food emanating from the small dining room (now closed, dark and empty), and the grumpy welcome I received from the night porter, were losing points for the Barrington Hotel.

Against all my judgements, not only my better ones, I bought a hamburger from the franchise in Victoria Station and consumed it in my sad little room. I berated myself for neglecting to pack a spare bottle of wine which would, at least, have masked the taste of the food. Even Turk seemed reluctant to finish the leftovers.

I slept badly, unused to the lights and noise of the city.

At breakfast, I still hadn't decided whether or not to attend the auction. In the end, the late February sunshine and the possibility that, for once, I had some buying power, swayed my decision. I'd spend the morning shopping in the West End, have lunch at a place where the sauces didn't come in squeezy plastic bottles, then meet up with the nice Mr. Parry in the afternoon to collect my cheque.

Chelsea's boutiques were as much of a fascination to me as the ceaseless tide of human traffic was to Turk. I marvelled at the exquisite couture, the beautiful handbags, the to-die-for shoes . . . I could have bought an entire new wardrobe. But I couldn't imagine wearing such elegant apparel in my little village – except, perhaps, for the occasional *diner à deux* at a smart Saint-Emilion restaurant, and there were no dinner dates in my diary for the foreseeable future. Eventually I plumped for a gorgeous pair of calf skin boots and wandered back towards Mayfair, trying to locate the only restaurant in town I could remember, hoping that it might still be there.

The brasserie on Stratton Street was still there alright. The food was still pretty good, too. As I sipped my aperitif, I tried to work out how many years had passed since my last visit. I stopped counting when I realised it was at least two decades ago and concentrated instead on the memory of the man who had paid for lunch on that hot June day, back in the big-haired, shouldered-padded '80s. Perhaps it was being here, in this place, that brought him to mind with such surprising clarity. I remembered almost everything about him – his face, his eyes, even the vanilla scent of his taut brown skin. We'd made love that afternoon, after our final exams, after our celebratory lunch at Langan's. I remembered it all, all except one thing: his name.

The realisation that I was enjoying an erotic reminiscence (if not a sexual fantasy) made me blush. As I emptied my glass, I looked furtively round the busy dining room to see if anyone had noticed. No one had. Silly girl, I thought, tucking in to my langoustine tails with happy enthusiasm.

There wasn't a squeezy bottle in sight.

After lunch, I strolled over to Saint James's Square and located Parry's HQ. An officious female receptionist led me to the boss's office and showed me in.

George Parry's physical appearance was every bit as polished and upper-middle class as his telephone voice. Save for the fact that he wasn't wearing a bowler hat, he looked the archetypal city gent. His clothes, tailored no doubt by the artisans of Saville Row and Jermyn Street, were authentically age worn. It was hard to imagine him being comfortable in anything other than a chalk stripe suit except, perhaps, a velvet smoking jacket with matching slippers. When he said hello, his smile was as bright as the silver links in his double cuffs. He replaced a wine bottle, which he'd been examining when I came in, in a small cabinet behind his enormous desk and invited me to sit down. As he did so, I caught the briefest glimpse of the label.

On the gleaming polished surface of the desk, between two piles of neatly stacked papers, sat two glasses of red wine.

'Congratulations, Madame Valeix,' he began, taking his seat.

'Oh, thank you,' I said, crossing my legs, 'how did we do?'

'Splendidly, splendidly. The hammer came down on your lots at nearly a hundred and fifty-eight thousand. Not bad, what?'

Not bad at all, I thought.

'Oh, that's wonderful,' I said, grinning like an idiot but unable to stop myself. 'Thank you. Thank you so much, Mr. Parry – for organising everything I mean.'

'Think nothing of it, madame. It's the least I could do for a friend of Andrew Maconie's. Anyway, the auctioneers deserve your thanks – they did a splendid job today, truly splendid.'

He slid a cheque across the desk. There seemed to be an awful lot of numbers written on it.

'Well, thank you for seeing me,' I said, folding the cheque and putting it in my bag. 'And thanks for ordering more of my wine, too.'

'Ah, yes,' he said, still smiling. 'Château Fontloube. I really must come and visit you the next time I'm in Bordeaux.'

'That would be . . . splendid!' I said, putting my mouth into gear before engaging my brain, and bumping straight into his favourite word.

He rose from his chair and handed me one of the tasting glasses.

'Are you staying in town?'

I nodded. 'Yes.'

'I wonder if I might prevail upon you to give me your opinion of this wine – I had it double decanted this morning. It's from a batch of late-'70s clarets from a client's private collection. He wants to know how it's drinking.'

Mr. Parry was testing me. A thirty-odd-year-old wine with any doubt about its readiness must be a Bordeaux from the Left Bank – something rather special, too. I brought the rim of the glass to my nose. The wine had concentration and finesse and something else: a wild, masculine edge.

I sipped.

'Mmm. A first growth from one of the *cru classé* villages at the top end of the Haut Médoc, perhaps?'

I took his smile for a hint of assent.

'A Pauillac maybe?' I ventured.

'Well done, madame!'

'. . . a deliciously ripe fruit,' I continued. 'Must be from a good year, not too hot but ending with a warm September.'

'Splendid, my dear. A straight set so far – go on . . .'

'I'd say that it's drinking very well now but could be left a little while longer.'

'You have an excellent nose and a gifted palate, madame. I shall certainly pass on your comments to my client.

'Now,' he continued, 'this sale has caused quite a sensation in our little world. I wouldn't be surprised if the commentators come knocking on your cellar door this summer. My team would like to order some of your 2008 – if we can agree on a price, of course. You might also want to look for a more . . . mainstream distributer, too. So, I've passed on your details to a friend of mine who buys for one of the big high-street retailers – I hope you don't mind?'

Don't mind? I could have hugged him.

'I can't thank you enough, Mr. Parry. Really, I don't

know how to thank you—'

'Nonsense, Madame Valeix. As I've said, Andrew was a friend of ours. He was a good man to work with – whether buying or selling. He was also a gentleman, and there aren't many of us left, let me tell you – certainly not in this business.'

He put down his glass and splayed his fingers on the surface of the desk. I noticed his wedding ring.

'I hope Mrs Parry appreciates you,' I said.

'What?' he looked down at his left hand. 'Oh, yes, yes. I hope so, too.'

'Have you been married long?' I asked.

He picked up his glass again and eyed its contents. 'Oh, since 1978. A superb year – lovely warm September I recall . . .'

Yes, I thought, and a damn good vintage, too.

'And do you have children?'

'Yes, two boys and a girl – all grown up now, of course. And seven grand-children at the last count.'

He raised the glass to his lips.

'You're a very lucky gentleman, Mr. Parry.'

He gave me a surprised look then said, 'Yes, I suppose I am.'

We finished our wine.

'So,' he said, getting up. 'Can you tell me the name of the château and the vintage, then? There's a prize for the correct answer . . .'

I still wasn't one hundred percent sure, but the glimpse I'd snatched of the bottle's simple, unfussy label swayed my guess.

'Château Latour . . . 1978?' I said, crossing my fingers.

'Bravo, madame! You are a true connoisseur.' He reached into the little cupboard and retrieved the bottle. 'Here,' he said, 'take this. You can drink it tonight in your hotel if they don't have anything decent on the wine list.'

That, I thought, is a certainty.

'Thank you again, Mr. Parry. And do come and visit when you're next in Saint-Emilion.'

'Splendid! I will most assuredly do just that, Madame Valeix. Well, goodbye then.'

'Goodbye,' I said, as Mr. Parry opened his office door. 'Incidentally, who does this wine belong to?'

'Ah, one of our oldest and most cherished customers. But there is such a thing as client confidentiality I'm afraid – let's just say that he has a very regal wife, and although he is one of the few people who call me George, I address him as "Your Royal Highness"'.

I scrutinised the man's face to see if he was pulling my leg. He was deadly serious.

That evening, in the half-empty dining room of the Barrington Hotel, as I ate steak-and-kidney pie washed down with the royal wine, I raised my glass and whispered quietly to myself, 'Well, here's to you, Andrew. As you always said: you have to take your pleasure where you find it.'

When I checked out, early the following day, the grumpy night porter was still on duty. I gave him a smile and a handful of banknotes, but all I got in return was the change and a look of expectant anticipation.

As I stuffed the change into my purse, I said, 'Ah, perhaps I should give you a tip . . .'

He looked away and mumbled something unintelligible.

'Smile at the world,' I suggested, 'and the world smiles back.'

I turned – on my expensive new heels – and made for the revolving doors with a wicked grin on my blushing face.

After checking out of the Barrington, I delivered the wine consignment to Parry's out-of-town warehouse. The journey down to Dover was as long as a day without bread. It seemed as though the cars and white vans that nudged their way along the six-lane motorway were stuck in a perpetual rush hour. Eventually the traffic came to a complete halt. The only vehicles that moved at all were the police cars and ambulances whose Doppler-shifted sirens howled past us on the hard shoulder. I had a bad feeling about what lay ahead. When, at last, we arrived at the scene of the accident, I fought the temptation to look. Instead, I gunned the jeep's engine and roared past, catching only a glimpse in the mirror of the sad tableau of roadside chaos behind me.

It was after six o'clock when we arrived in Calais. I needed a caffeine hit if I was going to drive through the night, so I came off the autoroute at Boulogne. My journey had taken me from the heart of Europe's busiest capital to a languid, genteel, near-deserted French provincial town. The closing-time hiatus, between the daytime crowd and the evening's restaurant goers, had emptied the streets like a curfew. Even the parking bays were empty.

We left the car near the ramparts and went for a walk. In the bistros and cafés that line the rue de Lille, waistcoated *serveurs* were busy wiping the day's grime from their tables and re-laying for the dinner service. The smell of onions frying in olive oil wafted from the restaurant kitchens. Somewhere a chef was roasting a leg of lamb in rosemary and garlic. At another brasserie, a bubbling stockpot of *soupe de poisson* belched its unmistakeable fishy aroma into the evening air. The sun was setting behind the buildings. A peal of bells from the cathedral tower rang clearly over the empty streets. I thought about the ten hours of driving between here and home, and decided to stay the night in Boulogne-sur-Mer.

Turk and I had just begun to search for a dog-friendly hotel, when Andrew's mobile started chirping in my handbag. I took a seat at a pavement café, hailed an espresso from the waiter and answered the phone. It was Mary. She sounded worried.

We said our hellos and asked after each other's health. When the formalities were over, Mary asked, 'Jean, are you sure you're alright?'

The coffee arrived. 'I'm fine,' I replied.

'I was worried about you. I couldn't reach you at home.'

I tucked the phone under my chin and unwrapped a small chocolate hazelnut. I was starving.

'No, I'm in Boulogne,' I explained, 'What it is, Mary? What's the matter?'

'My friend received a message for you.'

'A message?'

'Yes, you know . . . from Andrew. She said it sounded like a warning, Jean.'

'A warning? What do you mean?'

'I don't know exactly, but something isn't right. You should be careful.'

'Careful? What of, Mary?'

'I don't know, Jean. It's not clear – my friend's a medium, not a clairvoyant.' – was there a distinction? – 'Sometimes it's not what's said but . . . how it's said.'

'And the *message*,' I said, trying not to sound too cynical, 'was definitely for me?'

'Yes, Jean, he spoke your name.'

'What, he said "Jean"?'

'Aye, but he said "Miss Jean". Does that mean anything to you?'

The chocolate hazelnut stuck in my throat. I coughed. 'Yes, it was his nickname for me,' I said.

A second of silence slid past us.

'Jean, there's just no way that I or my friend could have known that.'

'I believe you,' I said; and I meant it.

We said goodbye. I drank my coffee.

I spent a terrible night in a portside hotel at the bottom end of the town. The sagging mattress, the dank smell from the harbour at low tide, and the flash and buzz of the neon sign next to my window made it almost impossible to sleep. All that, and the nagging question of what Mary's message meant, kept me awake until the early hours of the morning. Had I mentioned my pet name to her? Had she, perhaps subconsciously, relayed it somehow to her medium? I couldn't remember telling her that Andrew called me Miss Jean. Perhaps he had told her during one of his many phone calls from Saint-Emilion. As to what the message's warning meant, that was anybody's guess. I didn't believe Andrew was trying to contact me, but nor did I believe that Mary was lying. I was wrestling with this paradox when I finally drifted off.

I dreamt I was sailing a cross-channel ferry to the underworld, but I had to plug the holes in its wooden hull with corks that kept falling into the rising bilge water and floating off.

The day after our return to Fontloube, I gave the house a spring-clean and started to tick a few things off my ever expanding to-do list. By lunchtime I'd finished my chores, called the bank manager and booked the jeep in at the garage (for repairs to its damaged bodywork). The post lady arrived in her yellow van, delivered the mail and reversed back into the lane at speed; clearly she was late for lunch. Amongst the supermarket catalogues and adverts for car spares, mattresses and building supplies was a single letter. The scruffy brown A5 envelope was addressed in a familiar hand, and the letter inside was written in the same neat cursive script. I sat down on Clémentine's front wing, idly flicking the faulty passenger-side window open and shut, and read:

Dear Jeanne,

I was so sorry to hear of your sad news. I know you must still hate me and you are right so to do. But by Tuesday I should be able to pay you back all the money I took from you. I'm a little scared and sad and I feel all alone here. So I hope you can forgive your Aimée? I wanted you to have Andrew's poem – I think he must have loved you very much and I am sorry for having taken it.

Je t'embrasse affectueusement,

Aimée.

The second page, torn from a black Moleskine notebook, was written in Andrew's handwriting:

Kingfisher

I imagine this:
The river of a man's life
And a bird in flight,
From watery source,
Through deep gorges carved by time,
At the speed of light.

His path, seen through the
Burnished yellow of his eye
Is chosen so fast;
A kingfisher flies
With no thought for the present
To claim from the past.

Nearing the delta
He grows tired; you take my weight,
Feather-light and free,
Over vast waters
Towards a distant shoreline
We can barely see.

Eyes dim, hearing not
The sound of the crashing waves,
You are with me yet.
I remember your eyes
When they first looked into mine;

Blue the moment set.

The kingfisher gives
A glimpse of eternity
In a flash of blue;
Holds for a moment,
In perfect iridescence,
The essence of you.

A.M. 2008

At first I thought: poor Aimée, all alone in the world again, then: my God, the callous bitch wants to know if I've inherited.

I went to the study, put the letter and the poem safely in my filing cabinet and tossed the screwed-up envelope into the wastepaper basket.

Aspergers

They are not long, the days of wine and roses:
Out of a misty dream
Our path emerges for a while, then closes
Within a dream.
   - Ernest Dowson, *Vitae Summa Brevis*

After breakfast on Sunday morning, I went to my study to call Valentin and Paul, having decided once and for all to offer them both an apprenticeship at Fontloube. I'd just managed to find Valentin's home number in my little book when the phone rang.

I picked up. '*Allo,*' I said.

Strangely, during the caller's split-second hesitation, I knew exactly who was on the line.

'Hello, Jean.'

'Hi, Archie,' I said, delighted hear the boy's voice again so soon after the funeral. 'How are you?'

He paused. 'Same as usual, I think. But I'm in Paris, at the Gare du Nord. Do you know that the train from London to Paris only takes two hours and twenty minutes?'

'What? You're here in France?'

'Yes, Jean, at the Gare du Nord in Paris. I'm coming to Saint-Emilion this afternoon to help you blend the wine. You said I could come again in March.'

'Er, yes, of course, Archie, but that was last year – your mother wouldn't let you come back here, remember?'

'I know, but now that I'm eighteen she can't stop me from travelling, so I'm coming to keep my promise. I've checked all the timetables, and I should arrive in Libourne at five twenty-three p.m. But I can't get a train from there to Saint-Emilion because it doesn't run on Sunday evenings.'

What else could I say?

'Archie, I'll be waiting for you at the station in Libourne.'

There I was again, fetching another youngster from the station – another of Fontloube's returning swallows. This time the car park was empty, the arrivals hall deserted. Archie was one of only a handful of passengers disembarking at Libourne. We embraced awkwardly on the empty platform. He was quiet, almost withdrawn. On the way back to the car, I quizzed him gently about his visit. How had he known that I would be at home? Why wasn't he at school? Apparently, his Aunty Mary had told him I'd be there. But he wouldn't say why he was absent from school. It wasn't the spring break and the Easter holidays weren't until April . . . I surmised that he'd had a fight with his mother.

I asked if he was hungry. He nodded and gave me a broad smile. But as the shops that we passed on the way home were all closed, I was going to have to be quite creative in the kitchen when we got back.

The near-empty fridge contained no fresh ingredients for our Sunday supper. However, a solitary jar of salted anchovy filets provided the inspiration for one of my favourite store cupboard meals. In the larder I found pasta, tinned tomatoes, olives, a jar of capers and some dried chillies – everything I needed for a throw-together spaghetti puttanesca. I only had to hope that Archie would like it.

As I prepared the meal, Archie laid the kitchen table. Two plates, two knives and forks, two glasses, one bottle of wine . . . We chatted politely, as we ate the saucy pasta, about his recent holiday in Morocco and the driving test he'd passed on the second attempt. Eventually, I got him to talk about his school and his relationship with his mother and sister. Life at home and at school was, apparently, mundanely agreeable to him. In fact, he was confidently expecting to pass his international baccalaureate in the summer. So I asked again why he'd chosen to visit me now.

He thought for a moment, reaching down to stroke the dog's ears. 'I came because you invited me back for the *assemblage*, Jean.'

'I know, Archie, so you said – and you're really welcome, you know that – but it all seems a bit . . . sudden, that's all; showing up here out of the blue, I mean.'

'You mean that blue train that I took from Paris?'

Idiomatic expressions are a no-no for Archie, so I rephrased the question. 'Sorry, I mean that you arrived here suddenly, you know, without telling me you were coming.'

'Oh, I see. Well, it was something my dad said to me before he died.'

'Your dad?'

'Yes, he said: "When you go back to visit Jean, don't tell her you're coming or she'll worry too much, and she'll try and stop you."'

'Did he say anything else?'

Archie's eyes fluttered. He looked up at the ceiling.

'Yes,' he said, lowering his voice like a confession, 'he told me that you needed me to help you.'

'In the winery, you mean?'

'And with money and stuff.'

'Money?'

'Yes, he said that when I reached my eighteenth birthday I'd inherit quite a lot of money. He said it was up to me, but if I wanted I could invest in your vineyards. I didn't really understand what he meant at the time, but this term we've been learning all about share dealing and stuff in Business Studies, and now I understand—'

'Hold on,' I said, 'no one would want to buy shares in Fontloube. I was nearly bankrupt this year, you know.'

'That's what I figured,' he said. 'It's like what Warren

Buffet said, "The time to get interested in stocks is when no one else is". And he's one of the world's richest men, Jean.'

'Archie—' I began, then stopped myself with a sigh.

I told him about the wine auction and explained that, rather than taking his money, *I* should be giving *him* the proceeds from the sale. But his insistence revealed a passion that I'd not seen in him before. A young man I was very fond of – a potentially gifted winemaker with a photographic sense of smell – was offering to invest in my flagging wine business. I wasn't going to let the opportunity pass me by. In the end I agreed to give him a share of Fontloube equal to the value of the wine I'd inherited – on one condition: that he went back to England as soon as possible to finish his baccalaureate. He could come back in the summer when he'd got his results.

We toasted our joint venture with a second bottle of wine. As we brought our glasses together, his pale blue eyes blinked again, then settled on mine. A line from Andrew's poem came into my head: *blue the moment set.* My eyes are hazel, I thought; Archie's are blue. It's not about me. It's about him . . .

I went to the study, then returned clutching the poem.

'Read this, Archie,' I said, handing the piece of paper to my fledgling investor. 'Your dad wrote this for you, quite some time ago.'

I watched his eyes flicker disinterestedly down the page.

'I see,' he said, turning the paper over as though there might be more to read.

'Don't you like it?' I asked.

'It's okay. I don't really like poetry, Jean. I don't see the point of metaphors.'

'What do you mean?'

'Well, we've studied literature and all that, and poetry. We learned a poem about a huge tree in a field that was supposed to represent the entire natural world. I just didn't get it. I can't see the point of representing one thing by another.'

I twirled my last few strands of spaghetti, mopped up the last of the sauce.

'But you do it, Archie,' I said. 'You *think* it. You represent the smell of something by a particular colour, don't you?'

'Yes . . .' he said slowly, 'but I can't help it, Jean.'

'No, Archie, and nor can poets.'

Outside, we could hear the owls heralding the dusk. I swirled my glass, waiting for the boy to speak.

'So what does it mean then?' he said, at last.

'It means that your dad loved you very much young man – very much indeed.'

My plate was clean, and Archie had finished, too, leaving the capers and black olives in neat little rows on the side of his plate.

I stood up. 'Now,' I said, 'I cooked supper, so it's your turn to do the dishes. Okay?'

'Okay, Jean.'

It was the day when my jeep went for its re-spray. With the dents and scratches removed, the last reminders of Aimée Loroux and her influence on my life would finally be gone. The previous evening, the kitchen had been meticulously tidied and cleaned by my new lodger who was now still fast asleep in his bed. I prepared a pot of coffee. I was happy.

I heard a vehicle crunch to a halt on the gravel outside, then a car door bang shut. Who could it be, this early in the day? I opened the old oak door and looked out onto the courtyard.

A uniformed police driver was standing at ease next to a marked police Peugeot. He waited, watching me, without making any sign of greeting. The back doors opened. Captain Lefèvre and Lieutenant Dauzac emerged. Lefèvre hailed me as he shut the door, then approached the house, followed by his lieutenant.

I greeted my visitors and invited them into the kitchen. The captain seemed ill at ease. Both men remained standing as I scoured the cupboard in search of three matching coffee cups.

'Madame,' Lefèvre began after I'd stopped clanking the crockery. 'I have some . . . news about Aimée Loroux.'

'Oh,' I said, setting the cups down on the table, 'that's a coincidence – so do I.'

Lefèvre and his lieutenant exchanged glances.

'What . . . would that be, madame?'

Not for the first time, the man had made me feel like an errant schoolgirl.

'Oh, I received a letter from her. I was going to call you, you know, after the weekend.'

Lefèvre's expression remained neutral. 'May I see the letter, madame?'

'Of course, I'll just go and get it from the study. Please, do sit down.'

When I returned with the letter, the policemen were sitting at the kitchen table. Dauzac poured the coffee. I handed the note and the poem to the captain who read both pages, two or three times. 'Thank you, Madame Valeix, I will have to keep this,' he said indicating the letter and passing Andrew's poem back to me. 'Do you still have the envelope?'

The envelope? 'No, I threw it away I'm afraid,' I said, adding, 'Sorry.'

'Did you happen to notice the postmark?'

I thought about it. I had read the postmark.

'Yes, it was posted in Bordeaux. I'm sure it was.'

Lefèvre's expression darkened.

'Madame Valeix,' he said, 'Miss Loroux's body was discovered this morning in the estuary, on the shore of the Île Nouvelle.'

I sat down, barely able to comprehend what the man had just said to me.

'My God,' I said, 'on an island?'

'Yes, she was found at first light by the skipper of the Blaye to Lamarque Ferry. It looks as though the body had been washed downriver by the high spring tide.'

'My God,' I said, again. 'How did she—?'

'Ostensibly we're looking at death by drowning, possibly suicide. But due to certain features we're currently treating the death as suspicious.'

'Features?' I said, staring into the man's eyes. He shuffled awkwardly in his seat then glanced down at Aimée's letter. Again, he and Dauzac looked at each other.

'Initial tests show a quantity of opiate-based narcotics in her blood, and there was enough superficial bruising to indicate a struggle. With the strong tide, she could have entered the water as far upstream as the city or even Libourne . . . What we don't know is: did she jump, or was she pushed?'

'You think she could have been murdered?'

'We don't have much to go on except that, from what we have just learned, you are the last person to have had contact with her.'

Oh my God, I thought, am I a suspect?

'You don't think that I've got anything to do with this, do you?'

He looked embarrassed.

'I'm sorry, Jeanne,' – *Jeanne?* Were we now on first name terms? – 'but we will need to speak to you again, possibly at the *hôtel de police*. I would be grateful if you remained here for the next few days.'

'Of course,' I said.

'And, in the meantime, call me if you manage to retrieve that envelope, and I'll send someone to collect it.'

We finished our coffees then went out into the courtyard. Before saying goodbye, I mentioned that Archie was staying with me and that he was hoping to return to England soon. Lefèvre was polite but firm. He would be 'very grateful' if Archie stayed put, at least until the end of the week.

I was shocked and saddened by the captain's news, and more than a little anxious (in spite of my innocence) about playing such a major role in his enquiries. I saw no reason to change the day's plans, but Archie's return home would have to wait a few days. I took the keys to the 4x4 and my handbag and set off for Libourne.

After dropping the car off at the garage, I'd done a bit of shopping before returning home in a taxi. I'd decided not to tell Archie about my early morning visit from the police and set him to work, after lunch, cleaning the cellar in readiness for blending the 2008. We worked through until well after dark. I was delighted with my (or rather *our*) new vintage. Nature's onslaughts of that year – the bitter frosts, the devastating hail, the incessant rain in the early summer – had reduced the size of the crop, but the fruit that had been spared was rich and concentrated. So, too, was the wine.

It was after midnight when, exhausted by the day's blending, siphoning and constant sampling, we called it a day. I selected an ancient copy of Baudelaire from the bookcase and took it to bed. The book fell open at *Hymn to Beauty*. The poet's depiction of beauty as a Janus of good and evil (the fey with the velvet eyes, the monster from the abyss . . .) turned my thoughts to the frightened young woman whose cold, white body now lay in a Libourne police morgue. As I reached the bottom of the page, my eyes – and my mind – began to drift. I fell asleep thinking about Aimée. Where were you, Aimée? Where *were* you . . .? *Where* . . .?

She wasn't in my dream, but Mary was.

We were in a police interview room. Mary was holding a battered brown envelope.

'What's that?' I asked.

'It's a message from the spirit world,' Mary replied.

'What's inside?'

'You know what's inside, Jean.'

'I . . . don't think I do.'

'Sure you do – go on, guess.'

'Is it a letter?' I asked.

'No, it's not a letter. Try again.'

'A poem?'

'No, not that.'

'Money?'

'Och no, I'm afraid not.'

'A college prospectus?'

'Not that either.'

'Oh, Mary, I give up.'

'Go on, one more guess.'

'Oh, I don't know . . . it's empty. There's nothing in it!'

'Aye! Well done.'

She handed me the envelope. I tried in vain to read the scrawly handwriting.

'But it's just an empty envelope, Mary.'

'What's inside the envelope doesn't matter, Jean; it's what's on the outside that counts.'

Again, I tried to read the writing, but I fumbled and dropped the thing under the desk. I bent down to look for it on the floor, fearing that Turk had taken it, but Mary stopped me.

'It's not there, Jean.'

'Then where is it?'

'You know where it is, Jean.'

'Oh, please, please tell me,' I cried.

'Try the rubbish bin, Jean. The rubbish bin . . .'

My eyes flicked open. The Baudelaire lay open on top of the duvet. It was light outside. I could already hear the rumbling, grating noise of the municipal refuse van making its weekly collection at my neighbour's property, half way up the *côte*.

I didn't have time to shower and change, just pulled on my work clothes from the previous day and pattered downstairs. During my spring-clean at the weekend, I'd emptied all the bins and wastepaper baskets into black plastic bags and stuffed them into the wheelie bin on the drive. As I opened the kitchen door, two refuse collectors were hoisting the thing into the huge steel jaws of their lorry. They couldn't hear my shouts over the noise of the motor, and by the time I'd sprinted over to them, the black bags were already slipping efficiently into the machine's gullet.

I began by yelling the Anglo-French word 'stop!' then proceeded to shout a barely comprehensible explanation that my rubbish contained vital evidence in a police enquiry.

With a deft flick of a lever, one of the men brought the machine to a halt. The other man then reached inside to retrieve the bags. They drove on, wishing me a *bonne journée*, leaving me and my rubbish at the side of the lane.

It took me longer than I'd hoped to recover the brown envelope, but I found it in the end, at the bottom of the smelliest, dirtiest, most over-filled sack, covered in tomato sauce and olive stones. I wiped it clean with some tissue paper and examined the handwriting. An adhesive label had been peeled off, almost entirely, leaving a rough section of paper on which Aimée had written my address. Only the top right-hand corner of the label remained, and there, under Aimée's writing, I could just make out the name *Schinazi*.

I took the envelope to my study and called Captain Lefèvre to tell him about my find. I tried the number a couple of times, but his mobile phone was switched off, and I didn't leave a message. When I called the *hôtel de police*, I was told that Lefèvre and Dauzac were both out of the office. It was Tuesday. I wondered if the police were involved in whatever Aimée had alluded to in her note.

Next, I grabbed the Bordeaux telephone directory. There were two listings for the name *Schinazi*, both in districts on the east side of the city, close to the river. The first number I called was answered by a well-spoken elderly lady who, when I asked to speak to Monsieur, told me that she'd been a widow for over twenty years. I asked if she knew a Mademoiselle Loroux – or Gonzalès – but her confused response convinced me that Aimée had no connection with that address. I apologised for bothering her and hung up. The second number was unobtainable. 'Bugger,' I said to myself, looking down at my smelly, food-stained shirt and jeans.

In the afternoon we finished the work in the vat room and cellar. Although Archie was excited by his first foray into winemaking, I found it difficult to share his enthusiasm. And as I couldn't discuss my anxieties with him, I took myself to my room on the pretext of a headache to ruminate and fret on my own. My curiosity about where Aimée had been when she wrote the letter tormented me. In the end, I decided to have a look at the map and try to locate the two Schinazi residences. I went to the study and found a street map of the city. Sure enough, both addresses were near the Bordeaux quays, a few hundred metres from the river. I picked up the phone and tried Lefèvre's mobile for the third time, but again I was diverted to his voicemail.

I stared at the map. Aimée's words, like a line from an infectious pop song, looped inside my head: *by next Tuesday . . . I'm a little scared . . . I feel all alone here. . .* What was she scared of? What was supposed to happen on Tuesday – today, for God's sake? I had no doubt at all that she'd been murdered. I also had a nagging suspicion who was responsible – he might be calling himself Schinazi now, but his facial scar would always earn him the moniker *Le Balafré*.

I knew, too, that time was running out. If I couldn't talk to the captain, I would have to act. Perhaps I should drive to the city to test my theory. I didn't like the thought of bumping into Aimée's old acquaintances, but what the hell, I said to myself, you're only going to look, to observe . . . What can happen? In the end I made a deal with myself. I'd try Lefèvre's phone one last time. If he picked up, I'd tell him about my hunch, stop fretting and go and prepare some food. If not, I'd go to Bordeaux and see for myself.

The captain's phone was still switched off; Archie would have to make his own supper.

I said to Archie that I was going out for the evening to visit a friend and told him not to wait up for me. Turk and I climbed aboard Clémentine and, after a bit of a struggle to get her started, headed west – a tangerine car chasing a tangerine sun towards the city. Despite the beautiful sunset, a northerly wind had blown in from the Gironde, shaking the vine shoots in their trellises. A strong gust buffeted the little car as we crossed the Dordogne, causing the passenger-side window to flap open. Turk growled nervously, then stuck his snout into the fresh air and sniffed.

The first address – the little old lady's residence – was in a block of turn-of-the-century apartments in an affluent *quartier* near the university. I was reassured that old Madame Schinazi had nothing to do with Aimée, so I drove on to the other address which turned out to be an empty, boarded-up shop on a narrow cul-de-sac, parallel to the railway station sidings. There was no sign of any recent habitation. I sat in the car, staring glumly at the map in the dim glow from the interior light. My investigations appeared to have reached a dead end.

But what if Schinazi wasn't a person, I wondered. What if Schinazi was the name of a road? I scanned the list of street names listed alphabetically on the reverse side of the map – rue Saget, rue Saige, dozens of rues Saint-something-or-other, rue Ségur . . . but no rue Schinazi. I flipped the map over again and gazed at the labyrinth of city streets, hemmed in by the snake-like Garonne and its golden mile of quays. My eye fixed on the word I'd been searching for. There, under the western approach of the great Aquitaine Bridge, a vine row's length from the river, was a small, unassuming road: the Avenue Docteur Schinazi. Turk looked up at me, panting. I knew it was the place. I just knew it.

Mania

How given for nought her priceless gift,
How spoiled the bread and spilled the wine...
- Coventry Patmore, *The Angel in the House*

The Garonne's black waters flowed northwards, circumscribing the city and its twinkling towers on our left, carrying with it bottles and branches and dark, formless objects which kept pace with me as I drove along the quays. It was as though, like all this moonlit flotsam, I was being drawn towards the sea. But at the Place de la Bourse the road ahead was closed. The diversion sent me across the tramlines to the centre of town.

My detour took me close to Stéphane and Isabelle's apartment. He'd be working in the restaurant; she, reading bedtime stories to the children. What was I doing here, driving God-knows-where in search of God-knows-what? I considered for a moment that I was out of control. I should be at home now, putting myself to bed with a soothing nightcap and an improving book.

But then I thought about Aimée – the runaway daughter; the long-lost sister; the child who, not so long ago, would kiss her mother goodnight, just like Isabelle's kids, and drift into an innocent dream of magic and fairytales; Aimée the dead girl. Was she just another accidental casualty, or a victim of the most vile and wasteful of crimes? I needed to know. I *had* to know. I felt unstoppable, on a mission. I was doing this for Aimée and her family. Again I reassured myself that, after all, I was only going to look – what harm could that do?

Finally, after spending a frustrating ten minutes staring at a series of red traffic lights, I picked up a sign for the

Pont d'Aquitaine. At last, I was heading back towards the river and the Avenue Docteur Schinazi . . .

The road took me under the bridge into an out-of-town commercial zone of low-rise warehouses, storage depots and builders' yards. I drove the length of the street until a barrier, which marked where the road became a dirt track, stopped us from going any further. Still unsure about what exactly I was looking for, I turned the car round and crawled back towards the city. All the businesses we passed were closed and dark, their steel and wire gates securely locked for the night – all, that is, except one. Not far from the bridge, on the river side of the road, a gate had been left open. I brought Clémentine to a halt by the entrance and peered at a single-storey building on the far side of an open yard, fifty-or-so metres from the road. Two expensive-looking cars and a white panel van were parked outside. A dim, flickering light came from one of the building's windows. Someone was at home.

I drove through the entrance, made a u-turn back towards the road, then cut the engine.

'Stay there,' I whispered to Turk, then stepped out into the windy night, closing the door quietly behind me.

I had no idea what I was going to do. Should I creep up to the window silently, like an intruder? Should I bang on the door of the building and ask its occupant – probably just a nightshift caretaker – if they knew anyone called Loroux? Or should I crouch in the bushes and spy on people as they came and went? This really wasn't my forte, although I've never been quite sure exactly what is. In the end, I decided to approach the window quietly and see who was inside. When I was only a few paces away from the building (a shabby office built from a couple of joined-up portacabins), I could see that the light came from a television set. In front of an untidy table, sitting with his back to me, was a man in a swivel chair watching the news. I couldn't hear the TV, but the names that appeared on the screen were in Cyrillic script – an Eastern-

European caretaker then, I concluded. I'd seen enough. I didn't feel like interrupting the poor man's evening, nor did I want to startle him if he caught sight my ghostly face at the window. I was just about to turn and tiptoe back to the car when I noticed a packet of Lucky Strikes on the table – Aimée's brand. They might have belonged to the caretaker, but he looked more like a Gauloises smoker to me. I took another step towards the window. My gaze scanned the other items on the table – a few dirty plastic cups, a parcel tape dispenser, a cardboard box full of pens, a torch . . . Behind the table, running along the back wall, was a deep shelf. On its dusty surface were a couple of box files lying on their sides and a black sports bag. Next to the files was a small, well-thumbed paperback. I recognised the cover at once: *The Old Man and the Sea*. It was Aimée's book, the one that Andrew had given to her. My gaze went from the book to the cigarette packet and back again. I looked at the man's head, his grey cropped hair, his bald patch, his sticky-out ears . . .

I heard footsteps and sensed someone at my back.

In an instant of sickening shock, I was lifted off my feet and dropped onto my knees, forced there by the powerful arms of a man. His voice came to me from behind my head, his lips pressed against my ear. It was young man's voice.

'*Shush . . . ma chérie,*' the man hissed, covering my mouth with one hand, as the other closed round my neck. I contemplated biting into the bony flesh that pressed against my lips, but the smell of the man's aftershave mixed with his fetid breath made me retch. I clenched my teeth and tried to breathe, waiting for the gag reflex in my throat to subside. 'Well, well, if it isn't the Chatelaine in the 2CV,' he said.

Then, also behind me, another man spoke: 'You know her, Pope?'

'Yes,' – again that sibilant hiss – 'it's a friend of Aimée's.'

'Bring her inside, quickly. We don't want any fuckups

tonight.' The voice was Slavic, thickly accented, but mature and authoritative. The man spoke like a grumpy boss.

My attacker yanked me back to my feet and pressed my face against the window. The caretaker leapt from his chair, dragged his bulky form over to the door and joined us outside. 'What's this?' he said.

I looked at my captor's reflection in the window. The low brow and high cheekbone were joined, across the left eye, by a deep, pale scar. His mouth was twisted into a sinister rictus grin.

It was Scarface.

'This, *messieurs*,' he said, 'is Madame Valeix.'

Just then, Turk let out a shrill bark. Scarface span me round. Everyone looked at the little car on the other side of the yard. The dog was standing with his forepaws on the back of the rear seat, staring at us intently. Again he let out a yelp, then disappeared for a moment before returning to his former position.

Scarface twisted my arm behind my back and shoved me in the direction of the car.

'Wait,' said the grumpy boss. 'First you let a woman follow you here, then a dog. What's next, my little Pope? A whole fucking zoo?'

We stopped and turned again. I searched the other man's face for even the slightest sign of compassion but found none. 'Leave the dog in the car,' he said. 'We'll see to it later. Now, bring the woman inside.'

Scarface and the caretaker, like a couple of clumsy brigands, bundled me through the door, all three of us struggling and cursing. If the situation hadn't been so damned uncomfortable and utterly terrifying, it would have been comical.

The boss followed us inside. 'Tie her,' he said.

The fat caretaker gripped me in a reverse bear hug while Scarface set to work with the parcel tape, binding my wrists. Next they shoved me down on the floor in front of the table, taped my ankles together and tied my waist to the table leg with a leather belt, fastening it tightly behind my back. Finally, they bent me forward and attached my wrists to my ankles with more tape.

I managed to speak.

'You're going to regret this, Gentlemen,' I said. 'The police know that I'm here.'

The boss man's stare flicked from me to the mobile phone in his hand. He put the thing to his ear and waited a couple of seconds, then looked directly at me as he spoke into the mouthpiece. 'Are they still there? Good. No, no problems.'

He put the phone down on the table and knelt beside me. His trainers were muddy and wet.

'The *flics* are all on the other side of the city at the airport. They won't trouble us tonight. You are all alone, madame. Maybe later we can have some fun, eh?'

He looked round at his accomplices. All the three of them laughed.

'Enough,' he said. 'We have work to do.'

He stood and addressed the caretaker. 'We saw the signal from the ship. They have finished unloading. We must go now.'

He grabbed the sports bag and the torch, then he and the caretaker stomped outside. Scarface lingered, eyeing me mockingly. A smile slithered across his face as he casually produced a pistol from his waistband. I was defenceless, my hands were tied, but perhaps I could harm him with my spite. 'You killed Aimée,' I spat.

'Ha! You're crazy, Chatelaine—'

He was about to continue when the other men shouted for him to get a move on. Still grinning at me, he taped my mouth shut with a short length of parcel tape, then went to the door and followed his cronies out into the darkness. I remembered Captain Lefèvre telling me the boy's name: Grigor Popescu – Pope, apparently, to his friends. Well, Pope, I thought, crazy I might be, but you are a murderer.

Three blasts of a ship's klaxon rang out across the river, shaking the fragile walls of the building and leaving behind a vacuum of silence that emptied the room. The boss was right. I had never felt more alone, nor had I ever felt more afraid. There was a good chance that these men intended to kill me.

Squally rain pattered against the window pane. The door, which Scarface had left slightly ajar, rattled with each chilly gust of wind. A cold moisture, from the mouldy carpet tiles on the floor, had seeped through the seat of my jeans. Bound and gagged, lonely, frightened and cold; I'd had better days.

For some reason I thought about the eternity wedding ring and decided that, sometime soon, I would like pass it on to Andrew's daughter, Poppy. Then I thought about the others who relied on me in one way or another: Archie, at home, unsatisfied with his cold supper; Valentin and Paul, unaware that I intended to offer them both an apprenticeship; even poor little Turk, locked in the car, waiting for his mistress to return. And then there were those on whom I relied: Wendy Snook, Stéphane Lavergne, Captain Lefèvre ... all acrobats in my life's teetering human tower. It had been years since I'd thought much about death, but I wondered what would happen to them if I weren't here. More to the point, what would happen to me? I'd long since conceded that after I died I would simply cease to be. But what about Mary's spirit world? My father-in-law's Heaven? Archie's parallel universes? Perhaps they were all one and the same place. Perhaps that was what Andrew had seen when he took his dying breath – a divine light, guiding him to the next world. Or was he simply recalling a vivid memory of a glittering river and a gorgeous turquoise bird?

I didn't know; who can? All I knew was that right here, right now, the most important thing for me was living. I'd get through this, just like I got through my illness when death had been far easier to contemplate. I looked down at my bindings. I'd pull through. The only question was, how?

The door banged, the wind whistled through the gap, the

rain tapped harder on the window. I listened for the returning footsteps of the three men but heard something else: the sound, in the middle distance, of the 2CV's faulty window flapping in the squall. Next there was a frantic scratching at the door. After a few seconds, Turk cantered into the room.

When he saw me he hesitated, waiting for me to praise or greet him. But all I could manage from behind the gag was a barely audible whine. He appeared to take that as a sign of encouragement, put his front paws on my forearms and licked my face. I shook him off and tickled his muzzle and ears with my thumbs and fingers, teasing him with the tape that bound my wrists together. He took the bait and began nibbling my bindings with his sharp little teeth, tugging at the strips of tape – he always won these playful games of tug-of-war . . . He'd soon bitten through enough of the tape for me to separate my hands. I tore the gag from my face, then reached round to undo the belt buckle behind my back. I struggled to my feet. In amongst the pens on the table was a small pair of scissors which I used to cut through the tape that shackled my ankles.

'Come on, boy,' I said to the dog.

We trotted warily across the exposed tarmac plot between the office and the gate. There was no sign of the three men, but their vehicles were still there. I considered the possibility that Scarface was going to escape by boat. I threw myself into the car and grabbed my handbag, rummaging through its contents in search of the mobile phone and Lefèvre's card. Once I'd found the phone and turned it on, I realised that the battery was practically flat. I dialled the number. This time he answered. '*Allo.*'

There was no time for civilities.

'It's me, Captain, Jeanne Valeix. I'm at a warehouse by the river on the Avenue Docteur Schinazi . . . Scarface and his friends captured me . . . he killed Aimée, I'm sure of it . . . there's a ship on the river . . . come quickly, I think that he's trying to get away.'

'Madame Valeix,' Lefèvre said. He sounded appropriately concerned. 'Stay away from those people. Get out of there as soon as you—'

His voice disappeared along with the screen's greenish glow. I tried to switch the thing back on, but it was dead. I considered the policeman's advice in the light of Mary's supernatural warning, then immediately ignored them both. I'm always doing things like that. It's stupidity, I suppose.

I put the key in the ignition, left my bag on the seat and climbed out, leaving the door unlocked. This time Turk came with me. This time I was not going to get caught.

We went over to the office. At the side of the building was a patch of unkempt grass which might once have been called a lawn. In the dim light coming from the window, I could just make out a well-worn pathway leading to a line of scrubby trees. Beyond these was a dense wooded area that must surely border the river – and on the river was a ship . . .

I wasn't going to let Scarface get away. Until Lefèvre showed up, I would just have to find some way to stall him. We followed the path through the trees until it disappeared into the wood. The rain had stopped. The clouds obscured the moon. The way into the woods looked like the entrance to a black abyss. Fighting the urge to turn and run back to the car, I plunged on into the dark tunnel of trees with Turk keeping close at heel. Once my eyes had adjusted to the darkness, I could see the pathway ahead, rising to a ridge before descending again, presumably, towards the riverbank. We reached the top of the shallow slope. There before us, twinkling through the canopy of branches, were the lights of a huge cargo ship. The buildings and derricks on the opposite bank were dwarfed by the vessel's size. It loomed above us, high in the channel, a floating tower block of steel and smoke and lights. I looked down at the water's edge. At the end of a spindly wooden jetty, perched on a frame of timber struts, was a fishing hut. I'd visited one of these skeletal shacks with Olivier, one moonlit night a lifetime ago. They were built by local fishermen, whose torch-lit forays netted lampreys and crayfish. The occupants of this one though were not fishing. The men stood on a flimsy-looking balcony, overhanging the fast-flowing waters, watching a small motor launch making its way across the river from the direction of the ship.

I moved back to watch the proceedings from the cover of the trees. It soon became clear that the men were waiting for a delivery. When the launch had reached the jetty, the boss man dropped the sports bag carefully into the boatman's arms. The man examined what was inside the bag with a torch. Next, a smaller bag was passed up to the boss who, like the man in the boat, unzipped it and checked its contents. At a signal from the man above, the boatman delivered the rest of his consignment of six more bags.

The cloud had thinned. The moon appeared, and with it a ghostly white owl that fluttered almost noiselessly from a copse on our right. Its screech startled Turk, who bounded from our hiding place, barking at the bird as it flew downstream.

Despite the purr of the boat's idling outboard motor, those on the balcony had heard Turk's outburst. I tried to call him back to the bushes, but it was too late. The men had seen his pale white coat, conspicuous in the moonlight. Scarface dropped his bag and disappeared into the hut, then reappeared on the gangway, jogging towards the bank.

I turned and fled back up the slope, followed by the dog. I only had to cover about a hundred metres of ground, but with Scarface in pursuit it felt like a long, long way. En route I planned my escape: the car's not locked, the key is in the ignition; get in, lock the doors, turn the key and drive the hell out of there . . . We shot past the portacabins and the posh cars, then sprinted across the yard. I heard my pursuer shout something but couldn't catch what he said. He sounded close, though. Turk, in spite of his short legs, had made it to the car ahead of me. I opened the driver's door, let him jump in and then threw myself behind the wheel. The door slammed shut. I clicked the lock. My fingers gripped the ignition key and turned. I could hear my beating heart, my exhausted gasping and the starter motor's desperate howl. The silhouette of a man loomed into view in the rear window. I turned the key again, but still the engine wouldn't start. I looked in the mirror. The shadow slipped out of sight, then reappeared at the window by my left shoulder. The man tugged at the door handle and slapped the stiff fabric of the car's roof. I continued to turn the starter and watched, in panic-stricken horror, as he stooped slowly down, until his scar-disfigured visage was at the window, inches from my own horrified face.

'Open the door, Chatelaine,' he said.

I turned the key for the umpteenth time, still to no avail. Scarface stood up straight, stepped back from the car and raised his right arm. In his hand, pointing directly at my head, was the gun.

'I said open the door, Chatelaine. Unless you want to follow that junky whore friend of yours—'

Above the whine of the struggling starter motor, I heard a higher-pitched noise coming from the direction of the road. Scarface heard it, too. As he turned towards the sound's source, his face was illuminated briefly by the glow of a flashing blue light. Clémentine's engine spluttered into life, I yanked the stick shift into first and sped away, tyres squealing, towards the banshee howl of the approaching sirens. The ear-splitting crack that I heard next was not the sound of the car backfiring, but I drove on regardless, past and through the oncoming police vehicles in the road, swerving, skidding and finally colliding with a wire fence.

The car had stalled. Turk, who had fallen into the footwell, stared up at me with his head cocked to one side. An icy current of air was blowing down my collar where the skin was damp and cold with sweat. I rubbed my neck, then reached out to restart the engine. My fingers felt wet and sticky. I touched again the skin between my jaw and shoulder. The wetness was my own blood, trickling from an open wound. I noticed a bullet hole in the central facia of the dashboard. I could hear the beating of giant wings.

I blacked out.

Although my eyes were closed, I was aware of a searing white light shining in my face and something tugging at the collar of my jacket. I could hear two voices, one on either side of my head, and, flapping above me, the noise of a giant creature . . .

'It's only a scratch.'

What the hell was it?

'Only? How would you like to be shot in the neck?'

Some sort of monstrous flying devil, perhaps . . .

'Pass me that gauze, idiot. I mean it hasn't severed the artery. Look, there's the bullet hole.'

Or a huge winged angel . . .

'Oops, the wiper mechanism will be screwed.'

Perhaps it's that barn owl . . .

'Can we concentrate on the victim, Lieutenant?'

No, owls are silent in flight.

'She's coming round. Give her some room.'

God, it's so loud . . .

'Madame Valeix?'

I was sitting in the centre of Clémentine's bench seat between Captain Lefèvre and his lieutenant, Dauzac. I could feel a stinging pain on the right side of my neck.

'*Bonsoir*, madame,' Lefèvre said. The smile, lit from below by his torch, looked like a clown's.

'Turk! Where's Turk?' I said.

'He's in one of the cars, madame,' said Dauzac. 'Don't worry.'

'The ambulance has just arrived, Madame Valeix,' said the captain. 'Do you think you can walk?'

'I . . .' I stammered, 'I think so. But there's so much blood—'

255

'It's okay, the bullet only grazed your neck.'

Grazed?

I put my hand to where, by now, the pain was most acute and touched a padded gauze bandage. The blood on my fingers had dried.

I remembered the sound of the gunshot.

'Scarface!' I said, glancing at each of the officers in turn.

'It's okay,' Lefèvre said, again. 'We got him in the woods. The other men escaped on the motor boat but they didn't get far, what with the boys in the coffee grinder up there and the river police. Can you just confirm how many men you saw, madame?'

'Coffee grinder?'

'Yes, you know, the Police helicopter,' he said, looking upwards.

The noisy machine had drifted downstream, but the rapid beating sound of its rotors still echoed across the estuary.

'Oh, I see. Er, three of them – oh, plus the man in the boat: four.'

Lefèvre looked pleased. 'Excellent,' he said, 'no men overboard, then.'

A paramedic appeared behind him, and he stepped out of the car. I shuffled to the open door for the two men to help me to my feet. Dauzac sprinted over to a police car and returned with Turk. When Lefèvre helped me climb into the back of the ambulance, the clown's smile was still stuck to his face.

She was from Senegal, originally, the beautiful black nurse who had cleaned and re-dressed my wounds after the doctor had been in to see me. Her name was Florence. She'd given me a sedative, wished me a *bonne nuit* and turned off the light. Sleep had come quickly.

In the morning, my little nightingale returned with clean bandages and a breakfast tray of fresh black coffee, warm bread and a buttery croissant, all of which I wolfed down greedily. The room would have been large enough for three beds, but I was the only occupant. There were fresh flowers on the bedside table and, by sitting up in bed, I could see the white blossoms of a magnolia in a pretty walled garden outside. I hate hospitals, but this one was certainly much nicer than any of the others I'd stayed in. I asked the nurse if she knew how much the room would cost, but she told me not to worry because the police would pick up the bill. After a hot neck-down shower, I used the phone by the side of the bed to call home; there was no answer. I was wondering what had happened to the dog when the nurse returned, followed by my visitors: the captain, his lieutenant and a worried-looking Archie.

'*Bonjour messieurs.* Hello, Archie,' I said.

'Hello, Jean,' the boy said, shuffling slowly to the bedside and extending his hand.

I patted the quilt beside me and said, 'Oh, come and sit down here next to me, Archie, and don't look so worried – I'm fine.'

A look of concern had replaced Lefèvre's smile of the previous night. 'It's a miracle that you are fine, madame,' he said. 'What you did was very foolish, you know.'

Dauzac gave me a conspiratorial wink. 'Oh, I don't know, *Capitaine*, I think that Madame Valeix was incredibly brave.'

Sweet Dauzac. 'That's very kind of you, Lieutenant,' I said, 'but perhaps the captain is right. It was a strange kind of bravery – I think madness might be a better word for it.'

Lefèvre nodded, the smile returning. 'Yes, that's it, you are completely insane, Jeanne.'

The policemen and I all laughed, a little nervously, then I sighed and looked at Archie's furrowed brows.

'I'm not surprised that you were shot, Jean,' the boy said. 'You're six times more likely to get shot in France than in England and Wales. Still, compared to the risk of being shot in the United States, it's much less likely. So actually you're incredibly unlucky.'

'Either that, Archie, or incredibly lucky to be alive.'

His face brightened. 'Yes, I suppose so.'

Archie had brought me some clean clothes and my handbag. When the men had left the room, I got dressed, applied some makeup and said goodbye to the nurse and the bright little room.

In the car on the way home, the captain explained how he and his brigade were able to rescue me so quickly. Apparently, Bordeaux's drug squad had been carrying out a sting operation at the airport. They knew that a Romanian gang were bringing in heroin from Albania, and they knew when. They also knew how and where – or rather, they thought they did. But the Bordeaux boys had been hoodwinked. The drugs weren't, as they thought, coming by plane via the airport in Merignac, but by sea, in the hold of a cargo ship, beneath a thousand tonnes of Albanian timber.

With so many of Bordeaux's officers waiting to spring the trap in Merignac, Lefèvre's team had been called to assist another surveillance operation at a hunting equipment shop, just over the bridge in Lormont. Their job – to nab a small-time gun thief – had ended in a shootout and a manhunt. They'd only just caught the miscreant, with the help of the eye-in-the-sky helicopter, when I called. Lefèvre was only a five-minute drive away, but it would take his Bordeaux colleagues a quarter of an hour to get there.

In one night, the Libourne squad had caught the gang, rescued a hostage, and recovered twenty kilos of heroin and eight hundred thousand euros in cash. They'd also arrested an armed robber as well as the prime suspect for Aimée Loroux's murder. Dauzac summed it up: their commandant was very pleased with them.

No wonder Lefèvre had worn such a broad smile.

Back at Fontloube, I gave my statement to the captain – a story that I would have to repeat many times to Archie and his Aunty Mary, Wendy, the Valeix boys and the Lavergnes, and a few months later in a court of law, to a judge and jury. In order to secure a murder verdict, my testimony would be crucial. Now, that *would* be a long story, beginning with a chance encounter in a vineyard on a bright April day . . .

Kingfisher

Wine cheereth God and man.
- Judges, 9:13

Archie came back during the Easter holidays. On Thursday morning we visited the notary in Saint-Emilion together and signed the papers that would make Archie a partner in Château Fontloube. The lawyer asked if we wanted to change the name of the company – it would be easier and cheaper to do it then rather than later – and so Henri Valeix Père & Fils became Valeix & Maconie, two years to the day since I'd first met Andrew in his camper van. That afternoon, Archie and I went to the accountant's office in Libourne to collect a contract for Paul's apprenticeship. I'd offered a position to Valentin, too, but he'd declined – in a flood of bashful but heartfelt apologies – because, he said, he planned to go to catering school to train to be a chef.

Over the weekend we finished blending the 2008 vintage. We used a good proportion of the cabernets from the lower vineyard in the mix (Archie's favourite 'purple-silver' wine); and with what remained we blended a special reserve – something to squirrel away in the cellar for a decade or more. Who knows what future celebrations will call for a bottle, or two . . .?

For Easter Monday, I'd organised a celebratory picnic on the riverbank near Sainte-Terre. Stéphane and Isabelle were there with their charming children, and the Valeix cousins had driven down for the day with their girlfriends in tow (both healthy Corrézien girls – one pretty and buxom; the other no less attractive and clever to boot). We met in a grassy clearing on the river, spread rugs and cushions on the ground and unloaded a gastronomic takeaway from the back of Stéphane's car. I supplied the wine, including a magnum of vintage champagne that had been mouldering in the cellar for longer than I can remember. As well as his latest girl, Valentin had brought a tray of caramelised onion tartlets, a quiche Lorraine, and a rhubarb tart. He must be trying to impress me with his baking skills, I thought. As the others laid out the dishes, I poured the champagne, intending to make a toast.

Stéphane beat me to it. 'Here's to Jeanne and Archie!' he said. 'Oh, and you, Paul, of course.'

I sipped and looked across at Valentin, conscious that he might be feeling left out. He tossed his head back, swallowed the champagne, then looked directly at me, smiling the Valeix smile.

I sidled over to him. 'Not changed your mind about coming to work for me, then, eh?' I said.

'What, you mean spend my days tasting *grand cru* wines when I could be locked away in a burning-hot kitchen?'

I smiled. 'It's not all wine tasting, you know that.'

'Yes, I know, and I really do want to learn how to cook, you know, get my diploma and everything. I'm sorry, Jeanne.'

'Don't apologise; I understand. And anyway, who am I to tell you what you should be doing? Just make sure it's what you really want, that's all. You can't change your mind later.'

Paul, who was handing out the tartlets, came over to us.

'Well, you did, Jeanne,' he said.

'What do you mean?'

Valentin answered for his cousin. 'Yes, you know, first you were a student lawyer, then you became a successful winemaker, and now you're a super sleuth.'

I tried a mouthful of the delicious pastry.

'A sleuth?' I asked.

'Yes, like what's-her-name . . . Miss Marple.'

I narrowed my eyes at the boy. 'Which one?' I asked slowly.

'Eh?'

'Never mind, Valentin. Look, here's to you – want something badly enough and, you never know, you might just get it.'

Stéphane, who had been listening to our chat, swallowed his tart and put his arm round Valentin's shoulders.

'And carry on making pastry as good as this, my boy, and, who knows, you might be working in a kitchen like mine one day.'

I thought, aha, he's the one who Valentin is trying to impress. The poor lad must have been baking since before dawn.

After lunch, Isabelle and I relaxed in the sunshine, keeping one eye on the children, who were playing with Turk on the grass, and the other on Stéphane and the boys, flexing their muscles on the riverbank. The girls wandered past us arm in arm and disappeared into the woods that border the river. When they had gone, I told Isabelle all about my heroic exploits in Bordeaux, about how I was captured, how Turk helped me to escape, and how I was nearly killed. She listened, with horrified concern, to the whole story, then asked me to describe the captain in more detail – the man, she said, who had saved my life. I blushed slightly and started to say something, but Isabelle had noticed Archie sitting on a tree stump, a few paces downstream, reading a dog-eared college prospectus.

'What's that, Archie?' Isabelle called to him.

He shifted his position, sitting up straight with his knees and toes together, staring at the leaflet. 'Oh, just a thing . . .' he muttered, his right hand flapping gently like a vine leaf in the breeze.

'It's from the college in Libourne,' I told her. 'Archie can start there in September, assuming that he passes his baccalaureate this summer.'

'Oh, I'm sure you will, Archie,' she called to him again.

'Jeanne has told me what a bright student you are.'

The flapping stopped abruptly, and he clasped the prospectus in both hands. 'Thanks,' he said.

She turned back to me and said, 'I think it's wonderful what you're doing for Archie and Paul. You do know that Stéphane plans to give Valentin a work placement if he makes it to college?'

'No, I didn't. That's marvellous, Isabelle. Does he know?'

She put her finger to her lips and raised an eyebrow.

'Oh,' I whispered, 'I won't say a word. That boy's head is already far too big for his shoulders.'

Isabelle looked along the towpath at Valentin's date and her friend emerging from the woods.

'And who can blame him, eh?' she sighed.

Just then I heard one of the Lavergne children shout, *'Papa! Papa! Un martin pêcheur!'*

A bird hurtled past us at incredible speed, and by the time I'd said, 'Oh, yes, look! Archie! A kingfisher!' it had flown round the bend in the river and disappeared in a flash of electric blue.

I never did get to tell Isabelle how I felt about Captain Pierre Lefèvre.

Joy

My vines are weeping. It happens every spring. The awakening roots, warmed by the Easter sunshine, fill the stems with sap which gathers and drips from the pruning cuts at the tip of each cane. The French say that the vine bleeds, but I see tears, not blood, falling in gentle profusion to the recently turned soil, a soft shower of crystal droplets, each one created to twist and split a sunbeam into a sparkle.

Weep, vines, weep the winter's tears away. Soon you'll be like me, and there'll be no time for crying. You'll be too busy struggling against nature's mood swings to cry, battling with the frost and the hail, weathering the storms and the deluges of life. Summer is coming. And after the summer, the harvest. And then a succession of harvests (some good, some bad) carried in the flow of the future's endless river.

That river is rushing towards me now as I gaze across the broad, fertile valley. I'm seeing the vineyard's resplendence, as though for the first time; a long-worn veil has been lifted, to reveal a face whose beauty has never faded. What is this veil? Not my melancholy, nor my anxieties. No, I'm realising that for too long I've shared Aimée's utter disinterest in the future. The vineyard's future has been invisible to me, and so, too, has its beauty.

But now I can imagine the different stories that might weave themselves into this vine, the lives that might, one day, be shaped by this place, the infinite possibilities. I'm imagining the people who will struggle, year after year, to make this vineyard fruitful. I see their children, in grubby clothes, chasing colourful butterflies along the vine rows; the secret moonlit trysts; the haphazard encounters; the squabbles and reconciliations; the old folk, hand in hand, taking Sunday evening strolls; a grandmother, picking out the suckers from a vine trunk, cultivating her memories.

And I'm thinking about how, one day, my ashes might fertilise these merlots and cabernets. Oh, I know what death is – I buried three men in twelve years. Three men, whom I loved, lost and mourned, and mourn still. Three men, each with his own unfinished story: Olivier, my beautiful Olivier, who died far too young; Henri, his father, who left no heirs; and Andrew, who endured his last days in exile, separated from his family and his children. And then, of course, there was Aimée – dazzling, enchanting, fatal Aimée ... I know that my story must have its ending. But however and whenever I go – by accident or illness or in old age – I want my life to end, not with three little dots, but with an exclamation mark. In fact, I'm going to make bloody sure it does!

End.

From *A Devil in the Grape,* by Patrick Hilyer

I suppose I'm an old-fashioned kind of girl. Okay, so I'm not exactly a girl any more. I may still feel twenty-two, but I only have to look in the mirror to remind myself that a quarter of a century has passed since I came to Saint-Emilion. Still, all those years spent turning grapes into wine haven't been too unkind to me. Like my '95s, I think I've aged fairly well.

So, not old, but definitely old-fashioned. For me, the opera should be all gorgeous frocks, flamboyant scenery and men in tights. Not that I was complaining – I hadn't paid for the tickets after all. But a modern adaptation of Gounod's *Faust* set in the juvenile wing of a psychiatric hospital just wasn't my cup of tea. Hospitals are among the few things I can't stand – along with snakes, guns, early morning confrontations, goodbyes, pruning my vines . . . well, there are lots of things I dislike, but hospitals are the worst.

At least Pierre had been there, sitting beside me. Pierre Lefèvre: the man who'd saved my life, the softly spoken police captain whose thigh, when it touched mine in the near-darkness of the auditorium, had sent my pulse racing.

Admittedly, the opera wasn't all bad. The music was sublime, and by portraying Mephistopheles as a figment of Faust's drug-addled mind, the Austrian baritone had given a convincing devil. I shuddered, recalling his dark, gaunt features, blood-red eyes and the spike of crimson hair crowning his sallow, shaven head.

I empathised with Faust. There was a time when I had my own demons to cope with. One in particular, whom I called my evil gremlin, would never leave me alone. But, strangely, after being shot in the neck I haven't heard from him since. Now I talk to my Jack Russell terrier instead.

He doesn't talk back.

Of course, I empathised most strongly with the poor girl, Marguerite. I never did have children of my own, and now, halfway down life's one-way street, I've accepted I never will. A couple of years ago I resolved to help the young people around me, knowing that there are more than enough children in the world. Knowing is one thing; feeling is quite another.

I was delighted with the venue for our post-matinee dinner. Lefèvre had managed to get a table at Bordeaux's best − well, second-best − restaurant. Earlier, I'd been apprehensive, this being my first date since Andrew had passed away a year and a half earlier, but now I was beginning to relax and enjoy the evening.

Apart from at my partner's funeral, I'd worn nothing but a pair of old jeans and a flannel shirt for the past two years. This evening I had on a black dress, black heels and my last pair of sheer tights. The dress felt a tad more figure-hugging than the last time I'd dressed for dinner, and the shoes were killing my feet, but it felt good to be there in the restaurant's cavernous dining room, anticipating a delicious, gastronomic dinner surrounded by Bordeaux's bourgeoisie.

Lefèvre hailed the waiter and ordered champagne. I tried not to look at the stratospheric prices on the menu and, instead, took in my surroundings. Everything about the place merited the chef's two Michelin stars. The table, like the décor, was impeccable. No wrinkle dared show itself on the perfect white table cloth on top of which the squeaky-clean crystal glasses, linen napkins, and elegant silverware had been arranged with pinpoint precision. Pink roses, still bearing the morning's dew, formed the centrepiece. The assiettes de presentation, I noticed, turning mine over, were Limoges. The other diners, like us, were mostly in their forties and fifties. I reasoned that few young people or pensioners could afford such a swanky place.

The waiter served our drinks, and we toasted each other's health.

'A votre santé.'

Police Captain Pierre Lefèvre and I have known each other for three years but we've never settled on a mutually agreeable language. When speaking French we've always used the formal vous form of address which doesn't suit me at all. English is my preference – it's far less starchy.

Lefèvre took a sip of his champagne then looked at me, smiling.

'Merci, Jeanne,' – at least he'd stopped calling me Madame – 'and sorry for . . . you know.'

I understood the apology: we'd lost a murder conviction. But he had no need to thank me. 'No, thank you. You saved my life remember?'

He eyed the fizzy contents of his fluted glass. 'Oh, not really. You made sure everything worked out fine.'

'But if you hadn't turned up when you did—'

'—then we would not have made the drugs haul, I would not have got a promotion, and we would not be here enjoying these expensive aperitifs.'

Should I have offered to go Dutch? Oh please, I thought, don't let him be a cheapskate.

'Pride comes before a fall,' I said, teasing.

His smile faded. 'You know, in my line of work that is not an expression we like to use.'

He didn't need to explain. I'd been on the receiving end of a pistol barrel only once in my life but, for Captain Lefèvre, getting shot was a daily hazard.

'No, sorry.' I raised my glass. 'Let's drink to your success.'

The smile returned. 'And to yours, too, Jeanne.'

Now how the hell did he know about that?

I'd barely begun to peruse the list of delicious-sounding hors d'oeuvres when Lefèvre's phone buzzed.

'Let me take this call, then you can tell me how terrible the opera was.'

He picked-up, gave his name. His expression said bad news.

'Where? . . . In a what? . . . Merde. Okay, I will be there as soon as I— . . . No, I am in the city . . . What's the ad—? . . . But that's in the Dordogne, n'est-ce pas? . . . No, of course not, I can be there within the hour . . . No, he's still on vacation . . .'

He closed the flap of the phone and frowned. 'I am sorry, Jeanne.'

'What is it?'

'Something has come up. I have to go.'

'But you haven't eaten—'

'A body has been found, north of Libourne.'

Adrenalin replaced the empty feeling in my stomach.

'Oh, I see. Well, of course I understand.'

He'd already put on his jacket and waved a twenty euro note to signal for the bill. I stood up and picked up my handbag. Lefèvre flashed his police ID card at the waiter, mumbled his excuses and left the bank note on the man's tray. Then, as we made our way to the door, Lefèvre related the scant details he'd been given by his boss.

'A winemaker has been found dead in one of his vats, Jeanne. It does not look like an accident.'

My God, I thought, how awful.

'Oh, dear. Can you drop me off on the way?'

He stopped on the pavement outside.

'Er, there is not enough time. Perhaps you could come with me? I might need your expertise.'

Again, I felt my pulse quicken. Calm down, Jeanne, calm down.

'Well, of course, if you think I could help – if I won't be in the way . . .'

He was already striding towards the blue Peugeot with his phone pressed to his ear.

'Wait for me,' I called, running after him across the boulevard.

He stopped, put the phone to his chest. 'Do you know a winery called Château Lacasse, in Les Eglisottes?'

'No, I've never heard of it.'
'Good. Come on then, let's go.'

In less than half an hour we'd crossed the bridge that spans the sparkling waters of the Dordogne and were cruising along the four-lane Transeuropéenne highway past the town of Libourne. Lefèvre drove too fast. I glanced at the speedometer but had to look away when the needle skipped past one-forty – speeding is another of my pet hates. Even though he was a skilful driver, I was scared.

We came off the autoroute at Saint-Médart with the sun behind us. Long shadows, cast by the road signs, stretched across the exit road. Summer had passed so quickly. We crossed the River Isle, leaving behind the vineyards of the Libournais, and turned onto a narrow wooded lane. My heart rate settled, the gloom of dusk replaced the sunshine, and my mood darkened too.

I know what I'm like, what my *condition* is. It has a name, of course, but I don't like to use it and refuse to let it define me. Here's a clue: *when she was good, she was very good indeed, but when she was bad she was horrid.* Well, I've been like that ever since I was a little girl. They used to say it was manic depression, but nowadays even French psychiatrists call it *bipolaire.*

Anyway, the lithium tablets never agreed with me, and I stopped taking them years ago. Since then, as long as I keep a check on my flights of fancy and surround myself with those I love – especially when the black thoughts threaten to strike – I get along just fine. And after the fairly manic series of events in 2009 that led to my getting shot, I'd managed to stay away from anything, well, too exciting. Until then, that is; until the phone call that put paid to my romantic evening with the captain. The grape harvest was almost upon me, I'd been elected to join the Jurade – the hallowed Saint-Emilion brotherhood – and now I was racing towards the scene of . . . what? A

suicide? A murder? Oh well, I said to myself, just remember two things Jeanne: remain calm and keep smiling.

I was still forcing a smile when I began to wonder if Lefèvre had taken a wrong turn. I've always trusted policemen, but I was starting to suspect that this one had no idea where the hell he was going.

'Do you know this area,' I asked, peering out at the dark forest.

He slowed to navigate a crossroads.

'Er, yes, yes I do. My father used to fish here when I was a boy, and then when I was about fifteen or sixteen we would camp here near the lake, you know – friends from school.'

I pictured the captain as a boy scout. It wasn't difficult.

'I never knew there was such a wilderness right on our doorstep.'

'Yes, it is quite remote. These woods are part of the great forest of Le Double – hundreds of square kilometres of trees that go from here right across the Perigord. Good hunting, too – wild boar, roe deer, some muntjac.'

My thoughts turned to the captain dressed in huntin', shootin' and fishin' gear – a not unpleasant mental image. 'So, you're a keen hunter then?'

'What do you think?' he said, smiling. 'No, I read it in La Chasse in the dentist's waiting room.'

He took his phone from an inside pocket, flipped it open and pressed a couple of buttons.

'Okay, Jonzac, I'm in the woods a kilometre-or-so past the junction . . . On the left or the right? . . . Fine.'

Click.

He looked across at me. 'But it's not all trees; there is one huge vineyard in this section. Ah, here it is.'

The car slowed. There, on a rough verge, was a small hand-painted sign:

PROPRIÉTÉ PRIVÉE – DÉFENSE DE PÉNÉTRER

Keep out – not the usual advertisement that wineries put up to entice the passing trade.

We drove through the open gates, followed a winding, potholed drive, and there before us was the château, silhouetted against the orange glow of the western sky. With all its lights ablaze, the house resembled an enormous Halloween lantern. The windows in the tops of the two towers glowered at us threateningly; below them a row of stone mullions on the ground floor formed a malevolent scowl. If houses could speak, this one was saying: turn round and go home. Had I been on my own I'd have done just that because, although I was curious about the owner's demise, I was far from prepared for what we were about to discover.

From *A Devil in the Grape*

French Vineyards

by Patrick Hilyer

"a wonderful book, full of information and enchantment"
Heimburger's European Traveller

"great places to stay on French wine-producing estates,
from châteaux to B&Bs"
The Guardian

"a vicarious travel adventure"
Jancis Robinson OBE, Master of Wine

"enticing and indispensable"
Jonathan Ray, wines editor, Daily Telegraph

"recommendations from all the French wine regions"
Jim Budd, The Circle of Wine Writers

Made in the USA
Monee, IL
06 March 2022